BRINK OF WAR

A PROSECUTION FORCE THRILLER

LOGAN RYLES

SEVERN RIVER PUBLISHING

Severn River Publishing
SevernRiverBooks.com

This is a work of fiction. Names, characters, businesses, places, events and incidents are either the products of the author's imagination or used in a fictitious manner. Any resemblance to actual persons, living or dead, or actual events is purely coincidental.

ISBN: 978-1-64875-391-6 (Paperback)

ALSO BY LOGAN RYLES

To find out more about Logan Ryles and his books, visit

severnriverbooks.com/authors/logan-ryles

For my father, Tony
The best man I know

1

His name was Eberardo Alvarez Castillo, but to the locals, he was known as *El Diablo*—The Devil. Born to a Colombian mother and a Venezuelan father, Diablo snorted his first line of pure Colombian cocaine at eleven, and by fifteen, he was a street dealer, moving dime bags for the Medellín Cartel. At eighteen, Diablo watched that famed cartel go down in flames as pressure from American anti-drug interests finally brought the legendary Pablo Escobar into his grave, leaving a war zone of carnage—and opportunity—in his wake.

Moving drugs would never be the same, but for a man as resourceful and vicious as Diablo, the risk was worth the reward. By his thirtieth birthday, Diablo was a whispered legend amid the corrupt governments of South America. He was a kingpin. A killer. An alcoholic womanizer known for both extreme generosity and unmatched brutality, depending on his mood. Diablo was a drug lord in the truest tradition of the title, and he was also the man Reed Montgomery came to Colombia to kill.

From the inner edge of an open-air café, Reed watched as Diablo's armored Mercedes G-Wagon stopped at the curb and the man in the front passenger seat got out. He spoke quietly to the hostess, passing her a wad of colorful Colombian pesos and keeping his hand near the grip of the .45-caliber automatic holstered beneath his jacket.

The G-Wagon waited at the curb, exhaust clouding beneath the rear bumper. The windows were heavily tinted, but Reed didn't need to see inside. Every day for the past week, Diablo's G-Wagon stopped at this café on the way back to his hotel, and one of his bodyguards got out to retrieve his favored carnitas dinner. The food was prepared ahead of time by the café, and Reed would've poisoned it, but he knew the bodyguard sampled the dish to protect against that very point of attack.

Diablo was a careful man—and he should've been. Reed first encountered him eighteen months prior while working a recon mission in Colombia. The meeting was disastrous, ending with Reed backstabbing the drug dealer over a matter of a thousand kilos of cocaine. Immediately afterward, Diablo put a price on Reed's head, and more than a couple second-rate assassins had taken a pass at him.

That wasn't why Reed decided to exterminate the drug lord, however. He took the job because he was broke, and one of Diablo's rivals had offered him fifty thousand dollars to eliminate competition. Two birds with one stone, as Reed saw it. He'd sleep better with Diablo six feet under, anyway.

The bodyguard returned to the G-Wagon, and the SUV rumbled off. Reed watched it go, then noted the time on his wristwatch. Diablo was almost forty-five minutes early that day, which meant he probably had a prostitute waiting at his hotel. Twice in the previous five days, Reed had observed that protocol, eventually correlating an early dinner with the prospect of . . . well, dessert.

It was an important footnote. Reed had killed before in the presence of a prostitute, and it hadn't ended well. He didn't like involving innocent third parties, regardless of their occupation. Tonight wouldn't be his night.

Reed dropped twenty thousand pesos on the table for his coffee, then stepped back into the damp street just as the G-Wagon made a right-hand turn, routing toward the Four Seasons Hotel. Diablo lived in the mountains of Colombia's Antioquia Department and had ostensibly traveled to the nation's capital for vacation, but Reed knew better. Several other bad actors in the South American narcotics community were also present that week, and Diablo spent a lot of time at various restaurants, hotels, and private condominiums throughout the city.

Negotiating, Reed figured. Enjoying the city and conducting business in typical drug lord style—very slowly, with a lot of alcohol and naked women around. Any day now he would return to his mountain fortress, surrounded by an army of bodyguards and perhaps the best security of all —the vast emptiness of the Colombian jungle. If Reed waited too long, his window to complete this hit would close, and best-case scenario, he'd never get paid. Worst case, his employer would turn on him.

Reed waved down a cab, and in Spanish, instructed the driver to take him to the AC Marriott on Calle 85. The outdated Crown Victoria bumped over cracked and potholed streets on the way. Reed pushed his sunglasses closer to his face and said nothing until the car groaned to a halt in front of the ten-story building. Puddles gathered next to the sidewalks, and the air tasted humid as Reed stepped out of the car. It was overcast in Bogotá, with a cool breath of sixty-degree wind whispering amid the buildings. Typical August weather in the mountain city.

Reed took the elevator to his fifth-floor suite. He locked the door behind him and removed his sunglasses, completing a quick sweep of the room to ensure it was unmolested. For the duration of his weeklong stay, he left the Do Not Disturb sign on his door, and the maids had been only too happy to oblige. The room was dark and still, with a tangle of sheets on the bed.

He moved directly to the window and pulled the curtain back six inches. The sliding glass door opening onto the balcony was dirty, but Reed could still make out the mass of the Four Seasons Hotel rising out of the cityscape. Diablo's executive suite was situated on the top floor, one hundred fifty feet off the ground, with a curving balcony wrapping around one corner of the building. It was an easy shot for an average shooter, and Reed was considerably above average. But Diablo never used the balcony, and he kept the curtains closed.

A careful man.

Reed studied the balcony for another two minutes, considering the angles and the possibility of shooting through the glass. It wasn't bullet-proof, but it was still double-paned. Even if Diablo opened the curtain and exposed himself to view, Reed couldn't be sure of a clean shot. The glass would deform the bullet, destroying both accuracy and velocity. If Diablo was hit at all, he might survive.

And that couldn't happen.

Reed replaced the curtain and returned to the bed. From underneath it, he withdrew a long duffel packed with dirty clothes and a mess of tourist trinkets he'd purchased at street-side vendors to help disguise the real purpose of the bag—that of a rifle case.

The false bottom of the duffel concealed a compartment ten inches wide and eighteen inches long—large enough to house the disassembled Remington Defense CSR Reed packed inside.

The rifle was chambered in .308 Winchester and specifically designed to be broken down into three parts, each no longer than sixteen inches. In under sixty seconds, Reed fully assembled the weapon, unfolding the stock until it clicked into place, then slipped the barrel into the receiver and used the included torque wrench to tighten the barrel nut. The forward rail locked into the receiver with a satisfying snap, and just like that, the rifle was ready to fire.

It cost Reed only five hundred bucks to acquire the Remington off a particularly corrupt police sergeant. There were plenty of CSRs in circulation down here, and Reed seriously doubted any of the locals appreciated the weapon's true potential. Too bad he'd have to ditch the rifle following the hit.

Reed flicked the lens caps up on either end of the pre-mounted Leupold scope, then deployed the bipod and settled onto his stomach six feet inside the sliding glass door. The rifle's butt rested easily against his shoulder as he closed his left eye and squinted into the scope. Through the gap he'd left in the curtain, he had a clear view of Diablo's balcony five hundred yards away.

Reed adjusted the scope's zoom, then took a long breath and settled his cheek against the stock. He swept the crosshairs from left to right, surveying the entire width of the balcony. A glass wall guarded the edge, standing four feet tall and topped by a brass railing. Diablo was short—not much over five feet—but Reed only needed to see his head.

One shot. Five hundred yards. Diablo wouldn't stand a chance.

All Reed had to do was get him outside.

2

The last three years had been a whirlwind for Maggie Trousdale. Born to a fisherman and a cook deep in the swamps of southern Louisiana, she took life in the slow lane for most of her first thirty years—not graduating from Louisiana State University until she was twenty-six and taking just as long to finish her law degree at Baylor. By the time she returned to her swampy home outside of New Orleans and seriously began to consider what her career would look like, she was in her early thirties and still single.

That was when she made the fateful decision to meet some college friends for a birthday party at a local bar. The TV was playing newsreels of yet another Baton Rouge political scandal involving the recently resigned governor, and one of her drunk sorority sisters cheekily suggested that Maggie should take his place.

Everybody had a good laugh, but when Maggie woke up, the idea stuck. Awkward but passionate, Maggie had long felt she was destined for greater things. Her humble upbringing in the swamps had taught her the value of simplicity, but the twin diplomas on her wall represented the promise of ambition. The only thing she lacked was a cause to champion, and as she casually began to investigate the reality of politics in Baton Rouge, she found her cause.

The city was rank with corruption. Both political and corporate, the news stories were endless, covering dirty cops, unscrupulous bureaucrats, and shady prosecutors. How had the home she loved suffered so long without anyone challenging the status quo?

The political campaign Maggie launched was never intended to land her in the governor's mansion. She ran as an Independent, with the sole goal of shining a light on enduring corruption. The people of Louisiana had other plans. By the time Maggie realized what a wildfire she had ignited, it was too late to back out. She was elected by a landslide and went to work immediately to deliver on her campaign promises.

The investigations that resulted were the stuff of Hollywood movies. Maggie uncovered a sprawling pharmaceutical scheme threatening the lives of thousands, and the resulting roller coaster of breaking news shoved her into the national spotlight. In the space of less than two years, Maggie Trousdale advanced from hometown beer pong champion to corruption-crushing superstar on the national political stage.

And now she was about to meet the most powerful man in the Free World—the president of the United States, William J. Brandt.

Maggie smoothed her dress and self-consciously inspected her shoes as the Tahoe rumbled over winding Maryland roads. During her governor's campaign, she maintained a trademark boots-and-jeans wardrobe. The look earned her the nickname Muddy Maggie, a moniker one of her opponents intended as a barb, but it was quickly converted into a battle cry by her supporters.

Maggie loved the nickname, but it didn't feel appropriate to meet the sitting president wearing boots and jeans. A staffer in Baton Rouge loaned her the dress and heels, and Maggie even made an attempt at makeup. The entire ensemble made her feel like an imposter.

The Tahoe groaned on its suspension as the Secret Service driver turned off the highway and onto an asphalt road overhung by towering trees. The countryside was beautiful. Bright wildflowers adorned the ditches, and songbirds flitted among the trees. The bulletproof windows of the Tahoe blocked out the world, but Maggie imagined she could smell the warm breeze, and it made her feel a little less claustrophobic.

"Would you like some water, ma'am?"

The man to her right spoke with a Cajun drawl even heavier than her own. At six foot one and two hundred thirty pounds, James O'Dell was an imposing figure, but his stern demeanor failed to fully disguise the heart of gold hidden beneath his Louisiana State Police badge.

O'Dell was her personal bodyguard and had been the lead officer of her security detail for the majority of her term as governor. He was difficult to work for and didn't tolerate fools, but despite that, Maggie liked him. Maybe that was *why* she liked him.

She accepted a water bottle and sipped as the Tahoe passed through the heavily guarded front gates of Camp David. A wooden sign hanging from chains swung in the breeze, advertising the storied private retreat of the president, and Maggie couldn't help but take a moment to drink in the scenery. Her meteoric rise to stardom had left almost no time for her to appreciate the trajectory of her life. Deep inside, she knew she should feel lucky to be here, lucky to be governor, and lucky to be en route to meet the president.

Instead, she felt overwhelmed and out of place, like a con artist who had gotten in over her head and was about to be busted.

"First time at Camp David, ma'am?" the driver asked.

"Yes," she said.

The two Secret Service agents riding in front had barely spoken since collecting her at Dulles International Airport an hour and a half previously. The silence was both comforting and unnerving.

"We're proud to have you," the driver said. "You know, Camp David was originally called Shangri-La, which means 'heavenly place.' President Eisenhower renamed the installation in honor of his father and grandson, both named David."

"Installation?" Maggie asked.

"Camp David is a military installation, ma'am."

"Oh, I didn't realize." Maggie watched the passing forest as the SUV wound deeper into the camp, the smooth asphalt rising and twisting beneath the tires. Sunlight broke through the trees far above, raining down in golden glory over a field of fallen leaves.

It was easy to see why a place like this could be considered heavenly.

As they rounded another curve, a series of squat buildings came into view. They were plainer than Maggie expected, built in a cabin-style similar to what she'd seen the Army Corps of Engineers build inside state parks. A row of cars lined one side of the parking lot, and gardeners worked in flower beds next to what appeared to be the main building.

It was as picturesque as it was simple, and Maggie found herself reassured by both.

The driver guided them to the back corner of the parking lot, where a one-story cabin sat by itself, the front porch adorned with an expansive display of potted tulips. O'Dell slid out ahead of the Secret Service agents but still didn't beat them to Maggie's door. The driver swung it open, and she stepped out into the warm August air. The breeze was just as fragrant and refreshing as she imagined, and the sun on her bare arms eased her nerves.

"The president is ready for you now, ma'am," the driver said. He turned toward the steps, and O'Dell moved to follow.

The second Secret Service agent held up a hand, blocking O'Dell's path. "I'm sorry, sir. Only the governor is permitted beyond this point."

O'Dell's jaw twitched, a tic usually preceding a defiant outburst.

Maggie put a hand on his arm and gave him a nod. "It's okay." She turned to the agent blocking his path. "Is there someplace Officer O'Dell can relax? It's been a long trip."

"Of course, ma'am." The agent gestured toward the main building across the parking lot, and O'Dell begrudgingly followed, casting a suspicious glance over his shoulder.

Maggie followed the driver into the cabin, stepping through wide pine doors and into a sprawling atrium. It was cool inside and smelled of burning candles. The walls were adorned with oak planks, and a subdued chandelier hung from the ceiling, casting gentle light over a hardwood floor. Everything was spotlessly clean and fresh, but just as simple as the exterior.

The agent led her through the atrium, around a stone fireplace, and into the living room. Beyond an assortment of leather chairs and couches were floor-to-ceiling windows, polished so perfectly they almost appeared invisible. Outside, a covered porch overlooked the forest.

Maggie's escort stopped and motioned through the door. "The president is waiting, ma'am."

Maggie's stomach twisted, and she resisted the urge to swallow.

Here goes nothing.

President Brandt sat at the end of the wraparound porch and leaned back in an Adirondack chair with a glass of liquor in one hand. When Maggie stepped onto the deck, he stood, setting the drink down and starting toward her with a smile bright enough to illuminate a football stadium.

"Welcome to Camp David, Madam Governor."

Brandt looked tall on television, but in person, he was of average height. Trim and well built, and in his late fifties with more salt than pepper in his hair, Maggie had to admit he was a handsome man. Twenty years earlier, he may have even been a looker.

"Thank you, Mr. President. It's an honor to be here."

Brandt shook her hand and held her gaze. The smile continued on his lips but didn't meet his eyes, which stared deep into hers with a searching, piercing intensity that made her feel strangely exposed, as if he could read her thoughts.

"Would you care for a drink, Maggie? May I call you Maggie?"

"Of course, Mr. President."

Brandt moved to the table resting next to his chair and retrieved a spare glass. "Call me William, please. I come to Camp David to take a break from the presidency."

Maggie wasn't sure what to say to that, so she said nothing. She accepted the glass and took a perfunctory sip of bourbon as Brandt resumed his searching stare. The liquor was good, but it couldn't take the edge off her nerves.

"Good trip?" Brandt asked.

"Yes, sir. It was smooth."

"Great."

Brandt sipped his drink without breaking eye contact. The silence on the deck was near perfect, with only the distant chirp of a songbird to break it. The uneasiness in Maggie's stomach grew but was now joined by irritation. Brandt's incessant stare breached the appropriate and bordered on the annoying. Maggie didn't like to be toyed with—not by anyone—so she stared right back, unblinking, and she waited.

At last, Brandt nodded, almost as if he were nodding to himself. "Would you walk with me?"

"Of course, sir."

Brandt carried his drink, and Maggie was subconsciously aware of the agent from the door following them at a distance. Brandt's shoes crunched over gravel, one hand in his pocket, one hand cradling the drink. His shoulders were loose, but behind the facade of relaxation, Maggie detected an undercurrent of tension. Stress, maybe. Or calculation.

Whatever it was, it put her on guard.

He led her to a small parking pad near the cabin, where a golf cart rested underneath a shed. Polished wheels and gleaming chrome adorned the cart, and Brandt motioned for her to take the passenger seat.

He left his drink on the parking pad and flipped the ignition with a cheesy grin. "They call it Golf Cart One."

Maggie forced a polite laugh, rotating the drink in her hand awkwardly. She wasn't sure what to do with it.

Brandt drove down winding asphalt trails, taking them deeper into the trees. Maggie couldn't see any more Secret Service agents, but the stillness around them felt loaded, as though they were being watched.

"How are things in Louisiana?" he asked.

Maggie detected the tone of a polite question and decided to provide a polite answer. "Wonderful, sir. It's an honor to serve the state."

Brandt adjusted his grip on the wheel, his gaze flicking across the trail ahead.

Maggie noticed white knuckles, and her uneasiness returned.

Why am I here?

"I suppose you heard about Gardener?"

The president's question took Maggie off guard. Harvey Gardener was —or rather, had been—Brandt's vice president. Three weeks prior, a news story broke about questionable campaign funding used in Gardener's 2010 campaign for governor of his home state of Missouri. The press sank their teeth into the story with a ferocity reserved strictly for the juiciest political scandals, and two weeks later, Gardener resigned and disappeared. Another casualty of corruption.

"I heard," Maggie said.

"He was a good man," Brandt said. "Or . . . I thought he was. That's the thing about Washington, Maggie. You never really know people."

Brandt shot her another piercing stare. This time Maggie refused to indulge him, turning her attention to a chipmunk bounding through the leaves.

What the hell is going on?

Brandt pulled the cart off the road. "Here we are! My favorite spot."

Next to the road, Maggie saw a narrow, winding trail leading through the trees and up a hill. A hundred yards away, a small gazebo sat at the top, surrounded by trees and wildflowers.

I had to wear heels.

Brandt walked slowly, his hands clasped behind his back, his face turned toward the ground. Maggie saw the tension radiating from his posture and felt more of the same in her own stomach.

"I wanted to ask you about the Resilient Pharmaceutical case," Brandt said.

Of course you do.

Maggie didn't mind talking about the case. She'd spent most of the last year talking about it, touring national news media and holding press conferences. It was, after all, her claim to fame. But there were certain questions about the case she couldn't answer— certain details that could never see the light of day. Brandt's interest was probably innocent, but thus far, nothing about this meeting felt innocent.

"What would you like to know, Mr. President?"

Brandt stopped on the trail. "I want to know why you did it."

"I'm sorry, sir?"

"Why did you go after Resilient?"

"Because it was my job, sir."

Brandt grunted, studying a gnarled oak tree that leaned over the path.

He started walking again. "They tell me you have no political affiliations, no big contributors, no corporate partners."

"That's true."

"They tell me you ran your campaign on piecemeal donations."

"Under a hundred thousand, total," Maggie said. "We're very proud of that."

"That's quite an accomplishment. Especially for a candidate of your age."

Maggie chose to ignore the barb and kept walking.

"What are your ambitions at the end of your term?" Brandt said. "Reelection, I assume?"

Maggie watched a robin glide out of a tree and land among the leaves, it's auburn chest puffed out like a life vest. This was the question every news pundit, campaign partner, and voter wanted to know. And it was a question she wasn't prepared to answer. She'd give Brandt her standard response. "We're focused on Louisiana right now, Mr. President. We'll cross the reelection bridge when we come to it."

They reached the gazebo, and Brandt stepped onto worn planks, standing with his back to her and staring out at the forest. Maggie remained behind, still awkwardly holding the drink. She took a swallow, if for nothing else than to ease her nerves.

"You're probably wondering why you're here," Brandt said. His voice now assumed an undertone of command.

"I am."

Brandt's fingers twisted the wedding ring on his left hand. He took a deep breath, then turned around. "You're here because I want you to become the next vice president of the United States."

The glass almost slipped from Maggie's fingers. Brandt stared at her a long moment, then motioned to the bench seat that ran around the interior of the gazebo. Maggie took a seat, feeling a little dizzy, and Brandt sat across from her, crossing his legs.

"I'm . . . I'm not sure what to say, Mr. President."

Brandt dusted his right knee with one hand. "Why don't you say yes?"

Maggie's head spun. Of the two dozen possible reasons she'd guessed Brandt wanted to see her, this never entered the list. Not even close.

Vice president? Has the man lost his mind?

"I really don't think I'm cut out to—"

"To be a leader? The last two years tell a different story. I have eighteen months remaining on my term—the same as you. Of course I plan to run again. I'm thinking about the next five years, Maggie. I'm thinking about what my administration needs to be successful. And what it needs is a strong vice president. Somebody without baggage. Somebody the people can trust."

So, that's it. He's thinking about his campaign.

The answer was obvious, and Maggie wanted to kick herself for not seeing it before. Of course Brandt was thinking about reelection. After the Gardener scandal, he needed to distance himself from corruption as far as possible. What better way than to nominate Miss Anti-Corruption herself?

Maggie might be uncomfortable with her own celebrity, but that didn't mean she was blind to it. She set the drink down and sat straight-backed. Suddenly, she didn't feel so awkward anymore. She didn't mind being summoned to Camp David, or playing along with the president's lengthy and roundabout way of reaching his point. But she very much minded being used.

"With respect, Mr. President. I'm not a Democrat."

"You're not a Republican, either. You're that rare unicorn of American politics . . . a *successful* Independent."

"Yes, sir."

Brandt grunted. "And you don't want to hitch your wagon to a party."

"I just want to make a difference."

Brandt's gaze drifted off into the trees. When he spoke, his voice was dragged down by an exhausted undertone. "I'm going to be honest with you, Maggie. Off the record. Can I do that?"

"Of course, sir."

"Partisan politics are breaking our nation. I started this game a long, long time ago. I've seen . . . a lot of things." He faced her again. "We play this game of party line, but the truth is, there are only two parties in America, and they don't begin with the letters D and R. They're the parties of money and power, and the life of a politician is that of bouncing between the two, sacrificing one in the name of serving the other, always on a quest to somehow win them both. It's an ugly, endless cycle, and I've seen the machine break one starry-eyed rookie after another. Sometimes quickly, sometimes slowly, but always, in the end." Brandt folded his arms. "You don't reach the top with clean hands."

Maggie's stomach twisted, and she thought again about the Resilient Pharmaceutical case.

You have no idea, Mr. President.

"You can help me win reelection," Brandt said. "I won't pretend otherwise, but there's a bigger picture. Washington needs an outsider. Somebody without decades of political affiliations, favors, and skeletons in the closet. Somebody who can fight corruption today and help lay the groundwork for something bigger tomorrow. Muddy Maggie . . . for president."

Maggie didn't move. Brandt kept that piercing gaze on her, and she felt both ice and fire in her veins. She didn't know Brandt well enough to judge his true motives, but the manipulation was obvious. It infuriated her, while the irresistible appeal of his offer dangled over her nose like a chunk of red meat just out of reach of a dog.

Who was she kidding? Did she really pretend she'd never lain awake late at night and thought . . . maybe? Someday? The pinnacle of any political career. The ultimate office of the land. Nobody who tasted power could pretend they hadn't dreamed of it.

"Are you trying to buy me, Mr. President?"

The words popped out of her mouth before she could stop them, but Brandt didn't seem offended.

"I don't buy people, Maggie. I'm trying to recruit you."

"You barely know me."

"True. But I know counterfeits. I know fakers. I've spent years dealing with them, so I know when somebody is different. You're different, Maggie. You're the real deal. And I need that." Brandt interlaced his fingers. "You said you wanted to make a difference. I'm telling you, there's no better place on Earth to do that than from the White House."

3

Bogotá, Colombia

The prostitute left Diablo's hotel just after ten p.m. Reed knew because he'd seen the woman twice before, exiting the G-Wagon with her arm interlinked with Diablo's and fawning over him like he was the prince of the world. Reed stood in the shadows across the street from the entrance of the Four Seasons and watched her wait on the curb, dressed in a miniskirt with a windbreaker pulled over her shoulders and smoking a cigarette until her cab arrived.

Reed checked his watch as the car pulled away, then stepped across the street, splashing through a puddle left by the late afternoon storm that brought with it the humidity. Cradled under his arm was a cigar box wrapped in gold paper with a note attached. Housed inside the box was a Cohiba Spectre, a rare Cuban cigar made of eight different types of tobacco, each individually aged in a barrel before being blended into one of the most opulent and expensive smokes available.

Something Diablo would find irresistible.

The note attached to the box was written in Spanish, scrawled by the man at the tobacco shop Reed purchased the cigar from. Reed transcribed the message himself and allowed the shop owner to translate—a simple congratulations for successful negotiations, signed by Diablo's rival.

The man who hired Reed to kill him.

Reed approached the hotel's service desk and handed the concierge the box. "Para el señor Castillo," he said. His Spanish was weak at best, but the concierge accepted the box. Reed retreated out of the hotel, hailing a cab and directing the driver back to the AC Marriott.

Over the last four years, Reed had assassinated over three dozen targets, and in his experience, the key to success had a lot more to do with understanding humanity than it did any special tactic or equipment. Reed could've stormed the Four Seasons and gunned down the guards. He could've planted a car bomb on the G-Wagon, or, for that matter, planted a bomb in the cigar box.

Any of those methods would've likely worked, but none of them were certain, and all of them left Reed far too close to the target at the completion of the kill. Diablo was a careful man, but he was still human, and the weakness in his armor could be found at the intersection of his most comfortable environment and his most treasured vice.

Reed didn't need to force his way past Diablo's defenses. He only needed to give the drug lord a reason to let his guard down.

The cab dropped Reed back at his hotel, and he ascended to his room. Fully assembled beneath the bed lay the rifle, a magazine loaded with full-metal jacket, 150-grain cartridges resting near it. Reed locked the door and then proceeded to the bathroom, turning the shower to full blast and leaving the door open. Next, he flipped on the TV, flicking through the channels until he found a suitable action film, then ramped up the volume until the room was a mask of shower water and the screeching tires of a car chase.

He pulled the blinds back ten inches before sliding the balcony door open an equal amount, leaving just enough gap for a clear view of the Four Seasons. Diablo's balcony lay dark and empty, the blinds still pulled closed. Reed was unperturbed.

He retreated to the bed and withdrew the rifle, slipping a ten-inch suppressor over the muzzle and twisting until it was tight. The gunshot would still be loud—like the sound of a falling book hitting a tile floor—

but easily dismissible by other hotel guests, especially amid the roar of the shower and the commotion of the TV.

Reed settled onto his stomach at the end of the bed, ten feet inside the sliding glass door and safely sheltered by shadows. He slipped the rifle's magazine into place, then worked the bolt, ramming a single cartridge into the chamber. The stock settled easily into his shoulder, and his cheek rested against it.

Reed breathed. In . . . and out. For two full minutes, he didn't even look through the scope, focusing instead on calming his heartbeat, clearing his mind, and centering his body. Then he tilted his head toward the gun and closed his left eye.

The MIL-Dot reticle hovered over the stillness outside, giving him a clear view between the slats of his balcony railing at the city outside. Reed used his left hand to adjust the zoom, bringing the optic out to 8X, until he located Diablo's balcony, then zooming in to 24X.

The night was calm, and the view through the scope was crystal clear. Reed rested his trigger finger against the receiver and watched Diablo's window. The curtain was still closed, but he could see the flash of a television beneath its bottom edge.

Reed drew another long breath and relaxed his shoulders. He didn't mind waiting. He could wait this way all night long. But he didn't expect to.

It took half an hour for the curtains to flick back, exposing the blocky features of Diablo's bodyguard. The big man pulled the curtain back a foot, then leaned into the window, looking suspiciously to either side of the balcony. Reed centered the crosshairs over his face and waited. From this distance, the man's head appeared little larger than a coffee mug, but with ease, Reed was able to hold the crosshairs just a few inches above it, allowing for bullet-drop.

One press of the trigger, and Block-Face would become Hamburger-Face.

At last, the bodyguard pushed the curtain back and opened the door far enough to step out onto the balcony. He looked either way once more, as if he expected assassins to materialize out of thin air, then lit a cigarette.

Reed watched his arms move—the only indicator of his activity. He couldn't make out the faint glow of the smoke from this far away, but the body language was unmistakable. The guy smoked for a while, a faint haze gathering around his head. Then he waved his hand over the rail—probably disposing of the smoke—and turned inside. He didn't shut the door.

Reed flicked the safety off but kept his trigger finger resting against the receiver. Another three minutes passed in slow motion, hallmarked by Reed's systematic breaths. A cigar could be smoked inside, and Reed knew plenty of people did just that, but during his previous encounters with Diablo, he remembered the drug lord preferring to smoke outside in the fresh Colombian breeze. With an exquisite cigar at hand, who could resist the full experience?

Diablo appeared on the balcony. He wore nothing but a bathrobe, and his skin glistened with the residue of a recent shower. He stepped to the rail, then called something over his shoulder. A moment later, the bodyguard reappeared and offered Diablo a glass.

The drug lord's head dipped, and Reed made out the silhouette of the cigar. It wasn't a fake—Reed had sprung for the genuine article, even though he might have skimped and simply swapped packaging. Call it a last meal, or a twist of irony. After months of dodging Diablo's assassins, Reed wanted to hallmark this moment with a little of each.

This time, Reed made out just a flicker of orange from the much larger tip of the cigar. Diablo leaned his head back and breathed upward. Reed guided the crosshairs over the drug lord's neck, past his chin, and over his scalp to a point about eight feet above his head.

The Leupold optic affixed to the top of the rifle wasn't equipped with target turrets used to adjust windage and elevation, forcing Reed to adopt a shooting technique known as "holdover"—aiming above his desired point of impact to compensate for the drop of the bullet. Exiting the muzzle at a velocity of about 2,800 feet per second, the bullet would fly straight for almost one hundred eighty yards, but by five hundred, it would drop as much as a hundred inches, or a little over eight feet. Reed spent the better part of the afternoon calculating and recalculating the trajectory, adjusting for humidity and air density to ensure the perfect shot. It was complex math, but he knew it well.

Diablo now stood on the edge of the great unknown, smoking casually as if Hell itself were an afterthought. Reed laid his finger on the trigger as a gray cloud obscured the space above Diablo's head. He would wait until the drug lord stood still during his next puff. Flight time for the 150-grain bullet would be almost exactly one second.

Diablo raised the cigar to his lips, and the orange tip blazed as air was sucked through it. Reed squeezed.

The rifle snapped, smacking him in the shoulder, the noise lost amid the continued blare of the TV. For a split second, Reed's vision was a mess of sky and clouds as the optic shot upward, but he quickly brought it back down to the balcony, sweeping the length of the glass wall.

Diablo lay on his side, a blast of crimson coating the glass door behind him. A growing pool joined his body, and he didn't move. He just lay there, a wisp of smoke still rising from the fallen cigar.

Reed lifted his head from the weapon, sucking in a deep breath of gunpowder-flavored air. In mere seconds, the weapon was unloaded, disassembled, and hidden in the bottom of the bag. Reed flicked the TV off as somebody pounded on his door, fussing in distorted Spanish. He quickly removed his shirt, wet his hair in the shower, then wrapped a towel around his waist and opened the door.

The desk clerk stood outside, her olive cheeks a little flushed with irritation. As soon as she saw him, she switched from Spanish to English. "Señor, I'm very sorry. Your television is too loud."

"It's okay," Reed said. "I was just leaving."

4

The house in the swamp leaned a little to one side. Green slime grew up the north wall, and leaves littered the roof. The mile-long driveway was mired with holes and ruts, and the home featured no running water.

But for all of that, Maggie still thought of the disheveled lake house as her favorite getaway from the pressures of Baton Rouge. Built by her grandfather almost fifty years ago, and used by the entire family for summer vacations during her childhood, the property was now all but abandoned. It sat empty for the majority of the year, save for when Maggie found time to break away from the Capitol and steal herself away to the solace of the swamp.

Early in her term, the house was the sight of an attempted assassination, during which both of her on-site bodyguards were gunned down. Maggie shot the would-be assassin during his flight through the trees, but ever since then, O'Dell insisted on a five-man team whenever she visited the swamp. Louisiana state cops carried AR-15s as they patrolled the drive and the yard leading down to the brackish water of the lake, and O'Dell himself remained on guard next to the front door, his own rifle close at hand.

Maggie thought it was all absurd, but after so many stress-filled months as governor, the presence of a few cops was a small concession to make. At least she could escape the reporters, staffers, state politicians, and endless lobbyists. At least she could escape the office, just for a while. In that way, the mucky house by the lake was her own little version of Camp David.

"Remember that summer with the gator?"

Maggie's younger brother Larry sat next to her on the slouching back porch, overlooking the lake a hundred yards away. The moon glinted off the slimy water, and a distant fish flipped among rotting tree stumps.

Maggie sipped from a glass of Chardonnay. She remembered the gator, all right. The entire family—complete with cousins, aunts, uncles, and grandparents—had packed into the lake house for a long Labor Day weekend. Unbeknownst to the adults, Maggie and Larry had captured a two-foot adolescent alligator and kept it like a pet in one of the bedroom closets for the duration of the weekend.

The little guy was lethargic at first, but the longer they left him in there, the more active he became until he eventually escaped the closet and scrambled into the hallway. Upon reaching the living room, all hell broke loose. One of Maggie's cousins had married a city girl from Dallas, and she screamed like a ten-year-old on a roller coaster. Things got worse when Maggie's grandfather reached for a shotgun.

The alligator escaped, but there were still buckshot scars in one corner of the living room. Maggie and Larry were grounded for a month.

Larry chuckled, putting one arm behind his neck as he sucked on a cigarette. Maggie drained the wineglass and poured herself another, slumping into the cheap camping chair and enjoying the dull buzz in the back of her brain.

Since childhood, she and Larry had been inseparable, though they were different in almost every way. Maggie was bookish and a bit nerdy. Larry was outdoorsy and struggled in school. But those differences somehow bred respect, not distance, and that connection lasted through Maggie's whirlwind of a career. Months sometimes passed without a moment like this, drinking together or catching up, but Larry was always there. He was the first person she called when chaos overcame her in Baton Rouge—the first person she called after leaving Camp David.

"What should I do, Larry?" Maggie watched ripples play against the boat shed and thought about every decision she'd made since leaving law school. They were a lot like those ripples—building on one another and radiating across the swamp until they eventually drove her someplace unexpected.

Larry tugged on the cigarette. He always took his time answering questions, and she liked that about him. It made her feel like he really cared about the conversation.

"What do you *want* to do?" Larry said.

And there was something she liked less about him. He often answered questions with questions.

"Go home. Open a law practice. Maybe date somebody for a change."

Larry just grunted.

"What?"

He dropped the cigarette butt in a waiting ashtray and promptly lit another.

"*What?*" Maggie repeated.

Larry blew smoke between his teeth. "Nothing. I just wonder who you're trying to convince."

Maggie folded her arms. "What are you trying to say?"

"What are you trying to hear?"

"Answer my questions, idiot."

Larry grinned, and Maggie couldn't resist a chuckle. She sipped wine and threw one hand up. "You don't think I want to be out? Want to be home?"

"Honestly?"

"Of course."

"I really don't."

Maggie's wineglass hung midair. She glanced sideways at him, and Larry shrugged. She set the glass down and looked out at the swamp again. The quiet was near perfect, disturbed only by the distant boot falls of one of her sentries on patrol. She used to love this quiet. She used to long for it on busy days when it felt like she could never catch a break.

But now . . . it felt a little hollow. Like something was missing.

"You remember your first campaign rally?" Larry asked.

Maggie winced. She tried not to remember it. "It was awful," she said. "Terrible speech."

Larry nodded. "Horrendous. But that's not the point."

She waited for him to gather his thoughts. It took another two tugs on the cigarette.

"The spirit of those people when they left that rally . . . it was something special. They felt empowered. They felt hope." He nodded a couple times, as if to himself. "But more than that, I've never seen you like you are now."

"A stressed-out asshole?"

"Predominantly. But a passionate asshole. An asshole with a vision."

He ground the cigarette out in the ashtray and faced her for the first time. "You do whatever you want. But you weren't born to draft wills and catch catfish on the weekend. You have a way with people—both as a leader and as an adversary. It's somethin' special."

Maggie looked away, feeling suddenly awkward. She gulped wine and thought about the gator again.

Why are the best times always in the rearview?

"If I did this, it would change everything," she said.

"Yup."

"It wouldn't be quiet anymore. There would be people, news media . . ."

"Probably."

"And he's probably just using me. Just trying to get reelected. It might begin and end with the vice presidency."

Larry shot her a coy smile. "Or it might not."

He stood up slowly, stretching his lanky frame before giving her shoulder a gentle squeeze.

"Love ya, Mags. Whatever you decide, I got your back."

He disappeared inside, and a moment later she heard his old pickup growl to life, followed by tires fading down the drive.

Maggie sat by herself, watching the water. It was perfectly still now. No ripples disturbed the surface, but the gleam of the moon was blurred by the gunk floating on the water. Both peaceful and murky—beautiful and sordid.

Like life. Like politics. Like the opportunity lying at her feet.

A million people probably dreamed of a chance like this. To jump from law school to governor to vice president in under four years? An unthinkable rise. But at what price?

She thought about the swamps. She thought about her beloved hometown, LSU football games, and getting drunk with her cousins at college dive bars. Everything she loved most. What she always believed she wanted, and yet . . . she was already letting it go. Because someplace deep inside, from the moment Brandt offered her the job, she knew she was going to take it.

Larry might call it passion. A therapist might call it a power complex. Whatever it was, Maggie had tasted the life of a political superstar, and she wasn't about to relinquish it.

She reached into her jeans pocket and pried her phone out. The buzz in the back of her head was still there, but she wouldn't wait for the morning. She had to do this now, before she lost her nerve.

"Maggie?"

"Mr. President, I hope it's not too late."

"Not at all. I'm glad you called." Brandt's tone was all business but seemed genuine.

Maggie heard a door close on the other end of the line, then the president cleared his throat.

"Have you considered my offer?"

Maggie's heart thumped, and her fingertips felt suddenly electric.

"I have, sir."

"And?"

"And . . ." She sat up. "And I accept, sir."

"Excellent." Brandt sounded neither surprised nor exuberant. Just satisfied. "I'm pleased to hear that."

"I'm honored with the opportunity, sir."

"Have you told anyone?"

"Just my brother."

"Good. Let's keep it that way. I'll submit your official nomination to Congress tomorrow. With luck, we can schedule confirmation hearings for next week. You'll need to be in Washington, of course."

Maggie sat bolt upright. "Wait . . . next week?"

"Absolutely. We can likely have you in office by the end of the month. I don't expect any pushback from the hill."

"But . . ." Maggie's head spun. She wasn't sure if it was the alcohol or the reality of what she was being told. *This month?* She'd expected weeks to transition out of Baton Rouge—weeks to plan her move, consider a vice presidential staff, prepare for Washington . . .

Brandt's tone dropped a notch. "But?"

"It just seems very sudden, sir."

"Is that a problem, Madam Governor?"

Maggie felt the edge in Brandt's voice, and she lifted her chin. "Not at all, Mr. President. I'm ready to go."

5

"One hell of a shot!" The overweight Venezuelan behind the table leaned back, the stub of a cigar smoldering from the corner of his mouth.

Reed didn't miss the irony as he stood stiff-backed and slowly counted the pile of American currency heaped in front of him. Fifty thousand dollars sounded like a lot, but in person, it wasn't much to look at. Reed counted the five banded stacks of one-hundred-dollar bills before slipping them into his backpack next to a SIG Sauer P226 pistol, then he shouldered the bag.

"Gone so soon?" Massimo withdrew the cigar, smirking at Reed as if he were a hooker or a street-level coke slinger. Just another expendable contractor for hire.

"We done?" Reed asked.

Massimo rolled the cigar between chubby fingers. The two gunmen standing on either side of his chair sported AK-47s and body armor. Reed wasn't impressed. He could take them both with head shots from the SIG long before the clumsy rifles were untangled from their poorly managed slings.

"We don't have to be," Massimo said. "I could use a man like you. A man with . . . finesse. Is that the right word? My English is subpar."

Massimo's English was fine, even if his attempt at self-deprecating humor fell fatally short.

"We're done," Reed said. "I think that's best for everyone."

Massimo leaned forward, his brow furrowing. "Is that a threat, American?"

"Not at all. Just a perspective." Reed turned for the door.

Massimo chuckled. "What if I have another perspective? What if I think you're a liability?"

Reed stopped, one hand on the knob. "In that case, I'd say you should remember what happened to Diablo. And yes"—he looked over his shoulder—"that was a threat."

The room felt suddenly ice cold, but Reed didn't break eye contact with Massimo. He stared until the moment lingered closer to a minute, then left the building.

⸻

Reed walked six miles through Medellín, switching back on his route four times and twice taking sharp detours through congested markets before contenting himself that Massimo hadn't sent anyone to follow him. Without a doubt, if he remained in Colombia past nightfall, there would be a price on his head. Maybe because he threatened Diablo's successor. Maybe because he truly was a loose end.

Regardless, he doubted that Massimo would waste the time or expenditure in tracking him all the way back to Central America, where Reed had made a temporary home just inland of the Pacific coast in the tiny Honduran town of Nacaome. It would take three days to reach it, riding public transportation busses and trains, and slipping through checkpoints using a series of fake Panamanian passports. But Reed couldn't fly. He was on too many international watch lists, and anyway, being on board a plane restricted his ability to flee.

After clearing the second market, Reed changed clothes in a public bathroom, quickly cutting away the blond ends of his dyed hair and tugging a baseball cap over the resulting brown stubble. Jeans replaced the cargo pants, and a light windbreaker replaced the utility jacket. Only the pistol remained—tucked into his waistband—while the cash and the passports rode in the backpack.

He made the border with Panama by midnight and slipped through customs without issue after flashing a domestic passport. The pistol was easy to smuggle, as was the money. Panamanian border security was a lot more concerned about drugs than they were small stacks of cash or the occasional handgun. After what he'd seen in South America, Reed couldn't blame them.

He tried to sleep on the bus into Panama City, but Reed found it hard to sleep anywhere other than his makeshift Honduran home, and with Banks, his bride of ten months. He met her in an Atlanta bar only a year before while working as a for-hire assassin, hunting down what turned out to be her godfather. The resulting chaos of that job—what was meant to be his *last* job—spilled into a private war with an underground criminal organization and eventually resulted in the exposure of a pharmaceutical scam threatening the lives of thousands.

Reed dealt with that criminal organization and their scam the same way he dealt with anyone who crossed him—without mercy. Those guys had been hurting a lot of innocent people, but some of Reed's methods in destroying them were altogether too violent to be forgiven, and he and Banks had been on the run from the FBI ever since, bouncing around first South America and now Central America in an attempt to find a safe haven.

The Diablo hit was a last resort to keep food on the table. It turned out that after years of work as an elite killer, preceded by years of work as a Force Recon Marine, Reed wasn't much good at finding or keeping a day job. Life in the Latin world was inexpensive, but it wasn't free, and besides food and shelter, Banks needed medical care for an ongoing battle with Lyme's disease. With luck, fifty grand would hold them over for another twelve months, after which, well, Reed would cross that bridge when he came to it. The only thing he knew for sure was that Banks would be taken care of, no matter the cost. In a perfect world, Reed would be finished with killing and embrace some quiet, honest profession. He always thought he'd enjoy working on cars, but neither the FBI nor his own restless spirit would allow for that. For the time being, he was at peace with not being at peace.

The journey through Costa Rica and Nicaragua passed without incident, and in Tegucigalpa, Reed hired a local farmer to drive him down dusty farm roads the final two hours to Nacaome. The little town sat on the banks of the Nacaome River, where fewer than twenty thousand people called it home. Reed's rented shack lay on the outskirts, sitting by itself on the bottom edge of a mountain ridge surrounded by trees. Even by Honduran standards, the property was humble, but Reed enjoyed the seclusion. It made him feel a little safer from the ever-watchful eye of the FBI . . . at least for now.

He asked the farmer to drop him four miles out and then paid him in Honduran lempira while adding a generous tip. Then Reed repeated his laborious pattern of switchbacks and circles, ensuring he wasn't being followed before closing on the shack.

The driveway was empty when Reed arrived. The two-room house sat slouched under a Spanish cedar tree, the lot around it overgrown with jungle vegetation. Reed picked his way up a footpath, surveying the yard and listening for sounds from the home. All was silent . . . Deathly so.

He reached the front door and twisted the knob. It wasn't locked, and Reed took a half step back, placing his hand on the SIG. Jumping off the porch, he circled quietly around the house, avoiding exposure to the windows and still listening for sounds from inside. The rising slope of the mountainside turned sharply upward just behind the shack, leaving a narrow plateau just wide enough for a washbasin and a small flower pot Banks grew herbs in. Reed recognized Baxter's food bowl on the ground, but there was no sign of the aged English bulldog.

He put a hand on the back door, and again, the latch twisted under gentle pressure. Reed led with the SIG, keeping his finger stiff next to the receiver, and eased the door open. It swung on greased hinges, exposing the darkened interior of the main room—a living area on one side, a kitchen on the other, and a table in between. Reed cleared the room with a quick sweep of the pistol and hesitated in the door.

"Banks?"

No answer.

He moved quickly to the bedroom, brushing the curtain that served as a door out of the way, and still leading with the pistol.

"Banks?"

The bedroom featured a double bed and a pile of dirty clothes, but no Banks. No Baxter.

Reed's heartbeat quickened. Defensive instincts born of a thousand gunfights clicked into gear, and he dropped the backpack, retreating to the bed and reaching underneath it until his fingers touched the AK-47 wrapped in a blanket. In a split second, the weapon rested against his shoulder, a round ready in the chamber and the safety switched to the fire position.

Reed moved back to the living room, turning toward the door, and then he heard it—a distinct rumble rising from the road and growing steadily louder. It was as familiar a sound as Banks's gentle breaths or Baxter's incessant snoring. Reed stepped to the window, standing to one side and keeping his finger near the trigger as he slid the curtain back just far enough to peer into the fading light of the Honduran evening.

The Rally Green Chevrolet Camaro purred up the drive, its windshield clouded with dust, its fenders muddy and battered. One mirror was missing, and bullet holes crammed with body putty decorated the driver's side. Through the open driver's-side window, Reed recognized the blonde cloud of Banks's disheveled hair, and in the passenger seat next to her, Baxter's saggy face bounced with each pothole and rut.

Reed breathed out an exhausted sigh and slumped his shoulders. His heart still pounded, but some of the tension left his mind.

She's safe.

He replaced the AK but kept the SIG in his waistband as he stepped onto the front porch. Banks parked the antique car under the shelter of the Spanish cedar, and the door creaked open. He hurried down to meet her, and she fell into his arms. Her lips were soft and warm on his, her hand encircling his neck and pulling him close. For a long moment, neither of them spoke. They just kissed and held each other.

Then Banks's crystal blue eyes gleamed in the dying sun while a frown crossed her face. "You're late."

Reed looked away, somehow feeling awkward. Banks didn't know where he'd gone, or why, but she wasn't stupid. He told her he was going to get paid, and she knew he wasn't a thief. It would've been too risky to call while he was in Colombia. Anyone tracking him could've easily tracked the call. When the hit ran long, he was forced to leave Banks hanging.

"I'm sorry," he said at last. "Everything's okay."

Banks forced a smile. Her soft cheeks were flushed red, and when he stroked her face, her skin felt hot. Another Lyme flare, probably. The unbeatable disease would randomly ignite into a sort of fever, leaving her joints stiff and her skin hot while draining her energy. Banks endured without so much as a complaint, but it still crushed him to watch, knowing this was one battle he couldn't fight for her.

"You left the house unlocked," Reed said. "We've talked about this."

Banks pulled away, reaching into the back seat for a sack of groceries. Baxter climbed out, landing next to Reed's feet and turning his big, wrinkled face upward. Once upon a time, Baxter had been Reed's pet, but the bulldog had since reassigned loyalty.

"We needed food," Banks said. "I took what was left out of the change jar. It's not much, but . . . it'll do."

"Banks, I'm serious about the locks."

Her smile faded, and she turned toward the house. "I heard you already."

Banks stumbled onto the porch, and Reed watched her go. She'd lost weight since fleeing America. A year before, she'd been a little pudgy, but now Banks looked rail thin—almost malnourished. He hurried after her, holding the door open and pulling back the curtains to allow light into the home. There was electrical wiring in the walls, but it was faulty at best, and lately, they hadn't wanted to pay the power bill. At least the cash problem was solved for the time being.

Banks set the bag on the table but didn't turn to go into the kitchen. She stood facing the back door, hugging herself.

Reed heard her sniff, and he turned her around to see a tear shining on her cheek. "Hey . . ." Reed reached one battered thumb to her cheek, wiping a stray tear away.

She continued to hold herself, huddling a little.

"I'm sorry," he said. "I wanted to call. It wasn't safe."

She didn't answer. Reed ran a hand through her hair, stroking it back. Banks felt so small in his arms—almost like a child, battered and weak and worn down by a harsh life on the run.

"I shouldn't have mentioned the locks," he said. "I just . . . We have to be careful."

Banks faced him again. He saw something different in her face—strain, yes, but not sadness.

"It's not that," she whispered.

Reed brushed her cheek again. "What is it? What happened?"

Banks bit her lip, then she forced a small smile. "I'm pregnant."

6

"Madam Governor, how would you characterize the impact of your investigation of Resilient Pharmaceutical?"

Maggie shifted in the plush leather chair, staring out over a field of blue carpet that stretched between her and the high marble wall at the end of the room. A massive, V-shaped desk opened toward her, with United States senators positioned along each side.

She sat at a small, simple desk of her own, situated behind the V, with a microphone and a glass of water. A white nameplate mounted in front of her read: "Gov. Margaret Trousdale."

The senator who addressed her spoke with the speed and consistency of maple syrup dripping off a fork. He sat at the back of the V, kicking back in his chair, his fingers steepled in front of a triple chin. The esteemed John P. Wallinsby of Mississippi.

Maggie leaned toward the microphone. "I think the Resilient investigation will resonate with America for a long time. It's deeply troubling when one of our most trusted and critical industries is corrupted this deeply, but the only way you fix this stuff is by facing it. I'm proud of the work we did."

Wallinsby's sloppy lips smacked. "Allow me to rephrase, Governor. How would you say your leadership in the most successful organized crime bust in recent history has prepared you for the vice presidency?"

Maggie glanced around the room. A dozen senators were present, and only half of them paid her any attention. Most were busy playing with their phones, and she was almost sure one was asleep. Towering C-SPAN cameras faced her from either side, but even the camera operators seemed bored.

"Well, Senator . . . Leading the investigation against Resilient was certainly the greatest challenge of my life. My focus was justice for the people of Louisiana, and I propose to bring that same dedication to the Brandt administration. Corruption of any sort has no place in American politics, and that will be my policy, no matter my title."

Wallinsby's loose cheeks lifted into something a little more like a leer than a smile. His gaze drifted south of her face, and Maggie couldn't resist a soft frown.

Wallinsby drawled, "I have no further questions, Mr. Chairman."

The chairman leaned toward his mic. "The chair recognizes Senate Minority Leader Gallin of Colorado."

Maggie braced herself. Sitting across the political aisle from Brandt gave Mandy Gallin every reason to scorch her. If tough questions were coming, Gallin would bring them.

"Madam Governor, first let me say how refreshing it is to interview a fellow woman for such a prestigious role in our democracy. To begin our discussion, how would you say your achievements as a female in politics have prepared you for being one heartbeat away from the presidency?"

Seriously?

As she boarded her plane out of Baton Rouge a week prior, Maggie wasn't sure what to expect from her confirmation hearings. The vice presidency was the only presidential nomination that required review by both chambers of Congress, and the House took their turn first with three panels of hearings stretching over the course of four days.

Maggie was ready for brutal cross-examination, scalding challenges to her youth and inexperience, and relentless partisan pandering designed to align her with one party or the other. What she received was an endless parade of adoration, mixed with a steady diet of softball questions lobbed so slowly that Maggie could've shown up drunk and walked out a hero. Instead of undermining her résumé or forcing her into a political corner, congressional representatives from both sides of the aisle seemed more interested in wooing her into their corner.

It wasn't until senatorial confirmation hearings began and the dog and pony show resumed that Maggie finally understood: Congress had no *idea* what to do with her. Her reputation as a ruthless anti-corruption leader was bipartisan, and her national polling results were off the charts. Anyone who wasn't a sexist or a criminal loved her.

Sure, ninety percent of Congress probably hated her guts for both her success and her untouchability, but for the moment, at least, they couldn't appear to challenge her. Midterms were only three months away, and there was no political hay to be made out of attacking the superstar of the Resilient investigation . . . Only potential self-sabotage.

So here she sat, fielding another round of lazy invitations to sing her own praises. In one way, it was a relief. In another, it put her on edge.

When something feels too good to be true . . . it is.

Gallin completed her interview with two more softballs about Maggie's experiences in Baton Rouge, then yielded the remainder of her time to the chair.

Senator Mark Buchanan took the mic next, but instead of addressing Maggie, he faced his fellow senators. "I have just received word from our distinguished colleagues in the House that Governor Trousdale's confirmation has been confirmed by overwhelming vote. Rather than wasting any more of the governor's valuable time, I move to conclude hearings and expedite the people's work prior to lunch."

Maggie blinked, impulsively glancing at her watch. It was barely ten a.m.

"Is there a second?" the chair asked.

"Second," Wallinsby said with another jowled grin, his gaze still resting on Maggie's neckline.

"Objections?" the chair asked.

Nobody spoke.

"So moved. This hearing is adjourned. The chair thanks Governor Trousdale for her time."

A low murmur of voices filled the room as reporters migrated to the door and senators exchanged handshakes and slaps on the back. Maggie sat frozen in her chair a moment, then caught a grin and a wink from Gallin.

What the heck?

"Ma'am?" O'Dell appeared at her elbow, his hands crossed over his belt as he surveyed the room.

Maggie finished her water and followed him into the bustling hallway, where the army of reporters waited for a statement. She offered a few perfunctory words of gratitude to the Senate, then turned to find three suited men waiting for her.

"Madam Governor, I'm Agent Tom Jenkins with the Secret Service. We're here to relieve your protective detail."

O'Dell bristled like a skunk ready to detonate.

Maggie shook Jenkins's hand, then motioned him to follow her out. "You're welcome to tag along, Agent. O'Dell stays with me."

Jenkins exchanged a glance with one of his stone-faced colleagues, but he didn't protest. He led Maggie through another swarm of pressing reporters to where a Secret Service Tahoe waited outside. O'Dell hugged close to Maggie's side the entire way, glaring death at the reporters while pretending that Jenkins and his men were invisible. At the Tahoe, he held Maggie's door, then jumped into the front passenger seat before Jenkins could object. The agent waved a dismissive hand at the driver, then took the back seat next to Maggie.

As the SUV pulled away, Maggie peered up through the heavily tinted window at the gleaming dome of the Capitol. It rose above the city with Old Glory flapping in the breeze, the polished stone reflecting sunlight against a perfectly clear sky. For the first time since this whirlwind had begun with her visit to Camp David, Maggie felt the weight of what was about to happen descend on her shoulders, and it felt difficult to breathe. She reached for the window switch, but the bulletproof glass wouldn't budge.

"Can we get some air back here?" Jenkins said, and the driver flicked a switch.

"Where are we going?" Maggie asked.

"The president asked for you to join him at lunch," Jenkins said. "The White House kitchen is serving cod and rice."

Maggie's heart thumped. "The White House?"

Capitol Police cars swerved into place in front of and behind the Tahoe, blue lights flashing as they cleared the path for her along Constitution Avenue. She thought about every small decision that led her to this place. Any one of them, switched out for an opposing choice, could have led her someplace entirely different. Maybe someplace less stressful. Less terrifying.

But behind the strain and pressure in her mind, she felt fire—distant but growing. A rush of adrenaline and excitement. The touch of something spectacular, just around the corner.

I'm going to be vice president.

The Capitol Police pulled to the side to allow the Tahoe to roll through a fortified gate. Trees sheltered Maggie's view, but between the swaying limbs, she made out the stoic gleam of polished stone and a single column.

The White House came into view all at once. The four columns of the front portico facing Pennsylvania Avenue stood like iron guardians of the president's personal refuge. The driveway curved around the North Lawn, a single fountain shooting water into the hot summer air. Maggie's fingers tightened around the armrest, and she couldn't help gawking at the looming mass of the most famous house in the world. Out of the corner of her eye, she caught Jenkins watching her, but said nothing as the Tahoe rolled to a stop in front of the West Wing.

Jenkins said, "The president is ready for you, ma'am."

O'Dell hurried to get her door, and the driver shot Jenkins a questioning look.

"We'll need Officer O'Dell to remain with the vehicle, ma'am," Jenkins said softly. "He's not been cleared for White House access."

Maggie tore her gaze away from the presidential mansion. "Will you be the head of my detail, Agent?"

"Yes, ma'am."

"Terrific. Then I suggest you get busy clearing Officer O'Dell."

"Ma'am?"

"If I'm confirmed as vice president, Officer O'Dell will be joining my detail."

"With respect, ma'am, that isn't possible."

Maggie softened her voice but maintained an undertone of command. "Have you ever been shot at, Agent Jenkins?"

Jenkins's brow furrowed, but he shook his head.

"Have you ever killed a man?"

Another shake of his head.

"Officer O'Dell has. I don't pretend to be an expert on executive security, but it seems such experience would be an invaluable asset to your team. Don't you think?"

He may have tried to hide it, but Maggie noticed O'Dell's chest puffing out.

Jenkins said nothing for a long moment, clearly weighing his options. Then he nodded once. "Of course, ma'am. I'll see what I can do."

"Thank you, Jenkins. I'm in your debt."

Maggie piled out of the Tahoe. Her heels clicked against the smooth asphalt of the drive, and the Secret Service agent waiting at the door offered her a polite nod and held it open.

The carpet inside was royal blue, perfectly smooth, and the air smelled of lilacs. Maggie sucked in a deep breath of the air conditioning and had barely adjusted to the change in temperature before a short, wiry man wearing a black suit and a red power tie approached her and held out a hand.

"Madam Governor, Jason Coffman, chief of staff to the president."

Maggie accepted his hand, satisfied by a confident but not overbearing grip. Coffman had kind eyes that immediately eased some of the tension she felt.

"It's a pleasure to meet you, Mr. Coffman. I've heard great things about you."

"Likewise, ma'am. I hope you're hungry. The president is waiting in the Roosevelt Room."

Coffman led the way through a lobby and down a hall, nodding a greeting to half a dozen staffers along the way. All the walls were hung with presidential artwork, and the flawlessly clean carpets felt soft beneath Maggie's shoes.

Another Secret Service agent waited next to a wide door, pushing it open as Coffman approached. A massive conference table was revealed on the other side, with US military flags framing the Stars and Stripes along one wall.

President William Brandt sat at the table's end, reading glasses perched on his nose as he flipped through a sheaf of papers. He dropped the papers as Maggie entered, rising to his feet and offering his hand. "Congratulations, Maggie!"

"I'm not confirmed yet, Mr. President."

Brandt laughed. "If you don't know a sure thing when it's staring you in the face, you may not be the woman I thought you were." He motioned to the chair next to his, and Maggie took a seat.

Coffman disappeared through a side door, returning a moment later with a cart. A television rested atop it, and when Coffman plugged it in, the screen illuminated with a C-SPAN broadcast of the Senate Chamber. The clerk was busy calling the roll. Maggie's stomach tightened again.

"You like cod?" Brandt asked, dumping sugar into a cup of coffee and stirring it with a silver spoon.

"Absolutely, sir."

Brandt sipped the coffee. "That's not what your mother says."

Maggie sat up. "My mother, sir?"

"You'll have to forgive me, Madam Governor. I had Coffman reach out. We wanted to see if they'd like to be present for your swearing-in ceremony. Your mother is a delightful woman."

Maggie's cheeks flushed as she thought about her bustling mother. Rosalyn Trousdale was as simple and Cajun as they came, impressed by neither pomp nor circumstance. Maggie had little doubt that she spoke to the president's chief of staff no differently than she might address the bag boy at the grocery store.

What on earth did she say?

Maggie chose to roll with the punches. "If I'm busted, sir, I confess . . . I'm not the biggest fan of cod."

Brandt held his coffee and didn't reply. He watched her over the top rim of the cup with that same piercing, searching stare she'd seen before at Camp David.

"They're calling the vote," Coffman said, turning the volume up.

Maggie faced the TV.

The clerk leaned across his desk with an eighteen-inch sheet of paper laid out in front of him. He spoke into the mic, marking the sheet with a pencil as he called names. "Mr. Cadwell?"

"Aye."

"Ms. Colby?"

"Aye."

"Mr. Cole?"

"Aye."

Maggie's heart began to thump again as the clerk moved down the list alphabetically. Most of the senators present leaned back in their chairs, chatting quietly among themselves while a few wandered around the chamber. The clerk reached the F and G senators, and still nothing but "aye" votes had been cast.

Maggie caught the president watching her again, but she chose not to acknowledge him. Coffman was scratching on a pad of paper, making note of each affirmative vote, but by the time the clerk reached the Ps, Coffman stopped and leaned back, a smile creeping across his face.

"Mr. Parker?"

"Aye."

"Ms. Peters?"

"Aye."

"Mr. Roper?"

"No."

Maggie flinched before she could catch herself. The steady stream of "ayes" from the television had developed enough of a rhythm to make a negative vote crack like a bullet.

Quietly, Brandt said, "Matt Roper is the chairman of the Senate Intelligence Committee. He hates my guts. Don't take it personally."

The clerk continued down the roll, stopping at the end to inquire about six senators not present. After consulting his list again, he stood and approached the Senate president's chair. In absence of a vice president, the seat was occupied by the president pro tempore of the chamber—in this case, John Matlock of Minnesota.

Matlock accepted the final vote from the clerk and leaned toward the mic. "Are there any senators in the chamber who wish to vote or change a vote?"

His question was greeted only by silence.

Matlock cleared his throat. "In that case, on this vote, the ayes are ninety-three, the nays are one. The nomination of Margaret L. Trousdale of Louisiana to be vice president of the United States is confirmed."

Maggie's head went light. Hearing her own name over the television, coupled with that title, sent a strange blend of surrealness and elation through her mind. She found herself standing mechanically as Brandt extended his hand.

He spoke warmly, but when she met his gaze, his eyes were ice cold. "Congratulations, Madam Vice President."

7

It was always hot in the little house, even after nightfall. As the sun disappeared over the Pacific, Reed sat on the front porch of the shack and stared out across the glimmering lights of Nacaome, ten miles away. Hondurans were a lot more judicious with their use of electricity than Americans—perhaps because they could barely afford it—and only essential lights marked the town, leaving the sky beyond speckled by stars.

It was peaceful to look at, but the serenity didn't reach Reed's worn body. With his AK leaning against the wall next to him, he sipped black coffee from a battered mug and thought about the future.

They couldn't stay here. As much as he hoped this little shack on the back side of nowhere could be a semi-permanent address for him and Banks, that pipe dream was quickly fading away into the crush of an unstoppable force crashing into an immovable object. The unstoppable force? The pressure for him to always be on the run, barely ahead of the hounds that snapped at his heels. And the unmovable object? The reality that he was running out of places to go.

Banks knew it would be this way when she married him. Reed wanted to leave her in Georgia and embrace this life of a renegade on his own, but

Banks refused to be left behind. And maybe it was because he was tired, or selfish, or simply because he couldn't get rid of her, but Reed agreed. Now he wondered what sort of life he'd sentenced her to. And not just her . . . their child.

Reed tipped the mug back. The coffee had long ago turned cold, but he barely noticed. The strain in the back of his mind gnawed away at his consciousness like a rat burrowing its way beneath his skin—subtle, at first, then quickly becoming the only thing he could think about.

The front door of the shack creaked open, and Banks stepped out, carrying a steaming cup of tea. She offered him a tired smile, and despite the gauntness of her cheeks, Reed saw a little flush of color, untarnished by the stress that wore at them both. That was her magic and maybe the thing he first fell in love with. Banks wasn't stupid or simple. She saw the ugly side of life for what it was, but somehow, in spite of it all, she still saw the brighter side. She still kept that glow.

Reed got up to tuck the blanket around her shoulders as she sat next to him. He kissed the top of her head before resuming his seat, hoping she wouldn't notice the stiffness in his back or tension in his face. Reed lit a cigarette and flooded his lungs with the relieving cool of nicotine. It wasn't enough to erase the stress, but it damn sure helped.

"I was thinking about Clara," Banks said. She sipped tea, but her voice sounded a little hoarse.

"Clara, who?"

Banks laughed. "Clara Montgomery, you fool. Your daughter."

"Oh." Reed sucked on the cigarette. "So, we're having a girl?"

"How should I know? I just think it's a pretty name."

"Clara Morccelli is prettier," Reed said.

Morccelli was Banks's maiden name, and maybe it was still her legal name. Renegade weddings in the hills of Venezuela, unsanctioned by any government, didn't include name changes or new social security cards. It wasn't something Reed really thought about.

"No." Banks cradled her teacup. "I'm a Montgomery now. So is the baby."

Reed stared at her.

"What?" Banks said.

"You're just . . ." He searched for the right words, but nothing came to mind. Nothing described the way he felt when he looked at her. ". . . so damn beautiful," he finished.

Banks rolled her eyes, but her cheeks turned a little rosy. "You're so damn blind."

He placed a hand on her knee, and she slipped her fingers between his. Reed looked back over Nacaome, and his shoulders slumped.

"We have to go, don't we?" Banks asked.

Reed nodded softly. It was the obvious conclusion after leaving Colombia. Massimo would probably leave them alone . . . probably. Reed wasn't scared of either him or his ten-dollar thugs, regardless. But the greater problem with Honduras lay with the FBI. They would come, eventually, hounding him for every violent thing he did since leaving the Marine Corps years before. And even if the FBI was still too busy mopping up the fallout of the Resilient Pharmaceutical case, Honduras was no place for Banks. She needed medical care—enough to counteract the ravages of the Lyme disease.

The pregnancy only added fuel to that fire. Banks's health now held two lives in the balance, and the baby could be a lot more fragile than her.

"Where?" Banks asked.

Reed could hear the weariness in her voice, seeping out of her very bones. "West," he said. "Southeast Asia, I think."

The problem with running from the United States government was that most of the world would happily turn you in, if caught. Civilized, safe places with good medical care, such as Japan, Korea, Canada, or Europe, would extradite the pair of them in a heartbeat.

That left only two options—either developed nations that wouldn't extradite, or third-world nations, which were too disorganized to care either way. China and Russia featured an abundance of stable cities equipped with sufficient medical care, but neither country was particularly friendly to Americans, and both were secure enough to make flying under the radar all but impossible, long-term.

Third-world nations were even worse options. The chaos and instability that offered a smoke screen of concealment also promised plenty of mortal danger and a lack of the healthcare Banks needed. Had he been alone,

Reed would've lost himself in Africa or Asia months ago, but with Banks, the risk was too great.

That left them with only one real option: Southeast Asia. Underdeveloped, but not exactly third world. Allied with the United States enough to allow for the passage of Americans, but not so allied that local governments devoted much time to hunting down renegades. Mid-grade medical care, with premium care available for the right price. It wasn't a perfect option, but it would suffice.

"Is the food good?" Banks asked.

"The best, if you don't mind a little squid in your rice." Reed squeezed Banks's hand as the last light of the sun faded behind the mountains.

Banks's finger felt cold between his, and she didn't squeeze back.

"I'm scared, Reed. It's . . . not just us anymore."

Reed left his chair, settling down on one knee next to her and wrapping both her hands inside of his. He squeezed again, then reached up and brushed hair out of her eyes. "I'm going to protect you both," he whispered. "Whatever it takes."

8

Maggie hurried out of the Tahoe. O'Dell was at her hip and now dressed in the simple muted black of a Secret Service agent. His Louisiana state badge had been replaced by a federal government access card—a courtesy Jenkins insisted was probationary and would be revoked on the slightest provocation. O'Dell wasn't allowed to carry a weapon, but he stuck to Maggie like a tick on a hound, just as he always had.

Maggie cradled a leather briefcase as she hurried into the West Wing lobby, checking her watch. It was a quarter past nine, making her fifteen minutes late for the president's national security briefing. Maggie cursed under her breath as she followed an aide down the hallway, past the Roosevelt Room to the Cabinet Room. Down the corridor to her right was the Oval Office, facing the Rose Garden. In her twenty-four hours as vice president, Maggie had yet to set foot in the famed executive headquarters of the most powerful man in the Free World.

Showing up late to her first official meeting as VP wouldn't win her any favors.

Maggie reached for the door handle to the Cabinet Room, but O'Dell cleared his throat.

"Um, ma'am?"

He brushed his left cheek with two fingers, and Maggie followed the motion to her own face, where she detected a smear of syrup from breakfast.

She scrubbed it away with a quick pass of a napkin from the aide. "You're a lifesaver, O'Dell." She patted him on the arm, then pushed through the door.

The room on the other side was every bit as large as the Roosevelt Room, but less ornate. Wide windows opened up over the Rose Garden on the far wall, and a massive table stretched the length of the room, surrounded on all sides by high-backed leather chairs. Those chairs were occupied by the majority of Brandt's cabinet—secretaries of various government departments, representatives from the CIA and FBI, political aides, and military advisors.

All twenty of them went silent as Maggie entered, staring at her unabashed. Maggie's cheeks turned hot as she searched for an empty chair, quickly locating only one—directly beside Brandt. The president sat at the table's head, his fingers interlaced over a placemat, his gaze resting on her without expression. Maggie ducked her head and hurried to the chair, her heels clicking against the floor like gunshots in the quiet room. Nobody moved.

She settled into the seat and set the briefcase down, taking an impulsive sip of water from the glass in front of her.

"Sleep well?" Brandt asked. There was no humor in his tone.

"I apologize, Mr. President. We hit traffic."

The room remained icy silent another few seconds, then Brandt chuckled. "Welcome to DC, Maggie."

The laugh radiated around the room, but none of the cabinet members sounded very amused.

"We'll keep introductions short," Brandt said. "Maggie, meet General John David Yellin, chairman of the Joint Chiefs, Secretary of State Lisa Gorman, Attorney General Greg Thomas, and National Security Advisor Nick West. Of course, you've already met Jason."

Coffman offered Maggie a sympathetic smile. Of all the stone faces around the table, his was the only one that appeared human.

"It's a pleasure," Maggie said.

A chorus of grunts echoed around the table.

"We were just discussing my trip to UAE," Brandt said. "Have you been briefed?"

Maggie had. Her brand-new slew of vice presidential aides had shoved her headfirst into the business of the White House—and there was plenty of it. Rising tensions in the Persian Gulf, triggered by diplomatic conflicts with Iran, had prompted Brandt to plan a visit to the United Arab Emirates. In recent months, President Khalid bin Bakir had become the mouthpiece for the alarmist movement as tensions with Iran increased. Brandt's diplomatic visit to UAE was nominally calibrated to ease tensions and promote increased discussion. In reality, Maggie expected the president wanted to shut Bakir up before his distressed press conferences spilled into military action. *Air Force One* would depart Joint Base Andrews immediately following this meeting.

"Very good," Brandt said. "While I'm gone, you'll be placed under additional security protocols and be restricted to the greater DC area."

Maggie made a note on her legal pad. "Of course, sir."

Brandt motioned to National Security Advisor West. "Nick, can you bring the vice president up to date on the situation in the Gulf?"

West cleared his throat. He was an overweight man in his late fifties—balding, with round glasses. When he spoke, his voice was low and gravelly but carried an undertone of confidence that Maggie appreciated.

"Tensions in the Persian Gulf are at a historic high, Madam Vice President. Over the last three months, Iranian naval patrols have harassed international oil shipments, and in at least two cases, western-flagged tankers were illegally boarded while passing through the Strait of Hormuz. Twenty-one percent of the world's oil supply is shipped through the strait, passing between Iran and UAE along a channel only thirty miles wide. It's always been a sensitive geographic region, but Iran's aggression has put the Emirates on edge."

West turned to Gorman. The secretary of state looked to be about the same age, but unlike West, she was slim and well-kept, with dyed black hair and impeccable posture.

"The Iranians are testing their limits," Gorman said. "It's nothing new, but this time they aren't responding to traditional diplomatic pressures. The UAE, Saudi Arabia, and Kuwait are all on edge, and that's never a good thing for oil futures. OPEC is leveraging the problem into increased oil prices, and that makes this whole drama our problem. Average fuel costs here in the States have increased twenty-three percent since March, and if we don't get a handle on this soon, they'll keep rising into the fall."

Maggie made notes as Gorman ran through the situation with the efficiency of a woman very familiar with it.

"The Emirates are the key to the region," she continued. "Saudi will fuss, but all they really want is for the oil to keep pumping. Kuwait is more concerned about national security than anything. Nobody wants a war, but the Emirates are a different kettle of fish. This Bakir guy is seriously on edge. He's not been around long enough to know how to manage the Iranians acting the fool twenty miles off his coast. We need the Emirates to project a strong picture of solidarity with the United States before we can confront Iran. That's the core of the president's mission in Abu Dhabi."

Maggie's head spun as the influx of international diplomacy surged into her brain like a tidal wave. She felt a little sick to her stomach, suddenly realizing that with less than forty-eight hours on the job, the president was abandoning her in Washington.

General Yellin spoke next after a slurp of coffee. He was overweight, in his late sixties, with aviator-style glasses and the stern countenance of a man who'd spent half of the last century wearing a uniform. "While you're overseas, Mr. President, we'll be moving portions of the Fifth Fleet into active patrol off the southern coast of Qatar. We don't expect any funny business from our Iranian friends, but we prefer to be safe. We'll have firepower on standby, just in case we need to rattle their cage."

Brandt sat slouched back in his chair, stroking his chin with one finger and watching Maggie. Despite his fixation with her, he didn't seem to be really paying attention. He sat with his shoulders sagged, one finger drumming idly against his armrest.

"While the president is overseas, I'll remain in Washington to keep the administration running," Coffman said, addressing Maggie directly. "All we need from you is to stay close at hand in case anything should come up."

Maggie made another note. The conference room fell suddenly quiet, and she looked up. Everybody was making a fuss of checking smartphones and watches, but nobody made eye contact with Brandt. The president remained slouched in his chair, his gaze now glazed over.

Maggie tried to think of another note to write. She looked at the pad, and Brandt spoke suddenly.

"What do you think?"

Everyone looked up, unsure who Brandt was addressing. The haze in his eyes had cleared, and he now focused on Maggie.

"I'm sorry, sir?"

"What do you think?"

Maggie's spine tingled. "About what, sir?"

"About Iran. About the Gulf. About everything we're discussing."

Maggie consulted her notes to buy time. She hadn't expected to be asked her opinion and still wasn't sure exactly what she was being asked to express an opinion about. The president's trip? The price of gas? "Well, sir. I'm not sure I know enough about the situation to—"

Brandt sat up. "Maggie, when I ask for your opinion, I expect you to have one. America doesn't have time for you to waffle."

The president's words bit, and the room became as still as a graveyard.

Maggie squared her shoulders. "Yes, sir. We should do everything possible to avoid armed conflict. If a diplomatic approach, coupled with a show of force, will neutralize Iran's aggression, I stand behind it. But whatever the case, America must anchor the region. We cannot be bullied."

Brandt stroked his bottom lip. After a long while, he glanced at Gorman, who nodded once. "All right, everybody. I appreciate your time. I've got a plane to catch."

Everyone stood, and Brandt buttoned his suit jacket before exiting the room without another look at Maggie. She stood stiff-backed, still smarting from his rebuke but confident in what she had said. Brandt may be the president, but she'd never believed in pulling punches or second-guessing herself. If he wanted her opinion, well, he had it.

"Madam Vice President?"

It was Coffman. He gestured her into the hall as the cabinet filed out, and Maggie followed him to a quiet corner outside the Roosevelt Room.

Coffman produced a single sheet of white paper from his briefcase and passed it to her. "I've got your schedule for the next few days. I'm sure you'll want to find your own chief of staff, but until then, I'm here to make your transition as seamless as possible. I hope you don't mind."

Maggie accepted the sheet with a grateful nod, scanning the first column. Coffman had her booked for an appearance at Arlington National Cemetery the following day.

"State funeral," Coffman said before she could ask. "A retired Navy admiral passed away. I thought it would be a good look for you to attend."

"Of course," Maggie said. "What do I wear?"

Coffman opened his mouth to reply, but Brandt cut him off.

"Maggie, do you mind accompanying me to Andrews?"

She spun around, the schedule fluttering in one hand. Brandt stood just down the hallway, a briefcase swinging from one hand and two Secret Service bodyguards standing yards away. She hesitated, caught off guard by the sudden request.

"Please," Brandt said.

"Of course, Mr. President."

She handed the schedule back to Coffman, then smoothed down the front of her dress and followed Brandt through the corridor and out a side exit into the Rose Garden. Secret Service agents flanked them as Brandt ambled across a manicured lawn, stopping for a moment to finger a snow-white rose. Maggie stood awkwardly back, her hands clasped over her stomach. Even in early morning, it was uncomfortably warm outside, and sweat beaded on her forehead.

Brandt admired two more flowers before picking the fourth and tucking it into his coat pocket, then he hurried onto the South Lawn, Maggie and the agents trailing.

The hulking mass of the United States Marine Corps Sikorsky VH-3D, code-named *Marine One*, sat stoically on three identical orange landing discs, a Marine crew chief dressed in full-dress uniform standing at attention next to the door. The big chopper looked even larger the closer Maggie got. It dominated the lawn with its long rotor blades drooping toward the immaculate grass. Brandt paused at the foot of the steps, exchanging a stiff salute with the crew chief before hurrying on board. Maggie hesitated, unsure of the protocol for the VP, and was relieved when one of the Secret Service agents whispered to her, "You can go ahead and board, ma'am."

The interior of the helicopter was premium in every sense of the word. Brandt sat in a plush leather chair near the back, one leg crossed over the other as he propped his chin on one hand and stared vacantly out the window.

Maggie took a seat across the aircraft and buckled in as the crew chief shut the door and the rotors began to turn. It was cool inside *Marine One*, and she was amazed at how quiet it remained as the helicopter rose over the lawn with perfect grace. The pilot banked to the left, circling the White House before turning southeast toward Joint Base Andrews. Maggie allowed herself to gaze past the president, squinting into the rising sun as *Marine One* orbited the Washington Monument and the National Mall. The view was breathtaking, stretching out in front of them like a painting, both silent and serene.

"Beautiful, isn't it?" Brandt said. It was the first time he'd spoken since leaving the West Wing.

"Very much so, sir." Maggie kept her hands folded in her lap, still uneasy after the confrontation in the cabinet meeting. Brandt's changing moods were now bordering on mercurial, and in spite of herself, she was getting frustrated.

"It's fragile," Brandt said, still staring out the window.

"Pardon?"

"The nation . . . the grand experiment. It all looks so magnificent, but it's made of glass."

Maggie wasn't sure what to say, so she just nodded. For the duration of the five-minute flight, Brandt watched the passing scenery like a man headed to prison, drinking it in and sitting perfectly still. As *Marine One* touched down at Andrews, his countenance changed, growing serious again. He motioned for Maggie to follow him onto the tarmac, saluting the crew chief again on their way out.

Air Force One waited fifty yards away, gleaming in the morning sun like a polished show car. Its massive wingspan stretched almost two hundred feet across the runway, supporting gargantuan engines painted in royal blue. That same blue was mirrored on the belly of the aircraft, followed by a trio of red and gold stripes.

"How do you like my ride?" Brandt said, motioning to the plane.

"It's remarkable, sir." Maggie wasn't exaggerating. The plane was far and away the grandest aircraft she'd ever seen.

"It's brand-new," Brandt said, starting toward the foot of the airstair. "The Obama Administration commissioned the construction of two new aircraft to serve the president. The previous planes—the ones with the baby blue exteriors—date back to the first Bush administration. I'm the first president to use the new ones."

A Secret Service agent waiting at the foot of the airstair accepted Brandt's briefcase.

The president turned toward the sun again, smiling into the warmth and sucking in a deep breath. "Do you love your country, Maggie?"

"Absolutely, sir."

Brandt's smile slowly faded, and he faced Maggie. "Take care of her," he said softly.

"Sir?" Maggie's brow furrowed, but Brandt made no further comment. He hurried up the steps into the waiting aircraft, leaving Maggie standing in the blazing August sun. Secret Service agents stood at her elbow, asking her to step back as the giant plane turned slowly and began to taxi. She watched it prepare for takeoff, a strange sense of uncertainty and foreboding building in her stomach. There was something in Brandt's tone. It chilled her, despite the August heat.

Air Force One shuddered at the end of the runway, its engines roaring like unleashed monsters. Sunlight gleamed against white wingtips, and then the most famous plane in the world shot down the runway and lifted into the sky.

9

The morning was gray and muggy. Precedent demanded that Maggie arrive to the funeral in a long-sleeved dress and heels, but sweat trickled down her back as she stood at the leading edge of a small crowd, just outside the funeral tent.

The casket of Rear Admiral Frank D. Tipper lay on a stand over an open grave while eight members of the Navy's Honor Guard stood at attention with an American flag stretched over it. A full Navy band lined the hillside thirty feet away, and a firing party stood with rifles resting next to their legs, staring stoically into the murky morning.

Tipper's widow sat in the front row of family seating, her red eyes fixed on the casket as the Navy chaplain delivered the eulogy. She didn't cry, but Maggie could see the pain in her face—the complete weariness of a woman who had given her life to the Navy, almost as much as her husband.

"We read in the Book of John about many mansions that our Lord has prepared for us." The chaplain spoke confidently, projecting comfort into the crowd, even as the scepter of death hung over them like the grim reaper himself. Maggie listened but didn't really hear. She felt like a fraud for being distracted while attending such a sacred event, but she couldn't help thinking about Washington, the pressures waiting for her at the West Wing, and Brandt's cryptic farewell.

What did he mean, "Take care of her"?

"Our brother Frank rendered thirty-eight years of distinguished, selfless service to our great nation, and in the spirit of his faith, he protected our freedom through three brutal wars. The United States Navy is honored by his commitment, humbled by his sacrifice, and forever touched by his courage."

Maggie surveyed the small crowd, noting a knot of family, a perfunctory coalition of congressional representatives from Tipper's home state, and a few subdued reporters standing in the background, their cameras lowered. The stillness that guarded this place was reverent, and it added to the burden of uncertainty tugging on her mind.

What am I doing here? I don't belong in Washington.

The chaplain invited the gathering to pray with him, and Maggie ducked her head. Having grown up a Louisiana Catholic, she was unfamiliar with protestant funeral practices. She wasn't sure if she should join in the completion of the prayer with a spoken "amen," or if she should make the sign of the cross. She decided not to overthink it and tried to focus on the chaplain's words of comfort.

"Ladies and gentlemen, please stand for military honors."

Maggie looked to the firing party as orders rang across the still cemetery. Rifles gleamed in the muted sunlight as they snapped into the air. She couldn't help but flinch as seven shots broke the morning stillness, followed by the sharp snap of all seven rifles being reloaded in unison. Then another blast.

She saw the faces of the young men—just boys, really—pulling those triggers. They all stood tall and proud, dressed in spotless white uniforms as perfect as their practiced display of respect.

"Aim! Fire!"

The final blast from the honor guard ripped into the air at the same moment Maggie saw O'Dell twist beside her, his gaze snapping toward the lead agent of her protective detail. A flurry of movement erupted from the crowd, then two agents rushed Maggie, grabbing her by the elbows and shoving her toward the street.

"Ma'am, come with us!"

Maggie had no time to react or resist. Her feet lifted off the ground as they propelled her down the hill, breaking into a full run toward the waiting Cadillac limo fifty yards away. Maggie's heart pounded, and she searched for O'Dell. He ran behind her, one hand on her shoulder as he hugged her back with his body.

"Ma'am, keep your head down!"

A hand pressed the back of her skull as one of her heels caught on the curb and snapped. She grunted and almost tripped, but the agent on her right caught her and shoved her into the waiting limo.

"Go! Go! Go!"

The door slammed, and the car lurched forward. Maggie lay on her side in the back seat, still shaking and gasping for breath. O'Dell was gone. Two agents rode on the bench seat that ran the length of the cabin, both cradling submachine guns. Maggie tried to sit up, but the nearest agent put a hand on her shoulder and pressed down.

"Ma'am, we need you to stay down!"

The limo's engine roared. Outside, Maggie saw flashing blue lights and passing treetops framing a murky sky. She heard the back tires of the limo screech over wet pavement as the Cadillac completed a tight turn, then they hit a speed bump and she face-planted into the seat.

She choked and forced herself up. "What's happening?"

"Ma'am, stay down!" The agent pushed her beneath the window line again.

Sirens screamed, and the limo gained speed as the trees outside vanished. Maggie heard the rush of cars and caught a glimpse of Richmond Highway as it cut through the Arlington cityscape just north of the cemetery. Her hands shook, and she clutched the nearest armrest, forcing herself to breathe evenly.

Almost as soon as the frantic car ride began, the Cadillac screeched to a halt, and the passenger door flew open. Maggie heard the pounding beat of a helicopter's rotor, then strong hands closed around her arms and pulled her out of the limo.

"Ma'am, come with us!"

It was Agent Jenkins. He leaned low with one hand on her back, pressing her toward the raised bulk of the Pentagon Army Heliport, where *Marine Two* beat the air, ready for takeoff.

"Where's O'Dell?" Maggie shouted, tripping over her broken shoe.

Nobody answered, but two agents lifted her off the ground again, sprinting across the helipad and beneath the blast of rotor wash. The next thing she knew, she was inside the aircraft, being shoved into a seat and buckled in by yet another agent.

The crew chief slammed the stair door and screamed into the cockpit, "Get us off the ground!"

The helicopter shook as Maggie's mind became a numb blur of panic and confusion. One of the agents put a hand on her arm as the Sikorsky shot skyward, launching off the helipad far more aggressively than Brandt's chopper had the previous afternoon.

"What's happening?" Maggie shouted.

"Ma'am, please stay calm. We'll brief you as soon as we can."

The chopper's nose dipped, and Maggie's stomach flipped as they raced ahead. She braced her arm against the seat and pressed her face near the window, catching sight of the Virginia countryside flashing past in a blur of roads and buildings. She heard the thunder of more rotor blades and swallowed back a wave of nausea as another helicopter swung into view, barely a hundred feet away. It was small and gray, with the word "MARINES" marked on the tail and a large gun poking out of the nose. The gunship was so close, Maggie could make out the faces—stern and laser-focused—of the twin pilots riding inside. She looked to the window on the other side of the Sikorsky and saw an identical Marine chopper flying just as close.

"My God . . . my God. What happened?"

Before anyone could answer, a commotion erupted from the cabin. One of the pilots shouted, and the Sikorsky shuddered.

"Bogey! Rooftop, two o'clock. Engage! Engage!"

The Sikorsky banked hard left, the nose dropping. Maggie slammed against her seatbelt, bile erupting from her mouth as the left window of the helicopter dipped so low she saw asphalt and rooftops. At the same moment, she heard the thunder of automatic gunfire, and the Sikorsky trembled with the concussive blasts of the heavy cannon.

"Ma'am, hold on!" The Secret Service agent pressed himself into the seat next to her as the Sikorsky leveled out then spun counterclockwise. Maggie vomited again, unable to stop herself as sky, trees, and then the South Portico of the White House rocketed into view. The chopper dropped like a rock, pulling up only an instant before the wheels smacked into the South Lawn.

Maggie felt the jolt all the way up her spine. Already, the agent was unbuckling her and pushing her toward the door. More shouting voices called for her to hurry, and then she was outside, suspended between the bulky frames of two more agents and racing across the lawn.

Overhead, the scream of fighter jets ripped through the sky, flying so low she felt the tremor of their engines. Then she was inside the White House, crashing through the Diplomatic Reception Room and into the Center Hall.

Before she could object, a door was thrown open, and Maggie found herself inside an elevator. With the whine of an electric motor, the car began to drop, and Maggie choked again. Jenkins stood next to her. She wasn't sure when he showed up, but the stone-faced agent offered a small bottle of water from his coat pocket.

"We're almost there, ma'am. Please stay calm."

"What's happening?" Maggie shouted, half-choking on more bile.

Jenkins didn't answer as the elevator ground to a halt and the doors rolled back. Maggie felt dizzy from all the harsh movement, but once again, she couldn't argue with the push of agents propelling her down the long hall.

Maggie saw a massive steel door, ten feet high and just as broad, with armed Marines standing guard outside of it and dressed in full-combat uniforms. Still half-suspended by Secret Service agents, she didn't even have a chance to stumble on her broken shoe, but the agents moved slower as they reached the door. One of the Marines hauled it open, and Maggie was lifted inside.

"Close!" Jenkins barked.

A chair rolled across the carpeted floor and came to rest behind Maggie. One of the agents gently guided her into it as the massive vault door eased shut.

Suddenly, everything was still. Maggie gasped for air, listening to the agents around her wheeze a little as they holstered pistols and leaned against the wall.

Jenkins swabbed his face with one sleeve, then spoke into his wrist mic. "Gunner One, all channels. Saint is secure. I repeat, Saint is secure."

Maggie swallowed hard and accepted another bottle of water. She chugged it, then wiped her mouth with the back of her hand. "Jenkins," she said, looking up. "What the *hell* is going on?"

Jenkins exchanged a look with another man—a tall agent dressed in a dark suit with a muted tie.

He approached Maggie and spoke without raising his voice. "Ma'am, I'm Samuel French, director of the Secret Service. I need you to come with me."

Maggie exchanged a glance with Jenkins. She wasn't sure why, but her brief familiarity with him made her want his opinion. Jenkins nodded, then Maggie followed French down a hallway. Her head still spun, but now she felt vaguely disoriented, as though her equilibrium were disrupted. "Where are we?" she demanded.

"PEOC, ma'am. Presidential Emergency Operations Center." French held back a polished wooden door.

Maggie stepped inside and froze.

It was a conference room, much like the Cabinet Room in the West Wing upstairs, only this room was lined with TV screens and computers. Military aides crowded the corners, and the bulk of Brandt's cabinet surrounded the conference table. As Maggie entered, they all stood, and the room fell deathly quiet.

She stopped, brushing sweaty hair from her forehead. There was vomit on her dress, and she still wore a busted shoe, but Maggie didn't care. She stood in the doorway and switched from one face to the next, surveying the room. "What happened?"

Yellin and Gorman exchanged a glance, and National Security Advisor West dropped his gaze.

Coffman spoke from the end of the table. "We've lost contact with *Air Force One*, ma'am. We believe the plane went down."

10

With her feet rooted to the floor, Maggie stood at the head of the conference table just staring at Coffman. The room was as still as a tomb, as if the crowd of aides and cabinet members were frozen in time.

Then everybody started talking at once, military officials arguing with each other while Gorman clamped one hand over her ear and shouted into a phone. West cussed out a skinny man in an Air Force uniform, and Coffman slumped into a chair, his hands falling limp into his lap.

Maggie took a faltering step back. Her head spun, and the edges of the room turned black. She was suddenly very aware of how far underground she was, and the air felt thin. Shouting voices faded, and all she could hear was her own heartbeat pounding in her ears like a drum. One thought echoed over and over through her swimming brain . . .

My God . . . My God . . . My God . . .

Strong fingers closed around Maggie's elbow, propping her up. She locked her knee, unaware that she had stumbled, and her vision cleared. She looked up to see Jenkins standing at her side, his bold features creased into a frown.

"Are you okay?"

The fog receded from her brain, replaced by the storm of chaos around her. Maggie's mind became clear, and she yanked her elbow free. "Quiet!"

Her shout broke across the room, and everyone froze. Maggie ran a hand across her forehead, swabbing away sweat. She fell into the presidential chair at the head of the table and gulped down a swallow of water from the waiting glass. Nobody spoke, and Maggie sucked down another deep breath. Her chest felt heavy.

"Ma'am—"

"Shut up," Maggie snapped, cutting off the unknown aide. She turned to Gorman, pointing at the phone. "Hang that up."

Gorman mumbled something into the receiver before returning it to the table.

Maggie swallowed more water, then held out the glass toward Jenkins so he could refill it.

"No more shouting," Maggie said. "One at a time. Tell me what you know. General?"

General Yellin, the chairman of the Joint Chiefs, sat up, his bulging shoulders testing the limits of his Army uniform. "*Air Force One* went offline approximately forty-five minutes ago. We've been unable to restore contact."

"Where is it?" Maggie asked.

Yellin lifted a laser pointer from the table and gestured to a digital map spread across the massive screen at the end of the room. An aide adjusted the focus, panning across the Mediterranean and into the Middle East.

"GPS tracking puts the aircraft about here"—Yellin marked a spot with the laser—"just inside Turkey, along the border."

Maggie squinted at the map. "Wait. Along the *Iranian* border?"

Yellin nodded once. "That's correct, ma'am."

"What the *hell* were they doing that close to Iran?"

The skinny man in the Air Force uniform said, "Ma'am, the original flight plan—"

Maggie cut him off. "Who are you?"

"My apologies, ma'am. General Albert Porter, chief of staff for the Air Force."

"Great. Please continue."

Porter gestured to the map. "Our original flight plan for *AF1* included a brief stop in Berlin, after which the aircraft would turn south, flying over eastern Turkey and Iraq before landing in UAE."

"Your flight plan included a swing this close to Iran?" Maggie couldn't resist the incredulity in her voice, but Porter shook his head.

"No, ma'am. Prior to going offline, *AF1* drifted off course. We were unable to make contact with the pilots." Porter stood next to the map, gesturing with one arm to indicate the point at which the plane veered eastward toward Iran. "Our last point of contact is here, about fifteen miles west of the border." Porter marked the spot with his finger. It lay in the extreme southeast corner of the country, north of Iraq and west of Iran.

"When you say you lost contact with the flight crew, you mean . . ."

Porter's shoulders stiffened, but his head remained high. "Complete radio silence, ma'am. We were unable to make contact beginning about fifteen minutes prior to losing GPS signal."

Maggie turned to Yellin. "What are we doing to get a satellite image of the site?"

"Satellite imagery will be difficult. It's dark in Turkey, and that region of the country is extremely rural and mountainous. We've scrambled two Triton reconnaissance drones out of Muharraq Airfield in Bahrain, but they're still ninety minutes out."

"Don't we have any drones in Iraq?"

"Yes, ma'am, but they're mostly air-to-ground, strategic-strike aircraft. The sort of high-altitude reconnaissance birds we need are operated by the Navy."

"Double down on a satellite, then. I want a picture of that site, ASAP."

Yellin gestured to Porter, and the Air Force general moved to the corner of the room and reached for a phone.

"How long until we can have boots on the ground?" Maggie addressed the question to Yellin, but it was Secretary Gorman who answered.

"It's not possible to send military personnel into a sovereign nation. We'd need Turkish permission before any teams could be deployed."

Maggie glanced at Yellin. He looked pissed to be cut off, but he nodded.

"She's right, ma'am," Yellin said. "We have Force Recon Marines and Air Force Pararescue on standby in Iraq, but we can't deploy without executive approval, and ideally, we'd secure Turkey's support."

Maggie turned to Gorman. "So, where are we with the Turks?"

"I've been unable to reach Ankara, ma'am. Like the general mentioned, it's the middle of the night over there. I've spoken to the Turkish ambassador, and he's working to wake people up."

"Tell him to hurry up. This isn't a social call."

Gorman reached for her phone, and Maggie turned back to the table. "Is there somebody here from the Marines?"

A burly man with a flat-top haircut cleared his throat. "General Norman Tucker, ma'am. Commandant of the Marine Corps."

"General Tucker, who the hell did your helicopter fire on?"

Tucker's face remained impassive. "Are you referring to your escort, ma'am?"

"I'm referring to the gray chopper with the word *Marines* emblazoned on the side that opened fire in freaking Maryland!"

"We're still working out the details, ma'am. When the Secret Service received word of lost contact with *Air Force One*, we scrambled two Viper choppers to provide escort for *Marine Two*. During your return flight to Washington, we identified a threat and—"

"What do you mean, a *threat*?"

Tucker's upper lip twitched. "One of our pilots identified a probable shoulder-fired anti-aircraft weapon on a rooftop."

"You mean a rocket launcher?"

"We're not sure, ma'am. I'll have more details shortly."

"See that you do."

Another gray-haired man in an impeccable Navy uniform sat forward, interlacing his fingers. "Ma'am, Admiral Dan Turley here, chief of naval operations. With your permission, I'd like to put the Fifth Fleet on full alert. Tensions in the Gulf are already high, and it's imperative we maintain military control of the region—at least until we better understand what brought the aircraft down."

"Are you suggesting *Air Force One* was *shot* down?"

Turley broke eye contact.

Yellin stepped in. "We have no intelligence to support that belief, ma'am. But the admiral is right. We should put the fleet on full alert."

Maggie looked back to the map. The Gulf region stretched out across the screen, and she followed the border of Turkey down to Iraq, then Kuwait, then down the coast of Saudi Arabia to Qatar, followed by UAE.

And then Iran. Stretching from the Gulf of Oman all the way to the Caspian Sea, Iran dominated one entire half of the region. Her mind traveled back to her briefing with Brandt's cabinet the previous day. All the complex tensions and instabilities of the region now carried more weight than ever. Had Iran shot down America's most treasured aircraft?

No. She couldn't believe it. She *wouldn't* believe it. The implications were unfathomable.

"Put the fleet on alert," Maggie said. "But don't risk any confrontations. Not until we know what happened."

Turley reached for a phone just as General Porter returned to the table.

"We have a visual," Porter said, lifting a remote from the table. "It's not great, but we're working to improve it."

The wall-to-wall screen flashed, then turned dark. Somebody dimmed the lights, and Maggie made out the rough outline of Turkey, framed on all sides by darkness. The image changed as the satellite zoomed slowly in, but still, all was dark.

Maggie braced herself against the end of the table as the picture clarified, then zoomed and blurred, then clarified again. She caught herself holding her breath as the cycle repeated, slowly closing in around a cluster of tall, barren mountains.

"When the drone arrives, we'll have a night-vision image," General Porter said. "For now . . ."

He zoomed again, and Maggie leaned a little closer to the screen.

Then she saw it—vague at first, but steadily growing clearer. Marked by smoldering orange fire, the obliterated remnants of a massive aircraft littered a shallow mountain valley. It was a ten-foot section of a wing, followed by half of an engine cowling engulfed in flames. Shards of sheet metal and clumps of burning insulation spread over a crash site a thousand yards long—an endless field of debris obscured by darkness and smoke.

But amid the wreckage, one object remained clearer than the rest.

Resting by itself a hundred yards from the crash site, a large chunk of the aircraft's tail burned in the dusty darkness, providing enough glow for Maggie to make out a design painted on one side of the rudder. She pointed, and General Porter zoomed in.

The stillness in the room was perfect, so absolute that Maggie could've closed her eyes and pretended she was standing alone. Everyone stared at the screen in raptured silence, frozen as the blurry image flickered.

Painted across one side of the shattered tail, half-obscured by smoke but clear enough to recognize, was the flame-burnt emblem of the American flag.

Maggie spoke to Gorman through gritted teeth. "I don't care if you have to deploy the Marines. I want the Turkish president on the phone . . . *right now.*"

11

"I've got President Polat online for you, ma'am!"

Secretary Gorman motioned to the phone mounted in front of Maggie's chair. The room fell still, and Maggie gulped down more water. No matter how much she drank, her throat still felt as dry as dust. She hit the speaker button.

"President Polat, this is Vice President Trousdale. Thank you for taking my call."

"Madam Vice President." Polat spoke with an accent so oppressive Maggie had to piece together the words. She fumbled with the phone, and Yellin leaned in, helping to turn up the volume.

"May I express my sincerest condolences for this unthinkable tragedy," Polat said. "The Turkish people stand with our American allies in your grief."

Maggie glanced at Gorman. Prior to making the call, the secretary of state had briefed her on Polat. He was recently elected, taking office six months earlier after a protracted and contested Turkish election. Little was known about his political affiliations other than what was garnered from his campaign strategy, which could be summarized in a single word: ruthless.

Gorman warned Maggie that the president was an unknown quantity and advised caution. All Maggie could think about was reaching the crash site and searching for survivors.

"I appreciate your concern, Mr. President. I'm sure you understand we have a lot of questions about the crash."

Maggie left the sentence hanging and glanced to Gorman again. It was a baited comment, calculated to test the waters. The room remained quiet as Polat seemed in no rush to reply.

"The Turkish people take this tragedy very seriously," Polat said. "Whatever the cause, I assure you, we will find it."

Maggie's brow wrinkled. Polat's comments seemed every bit as calculative as her own. But more than that, she didn't like the level of control he had assumed over the situation.

We will find it.

Time to go on the offensive.

"America appreciates your assistance, Mr. President, but we'll find the answers ourselves. The leader of the Free World just went down over *your* sovereign soil. I'm sure you can appreciate our concern for a conflict of interest."

Gorman flinched, but Maggie remained fixated on the phone. She was aware of the edge that had crept into her words, and she was okay with it.

Polat gasped. "Surely you are not implying that *we* are responsible for this tragedy? The people of Turkey are fervent allies of—"

"I'm implying nothing, sir, other than America's dedication to finding the truth. I've already deployed reconnaissance forces to reach the crash site and begin search and rescue. Your cooperation with our people is greatly appreciated."

The line went deadly silent. Maggie held her breath and felt Gorman's stare resting on her. The secretary of state had recommended that she ask permission for American troops to access the site. Maggie felt a more direct approach was better. The possibility that *Air Force One* may have been shot down still rang clearly in her strained mind. If this were an act of war, she couldn't afford to pander.

"You deployed US forces into Turkey?" Polat's accent faded slightly as his voice assumed a monotone.

Maggie felt a tingle up her spine. "That's correct, Mr. President."

Maggie thought she heard teeth grinding across the receiver.

"Madam Vice President, you will immediately withdraw your troops. The Turkish people do not require your assistance."

Maggie's blood surged. "That's *our* plane burning in *your* mountains, Mr. President. For all we know, it was brought down by force. We have a right to access the crash site and—"

"Turkey is a sovereign nation! Your soldiers have no rights here. You will order them to stand down, immediately."

Polat's monotone was completely gone now, boiling instead into a blistering surge of angry spluttering. Maggie wanted to look to Gorman for help, but she could still feel the secretary's cold eyes on her.

Somehow, this was her fault.

Maggie gripped the edge of the table. "And if I don't?"

"If you don't, Turkey will have no choice but to interpret your actions as an act of war. I advise caution."

Maggie sucked in a breath to respond, but then the line went dead. Her gaze snapped up to Gorman. "Did he just hang up on me?"

Before Gorman could answer, General Yellin broke in. "He can bluster all he wants, ma'am. With your authority, we can deploy troops within the hour. They can't deny us access to our own crash site."

"Except they *can*," Gorman snapped, smacking the table. "This is why I advised caution. Polat is an unstable personality, and the entire region stands on the edge of a knife. We tell him we've got Pararescue on the way, and all he hears is US troops deploying right onto the border with Iran. It puts him in the position of appearing to ally himself with our armed forces. How do you think Iran would respond?"

"That's a great question," General Yellin growled. "One I'd love to hear an answer to." He turned to Maggie. "Let's not ignore the elephant in the room. We have to acknowledge the possibility that *Air Force One* was brought down by Iranian aggression."

A low chorus of angst rumbled through the room, followed almost immediately by murmured conversation. Maggie's head began to spin, the fog now accompanied by a throbbing headache. She placed one hand against her forehead and began to rub, fighting through the chaos around her to reach some place of mental clarity. Nothing could prepare her for this—not law school, not Baton Rouge, not the Resilient investigations. Nothing could set the stage for the fear and uncertainty that now seeped into her blood.

She was thirty-five. A politician for less than three years. And just like that, she was sitting at the end of the conference table in the presidential bunker, crushed under the weight of an irrefutable reality: this was on her. Whatever happened next, whatever she chose to do—or not do—was all on her shoulders.

A door clicked, and feet thumped. Maggie was vaguely aware of a soldier in full-dress uniform leaning close to General Tucker's shoulder, passing him a sheet of paper. They shared a whispered conference, then the man left, and Tucker sat frozen, fixated on the paper.

The old Marine made his way around the end of the table. He stopped next to her chair and stood straight-backed, the picture of strength and confidence, but what she saw in his face told a different story.

"Ma'am . . ." Tucker hesitated, the sheet clamped between his fingers. He swallowed hard, and when he next spoke, his voice faltered. "There's been a mistake."

Maggie tore the sheet out of his hands and scanned the top page. It was an email addressed to some Marine colonel. She breezed past the salutation and moved straight to the content.

. . . preliminary conclusions of our investigation state that on 23 August, Marine Viper escort craft, piloted by First Lieutenants Hill, Tyson H., and Keller, Jacob R., opened fire on a rooftop figure they believed to be armed with a shoulder-fired anti-aircraft weapon. Initial investigations of the building revealed no presence of such weaponry, but a tripod-mounted telescope was found next to the body of Maryland resident Joshua R. Simmons, 72.

The report continued for another two paragraphs, but Maggie stopped reading, and her fingers trembled as she looked up. "We shot an old man with a telescope?"

Tucker stared at the wall. "It was reactionary, ma'am. The escort helicopters were under standing orders to use any force necessary. The pilot identified an apparent threat and took action. I assume full responsibility."

Maggie looked at the paper again, and suddenly, all she felt was anger. It boiled up inside, crushing like a tidal wave of restrained frustration. She crumpled the paper between her hands and blocked out the chaos around her, shrinking for a moment into a hole.

My God . . . What do I do?

"Turn on CNN!" somebody shouted.

A bustle erupted at the end of the table, and somebody grabbed the remote for the big screen. Red and white illuminated the room as "BREAKING NEWS" streaked across it.

A monotone voice rumbled as the room fell quiet, all eyes fixed on the screen. "We interrupt this broadcast to bring you the following . . . Unconfirmed reports from sources deep in the Brandt administration now state that *Air Force One* has been shot down while the president was on board."

Maggie stood up, the chair shooting out behind her as she crammed the wadded-up email against the tabletop. "How do they know that?" she shouted.

The screen switched to an anchor sitting at a desk, and behind the reporter was a wide digital screen displaying a map of Turkey.

"*How do they know?*" Maggie repeated.

The anchor rattled through a monologue about the rumored crash in the Turkish mountains, and no one responded.

Then the chaos returned, louder than before, consuming the room as everyone pointed fingers and battled to be heard. The angst that had boiled under the surface only moments before now surged to the top, flooding the room with an indistinguishable rush of slamming hands and snapping voices.

Maggie's head descended back into the fog, and for a moment, she wanted to just stay there. She wanted to run out of the room and not stop running until she was back in Louisiana—back in the little house by the lake, all alone, with nothing but the damp wind on her face and the gentle rustle of wildlife in the swamp vegetation.

She cursed herself for ever taking the White House phone call. Cursed herself for journeying to Camp David. Cursed herself for ever thinking, even for a moment, that she had what it took to step into this madness.

But I'm here now. And nobody else will do it for me.

"Quiet!" Maggie shouted. She ran a hand through sweaty hair, then pointed to the door. "If you're not Secretary Gorman, General Yellin, Attorney General Thomas, or Chief of Staff Coffman, I need you out of this room, immediately." Nobody moved, and Maggie snapped her fingers. "Now, people. Please."

A slow shuffle preceded a caravan moving out of the conference room, tailed by Agent Jenkins. He nodded once at Maggie before shutting the door gently behind him. Maggie could hear conversation resuming in the next room, but as soon as the doors shut, it was muted.

She poured herself a glass of water and drained it. "Can we bump up the AC in here?"

Coffman hurried to his feet, adjusting the thermostat before taking a chair nearer to Maggie. She folded her hands and forced herself to breathe slowly.

It's on me now. It's on me.

"Mr. Attorney General, I don't want to ask what I'm about to ask . . ."

Attorney General Greg Thomas sat a few chairs down on her left, leaning over a notepad. He slowly rotated a pen in one hand. "You want to know what happens next . . . regarding the executive office."

"That's correct."

Thomas looked at his notepad as if he were consulting notes, but the page was blank. "Well, ma'am. As you know, upon the president's passing, the first order of business would be to inaugurate you as president in order to protect continuity of government."

Coffman broke in, his voice faltering. "But we don't know he's dead!"

Maggie saw dry streaks on his cheeks. She wanted to share his pain, but the pressure of the moment was too great.

"Jason's right," Maggie said. "We can't assume President Brandt is dead. We need to know that for sure. General Yellin, what can we expect to see with your drones?"

Yellin heaved his old body forward. "It's impossible to say. We'll have night-vision-enhanced footage of the crash site within the hour, and presuming the site is rural enough, I'll feel safe ordering the drones close to the ground for a better look. Tomorrow we'll also have daylight satellite footage, but even then, it's very unlikely we'll be able to . . ."

"Identify remains?" Maggie said.

"Yes, ma'am."

"So, you need boots on the ground?"

Yellin nodded, but before he could comment further, Gorman broke in.

"Ma'am, I must *strongly* urge you against deploying troops without permission. Turkey has made it clear that our people aren't welcome. With Iranian tensions at an all-time high, and the crash site so close to the border, we could very well trigger a war."

"We may already *be* at war," Maggie said. "If *Air Force One* was shot down by the Iranians, *that* was an act of war."

"Absolutely," Gorman said. "But we don't know that, and the last thing we'd want is to initiate an unnecessary conflict. If the Iranians shot down our plane, war is coming, regardless. It costs nothing to be cautious."

"With respect, Secretary," Yellin said, "waiting costs us plenty. It gives our enemies time to regroup and plan their next move. It makes us look weak. It gives our allies time to waffle. If there's even a chance that *AF1* was shot down, we need to act *now*."

Gorman blustered, but Maggie held up a finger. "What do you have in mind, General?"

"There's only one option." Yellin folded his arms. "We have to retrieve the flight recorder from the crash site. It's the only possible way to know for sure what happened, and to get it, we need boots on the ground. A reconnaissance team deployed from Iraq or air-dropped right on site would be ideal. That region of Turkey is extremely rural. It's very unlikely that the Turks have people in place yet. If we move now, we can get in and out before they know a thing."

Gorman was already shaking her head. "That's not an option, General. The diplomatic risk is far too great. And with respect, ma'am, I'm not sure the acting president has authority to deploy troops into a sovereign nation without congressional approval."

Everybody looked to Thomas.

"That's really a question for White House counsel, ma'am."

"We don't have *time* for congressional approval," Yellin snapped. "And even if we did, it would blow the security of the entire operation. We need people on the ground *now*."

Maggie traced the watermark left by her glass on the table, ignoring the seething bile in her stomach. She looked to Thomas, and he simply folded his arms.

"I can't advise you on the legalities, ma'am. It may be best for me to excuse myself from further conversation."

Maggie held up a hand. "Let's all stay calm. First order of business is to clarify my powers as acting president. Next, I should address the people. However the hell CNN found out about this, the cat is now out of the bag. America needs to know somebody is at the wheel. There's going to be panic."

Coffman's voice was raspy but strong. "I agree."

Maggie picked up the phone and hit zero for the operator. The calm voice on the other end was female and spoke with an East Coast accent.

"Send in Director French and Agent Jenkins, please," Maggie said. She hung up, waiting until the two Secret Service agents appeared, both looking as unflappable as ever. "I need to address the nation, Director French." Maggie rose from the chair. "I prefer not to do that from a hole. Is it safe to leave the bunker?"

Jenkins stiffened at the request, but French nodded. "Yes, ma'am. We've cleared you to return to the residence, but we're going to keep you on-site for now."

"That's fine. Please accommodate Mr. Coffman with his arrangements for a video conference."

"Of course, ma'am. That won't be a problem."

Director French turned to the door.

"One last thing," Maggie said. "Could you find Officer O'Dell for me? I'd like to have him present."

French hesitated. "Ma'am, I think—"

"We've been through this, Mr. Director." Maggie kept her voice calm. "Please bring him."

"Of course, ma'am. Right away."

The two agents left, and Maggie glanced at the TV screen. Somebody had muted the broadcast, but a running tape at the bottom of the screen repeated the same breaking news headline:

"AIR FORCE ONE SHOT DOWN. PRESIDENT DEAD?"

Maggie watched the tape scroll through twice, and all she could think was, *God, don't let us be at war.*

12

Maggie spent only a few minutes scrubbing sweat off her face and changing into a fresh dress before joining the cavalcade of Secret Service agents waiting to escort her to the press briefing room. Over a dozen of them clogged the hallways around her, led by Coffman, French, and Jenkins, with several of the agents sporting bulletproof vests and submachine guns.

Coffman passed her a two-page document. "I prepared a statement for you, ma'am. The press is ready in the briefing room."

Maggie scanned the pages, then handed them back. "Thanks, but I've got this. Is the briefing room where the press secretary works?"

Maggie was familiar with the enclosed rectangular room lined by reporters. She'd never visited it personally but had viewed it plenty of times on TV. It was small and sheltered, like a hole.

"Don't worry, ma'am," French said. "The briefing room is completely secure."

"That's not what I'm worried about," Maggie said. "The president of the United States was just attacked. The people need a stronger image. Move the press corps onto the South Lawn. I'll deliver an address from the portico."

French and Jenkins exchanged another one of their looks, but Maggie wasn't waiting for permission. She started down the hallway and back to the elevator as Coffman jogged to keep up.

"We need to project confidence, ma'am. But empathy is also critical." Coffman's voice was all business now.

"Are you telling me I'm too brash?" Maggie asked.

"No, ma'am. I'm just advocating for my prepared statement. I think it strikes a strong balance."

Maggie took the statement back as agents packed into the elevator around her. She read through the opening paragraphs again and then shook her head. "This is too polished. When people are shocked and afraid, they want sincerity, not perfection. I'll run off-the-cuff."

She handed it back and straightened her jacket. It was still difficult to breathe, but rising out of the depths of the PEOC made it easier. As the elevator rolled open and she stepped back into the residence, a storm of activity and semi-chaos surrounded her. White House aides scurried around like an army of ants, shifting furniture and carrying camera equipment through the hallway and into the next room.

Maggie shot French a sideways look.

"We've prepared a spot for you in the Blue Room," French said. "The cameras will have a clear view of the South Lawn through the windows. It's the best we can do, ma'am."

Maggie pushed past an aide and into the stretching oval of the Blue Room. It was a massive space with towering walls reaching to high ceilings. A semi-circular wall lined with windows faced through the South Portico onto the lawn, where gray clouds still blocked out the sun. The podium waiting in the middle of the room was inlaid with the presidential seal and was already surrounded by cameras and lights.

Maggie turned back to French. "Fair enough, Director. Did you find Officer O'Dell?"

French spoke into his wrist mic, and almost immediately, O'Dell burst into the room. There was mud on his suit, and his iron gaze was twisted into an anxious glare. When he saw Maggie, the tension faded from his shoulders.

"Ma'am, are you all right?"

O'Dell's Cajun warble reminded Maggie of hot summer days around giant pots of gumbo, and it gave her a little comfort.

"I'm fine, O'Dell." Maggie grabbed his elbow and pulled him to one side, out of earshot of the others. "Stick close. I may need you later."

O'Dell didn't ask questions. Maggie patted him on the arm, then turned toward the podium.

A young woman carrying a silver tray laden with makeup approached her. "Ma'am?"

Maggie surveyed the lot and selected a hairbrush, sweeping it through her hair twice.

The woman glanced impulsively at the rows of bottled foundation and mascara. "Would you like anything else?"

"I'm all good, thank you."

Maggie moved behind the podium and adjusted the microphone. Her heart began to pound as rows of press corps crowded the room in front of her, all managing cameras on swivels and high-powered lights on stands. Maggie's stomach churned, and her fingers went cold. She'd delivered dozens of press conferences during her time as governor, but never to this many reporters. Never to the entire nation.

She pushed back the nausea and looked for Coffman. He stood in the corner of the room, his strained face peering at her between the lights. She gave him a nod, and he motioned to a man behind a bank of computers, then held up an open hand.

Five . . . four . . . three . . . two . . .

"Good afternoon." As soon as she spoke, Maggie wondered if it *was* afternoon. Was it still morning? She had no idea. Her knees locked, and she suddenly felt overwhelmed and dazed, as though she didn't know how to speak. She glanced beneath the podium, looking for water. There was nothing, so she dry-swallowed and looked up again.

"By now, I'm sure you've all heard rumors that President Brandt's plane has crashed while en route to Abu Dhabi. While the situation is ongoing and under development, I can . . . ." Maggie hesitated, then looked to Coffman.

He nodded once, making a fist and shaking it encouragingly.

"I can confirm that *Air Force One* crash-landed in eastern Turkey about three hours ago, and we believe the president's life may have been lost."

The Blue Room was perfectly quiet. Lines of reporters sat frozen, watching her without blinking, pens hovering over notepads, mouths hanging half open.

Maggie gripped the podium to steady herself. A dozen body language experts and political advisors were probably in panic mode. Standing silent, in obvious uncertainty, sent all the wrong signals. It made her look vulnerable and out of control.

But Maggie's gut told her a different story. The people needed to believe in her. They needed to see a human, not a cardboard cutout repeating all the right phrases. They needed to know she was suffering with them.

"At this time, per constitutional protocol, I am assuming the role of acting president of the United States while we uncover the truth of this tragedy. I want to assure you that national security and continuity of government are still the top priorities of the Brandt administration, and there is no reason to believe our homeland is in danger."

Maggie allowed her forearms to flex as she gripped the podium.

"I won't waste your time with political smoke screens or vague promises of retribution. The truth is, we have no idea what happened or who is responsible. But what I can tell you, and what I'll tell the world, is that we've been here before. We've faced senseless violence and unprovoked attacks many times, and we've risen from the ashes, stronger and prouder than ever." Maggie felt a tear in her eye, but she didn't try to stop it. The anxious pain she felt radiating through her chest was real. But so was the resolve. "God bless America," she said. "God bless you all."

Maggie turned from the podium and hurried quickly out, ignoring the swiveling cameras and bustle of reporters rushing to their feet. O'Dell met her at the door, and Coffman hurried to make closing comments before catching up with her.

"That was good," Coffman whispered. "Just right."

Maggie nodded, conscious of the open doors and unknown spectators clustered around her. "Take me to the office," she said. "We've got work to do."

13

Coffman led her back to the West Wing. Along the way, they hurried past crowds of disheveled aides, many of whom were red-eyed with tear-stained cheeks. Again, Maggie found herself longing to be empathetic, but she simply didn't have the time. Her mind was already grinding into the next gear: manage the crisis.

Outside the Oval Office, Coffman put his hand on the doorknob, then hesitated. "Would you . . . like a minute?"

"A minute?" Maggie asked.

"You know. Since it's your first time."

"It's still his office, Jason. Until we know otherwise."

Coffman pushed the door open. Maggie stepped in, breathing in a deep lungful of fragrant air. Daylight streamed through windows covered in sheer curtains, spilling over the Resolute Desk and more royal-blue carpet.

Maggie stopped for a moment to take in the view, but she didn't really register the gravity of where she was standing. Today, it was just another room. Another place to work.

O'Dell shut the door, and Maggie turned to Coffman. "I need you to be blunt. Who can we trust?"

Coffman blinked. "Ma'am?"

"I have a plan to recover the flight recorder, but it's delicate. I need to know who can be discreet."

Coffman considered for a moment. "General Yellin is pragmatic. So long as his patriotism isn't compromised, he'll do anything. Secretary Gorman is a little more by-the-book, and she prefers a softer touch. If you're going to violate Turkey's intrusion policy, I recommend you leave her out of it."

"What about Attorney General Thomas?"

Coffman made a noncommittal shrug. "He doesn't like sticky situations. Frankly, he can be a bit of a flake."

"I got that impression downstairs. We'll cut him out. Get Yellin in here, pronto, along with the director of the CIA and the director of the FBI. Then I need you to seal off the room. Nobody disturbs us until further notice. Clear?"

Confusion clouded Coffman's face, but he moved to the door, already dialing a number on his cell phone. As soon as the door closed, Maggie turned to O'Dell. He shifted uncomfortably on his feet but didn't comment.

"Do you trust me, James?"

O'Dell seemed mildly offended. "Completely, ma'am."

Maggie chewed her bottom lip, then nodded slowly. "Good. Because I need your help."

14

Yellin arrived first, bustling in with a briefcase in one hand and a cup of coffee in the other. His Army uniform was as impeccable as ever, but Maggie saw dark bags building beneath his eyes. She invited him to sit on one of the couches in the Oval Office, then waited until a rail-skinny man with a polished bald head and rimless glasses followed Coffman into the room.

"Madam Acting President, may I introduce CIA Director Victor O'Brien."

Maggie took the director's hand, finding it icy cold and stiff. He offered her a perfunctory greeting, and she motioned for him to have a seat.

"FBI Director Purcell will be here shortly," Coffman said. "He was across town."

Maggie settled into one of the chairs facing the couches and waited until O'Dell had shut the door. "Gentlemen, I won't waste your time. I called this meeting because it's paramount that we recover the flight recorder from the crash site and search for possible survivors. Regardless of Turkey's position on US intrusion, I'm prepared to make that happen."

Yellin indulged in a satisfied grunt, but O'Brien said nothing. He scrutinized Maggie as though she were a painting—evaluating her. Measuring her.

"Mr. Director," Maggie said, addressing O'Brien. "Do we have any leads on who may have brought down our plane?"

Behind those rimless glasses, Maggie saw wheels turning—calculating a political answer. It told her a lot about the man.

"It's far too early to say. I've got my people working overtime on any possible lead, but we simply don't have any data to start with. We really need the flight recorder to determine whether the plane was shot down or simply crashed."

"Do you have assets in place to make the recovery?"

O'Brien winced and shook his head. "I'm sorry, ma'am. Any assets the agency might have in the region are strictly non-operators. Not the sort of search-and-rescue people you need."

Maggie expected that answer, but she wanted O'Brien to say it himself. It was important for Coffman and O'Dell to understand the inevitability of her plan.

"General, how quickly can you have boots on the ground?" Maggie asked, turning to Yellin.

The chairman of the Joint Chiefs sat forward. "We can have Air Force Pararescue on-site in under three hours. Planes from northern Iraq are already fueled and ready to take air, but . . ."

"But?"

"But it'll be a problem getting my people out again. The crash site is deep inside the Turkish mountains, about ten thousand feet above sea level. Roads are almost nonexistent, and the terrain is punishing."

"What about helicopters?" Maggie asked. She already knew the answer, but again, she needed it to come from somebody else.

"Black Hawks could reach the site without a problem, but there's no way to make that subtle. If we put birds in the air, the Turks will know. Even Pararescue is likely to be detected."

Bingo.

"You're worried about a military standoff?" Maggie said.

Yellin pursed his lips. "I disagree with Secretary Gorman's assessment of Turkey's sovereignty, in this case. But the proximity of the crash site to the border with Iran is concerning. Without Turkish support, we run a very real risk of leaving troops stranded at the crash site."

"What about spec ops?" Maggie said. "Somebody to sneak in and sneak out."

Tension played across Yellin's face. Even as a proud member of the Army for most of his life, the general was still something of a politician. Maggie guessed he was contemplating the personal risk of deploying troops, off the books, into a foreign country. And perhaps, more importantly, giving his approval to do so in front of witnesses.

"It's a possibility, ma'am, but we'd need some time. And there's still substantial political risk if our people were identified. It's worth mentioning."

And here we go.

Maggie interlaced her fingers. "What about somebody off the record? Somebody . . . not connected to the Department of Defense."

The general exchanged a look with O'Brien, then set his coffee cup down. "Ma'am . . . with respect. This isn't like Hollywood. We don't have—"

"I'm not talking about *your* people. I'm talking about one of mine."

The door clicked, and Maggie looked up to see Jenkins letting in another man in a black suit. Unlike O'Brien, this man was heavyset, with thinning gray hair and stumpy legs. He carried a briefcase, and Maggie rose to greet him, clasping her fingers around his chunky hand.

"FBI Director Bill Purcell," Coffman said.

"It's a pleasure to meet you, ma'am," Purcell said, his chunky cheeks shimmering with sweat.

Maggie motioned for him to sit, then resumed her chair. An evident tension now hung in the air, and she wasn't sure if it was due to Purcell's arrival or her previous statement. Either way, she decided to plunge right in. "Director Purcell, can you tell me where Reed Montgomery is?"

Dead stillness filled the room.

Purcell wiped his lip with one thumb. "Pardon, ma'am?"

"Reed Montgomery. Do you know where he is?"

Purcell looked to O'Brien, and both men looked to Yellin. Then Purcell cleared his throat. "You mean the domestic terrorist, ma'am?"

Maggie left the couch, stepping behind the Resolute Desk and turning her back to the men. She looked out over the lawn and interlaced her fingers behind her back. "He's not a domestic terrorist," she said. "He's a former Force Recon Marine with an unfortunate history of bad decisions and a penchant for violence. During the Resilient Pharmaceutical investigation, Montgomery was my chief investigator. Part of the deal was for him to receive prosecution immunity, but the US attorney responsible for making that happen backstabbed him. Now, Montgomery is in the wind, hiding with a woman named Banks Morccelli. But why do I feel like you already knew that?"

Maggie looked over her shoulder, and Purcell avoided her gaze.

Yellin spoke next. "I'm not sure I understand the connection."

Maggie circled the desk again, leaning against its front edge and folding her arms. "The connection is that Reed Montgomery may be the perfect man to recover that flight recorder. I've personally witnessed him tear apart a criminal empire like it was made of Legos and barely break a sweat doing it. The man is ruthless, highly trained, and relentless. Best of all, he's completely off the books. If the Turks catch him, we can disavow him without trouble."

Purcell scratched one ear, sweat beading on his forehead. "Respectfully, ma'am, I can't condone or enable the use of a national criminal for any sort of state-sponsored mission. It's simply not legal."

"So, you *do* know where he is . . ."

"I didn't say that."

"But you do."

"We do," O'Brien said, his voice dry and toneless. He sat at the end of the couch and ignored the semi-panicked glare Purcell shot his way. "He's hiding in a little village on the west coast of Honduras. Has been for a few months now. Not long after the Resilient investigation, my agency picked him up in Venezuela, along with Ms. Morccelli. We've tracked him ever since."

Maggie looked to Purcell. "So, you know where he is, but you haven't arrested him?"

O'Brien took control again. "Reed Montgomery is, as you say, a dangerous man. Something of a rabid dog. In my experience, the best way to manage a rabid dog is to give it space. Unless or until . . ."

"Unless or until?" Maggie said.

"*Unless* he becomes useful, or *until* he becomes a threat, ma'am."

Bingo.

Maggie resumed her seat. "He's become useful, Mr. Director. Now it's time to bring him home. Does anyone here have assets on hand to transport Officer O'Dell to Honduras?"

An invisible game of hot potato passed around the room, stopping at O'Brien.

He removed his glasses and rubbed his eyes. "We could move him on one of our SAC jets," he said. "Keep it off the record."

Yellin broke in. "Ma'am, I should stress that there *are* other people we could send. People properly equipped to—"

"Nobody is better equipped than Officer O'Dell. Montgomery knows him, and he'll believe him when he makes my offer."

Nobody spoke, but the question was obvious.

Maggie folded her hands. "I'm prepared to hand Montgomery a full presidential pardon in exchange for recovering the flight recorder, along with any crash survivors." Maggie looked out the window, feeling the crushing weight of responsibility dragging down on her shoulders. "No one will be happier than I if President Brandt survived, but we have to assume he didn't, and we can't fight a faceless enemy. We need that flight recorder, and Reed Montgomery is our best hope of getting it."

15

The man stood by himself in the room, heavy curtains pulled over all of the windows, save the last one—a narrow pane just wide enough to let a beam of sunlight spill over plush carpeting.

Through that window the man could see the bulk of the Washington Mall stretching out in front of him like a massive rectangular golf course. At the end of it all rose the majestic bulk of the US Capitol, its dome outlined against a sky still roiling with clouds.

So refined. So elegant. So fragile.

The soft ring of a phone filled the hotel room, and the man lifted the device from his pocket, pressing the answer key without checking the number. Only one person ever called this phone.

"Yes?"

"You won't believe this."

The man on the other end sounded out of breath and strained, as if he had just jogged a flight of stairs or was forty pounds overweight.

"What?"

"She's using Reed Montgomery."

The man in the hotel room frowned at the Capitol, fingering his lower lip. "Montgomery? Wait . . . The domestic terrorist?"

"Exactly. She's gonna offer him a presidential pardon in exchange for recovering the flight recorder."

"I'll be damned . . ."

"It's not something I could stop. The woman is impetuous!"

The man in the hotel rubbed his lip again. "What about Iran? Has she mentioned them?"

"Not while I was there. She's fixated on the flight recorder. I guess she wants to know for sure before things escalate."

"Well, we won't give her the time. Turn up the heat. Leak something else to CNN if you need to. Keep her on edge."

"Right. No problem. But what about Montgomery?"

"Let me worry about that."

"If he recovers that flight recorder—"

"He won't. Take it from me. He won't live long enough."

16

O'Dell left for Joint Base Andrews immediately after the meeting, taking a wad of discretionary cash and a handwritten note from Maggie. She knew the odds of Montgomery responding to a personal request from her, under any circumstances, were near zero, but she hoped what she wrote would help sway him.

From Andrews, O'Dell would board an unmarked Gulfstream jet operated by the CIA's Special Activities Center and fly directly to Tegucigalpa. With luck, he'd reach Montgomery's Honduran hideout by nightfall and locate the renegade killer soon after.

All Maggie could do was hope, but right then, she didn't even have time for that. The White House was a disaster zone full of aides, shouting media, and government officials who seemed unsure how to function in the absence of their president.

Maggie sat at the head of the conference table in the Cabinet Room, listening as Coffman read from an iPad, rattling through a checklist of priorities. Her head still buzzed, maybe from stress or simple exhaustion, but it was only two in the afternoon, and she still had a minimum of eight hours to go.

"We need to communicate with our allies," Coffman said. "Secretary Gorman, do you have a report for the acting president?"

Gorman brushed graying hair behind one ear. "Ma'am, I've already spoken with Prime Minister Bradley and Chancellor Shultz. We—"

"I'm sorry, Secretary." Maggie flushed a little. "I'm not familiar with those names."

Coffman subtly pushed a sheet of notepaper toward Maggie. It was inscribed with names and titles, beginning with those Gorman had mentioned.

Bradley — PM, UK

Shultz — Chancellor, Germany

Maggie motioned to Gorman. "Please continue."

"As I was saying, ma'am, I've spoken with leaders in the UK and Germany. They both expressed condolences and assured us of military support should conflict break out. I haven't yet had a chance to speak with Canada, France, Israel, or Japan, but my office has received memos from all four conveying the same. Default statements, of course, but helpful for the American people to know we don't stand alone."

"What about Russia?" Maggie asked.

Gorman shook her head. "Nothing, ma'am. That isn't altogether unusual. It's after ten p.m. in Moscow."

Maggie suspected Gorman's comment was meant to be reassuring, but the attempt was pretty transparent. News of *Air Force One*'s demise had leaked three hours prior. Moscow had plenty of time to respond if they'd wanted to.

"What's your read on the Russians?" Maggie asked.

Gorman hesitated, and Maggie could tell she was cherry-picking her words.

"Bluntly, please," Maggie said.

"I don't trust Moscow, ma'am. President Nikitin has been in office for less than eighteen months, and we don't know a lot about his diplomatic policy. Thus far, Moscow has behaved as Moscow always has—in their best interests. But I advise caution. I would wait and see if they reach out."

"Keep me briefed. What about Iran? Have we heard anything out of Tehran?"

"Not directly. I reached out to the embassy and requested an immediate meeting, but they haven't replied yet. If I had to guess, they're playing things slow."

"Lean on them a little," Maggie said. "I'd like to be present if you meet with the ambassador."

"Of course, ma'am."

Maggie glanced at Coffman, and he consulted the iPad.

"There's only one more thing." He drew an exhausted sigh and set the tablet down. "We're seeing pretty radical instability in the market. The NASDAQ is down fourteen percent, which we expected. It dropped sixteen percent after 9/11. But fuel prices are starting to balloon. The average price of gas has increased eighteen percent overnight and is projected to rise moving into next week. There have already been reports of pumps running dry."

"Why?"

"Reactionary market rush, ma'am." The voice came from the end of the table, and Maggie looked past the row of military advisors and secretaries to see a petite woman with sharp cheekbones. The nameplate in front of her read "Stacey Pilcher, Secretary of Transportation."

"Anytime there's a national emergency, people buy gas just like they'd buy milk or eggs. That surge in demand triggers price gouging from the fuel companies. Usually, we don't see more than eight or ten percent, but with the existing instability in the fuel market caused by tensions in the Persian Gulf, things are snowballing. If the situation isn't managed, we could see another twenty percent increase by the weekend."

"Twenty percent . . ." Maggie's head spun. "What does that mean? What are the externalities?"

Pilcher made a noncommittal tilt of her head. "Impossible to say. Short term, you're looking at a lot of media bluster, some empty gas stations, and maybe some random acts of violence triggered by panic. My greater concerns are what will happen if the situation remains unchecked. We could be looking at supply chain disruption, protests, and inflation. It's all dominos. One thing triggers another."

"What are our options?"

"You could open the strategic reserves—release some oil to help manage costs. But frankly, that's kind of like a Band-Aid. The only long-term solution is to remove the stimulant driving the panic. If it were me . . ." Pilcher stopped herself, fixating on her notepad and shifting uncomfortably, as if she'd said more than she intended.

"What?" Maggie pressed.

Pilcher looked up. "If it were me, ma'am, I'd focus on solving the crash. The panic won't fade until the people know they're safe."

Maggie looked to Coffman. He nodded once.

"I concur," Coffman said.

"Thank you for your input, Madam Secretary. Please monitor the situation and notify me if you think we should tap into the reserves. Was there anything else, Jason?"

"That's all for now," Coffman said.

"Great. I'll be in the Oval if anyone needs me."

Everybody stood in unison as Maggie moved to the door, Coffman and Jenkins at her elbow. The short walk to the Oval Office was already becoming routine, but she still felt like an intruder.

Maggie put one hand on the door and stopped. The hallway around her was momentarily still. The rare pause in the chaotic pace felt too good to break, and she took a few seconds to drink it in.

"Give it to me straight. Am I screwing this up?"

Coffman straightened. She saw the same exhaustion in his face that she felt in her core, but there was strength there, also. Strength and compassion.

"Not at all, ma'am. You're doing great."

She twisted the knob. "You're a good liar, Jason."

Sunlight spilled in from the Rose Garden as Maggie opened the door, squinting in the blaze. She stepped toward the desk, then stopped mid-stride as she was suddenly aware of a tall man in a charcoal-gray suit rising from the couch.

He turned toward her, offering his hand. "Madam Acting President, thank you for meeting with me."

Maggie stopped, then looked to Coffman.

Brandt's chief of staff stood frozen in the door, his face dropping to consult the iPad. He flicked across it, then flushed. "I'm so sorry, ma'am. This was one of President Brandt's meetings. We neglected to cancel."

The man in the suit looked from Coffman to Maggie, and his brow wrinkled into a frown. "I'm so sorry. I double-checked with my office, and—"

"It's fine," Maggie said, collecting herself and offering her hand. "Maggie Trousdale."

The man took her hand. "Lance Sanger, ma'am. Chief executive officer of Flashpoint Defense."

"The mercenary firm?" Maggie asked.

Sanger indulged in a wry smile. "We prefer the term *private security contractors*, ma'am."

"Of course." She withdrew her hand but made no effort to take a seat, leaving Sanger standing awkwardly next to the couch. He didn't seem perturbed.

"I was scheduled to meet with President Brandt to offer Flashpoint's assistance with any Middle Eastern security measures America may require. Of course . . . things are different now."

"I'm afraid they are, Mr. Sanger."

Sanger pocketed his hands and evaluated Maggie, just how Brandt had. But unlike Brandt, Maggie detected none of the stormy uncertainty in Sanger. He stood confidently with squared shoulders but no condescension.

"I'm very sorry, ma'am," he said at last. "President Brandt was a personal friend of mine. We were business partners for a time. When he launched his campaign, I was a primary contributor. America has lost a brilliant leader."

Maggie held her head high. "He may still be alive, Mr. Sanger. The situation is developing."

"Of course."

Coffman cleared his throat gently, making a show of checking his watch.

"Well, I won't take any more of your valuable time," Sanger said. "But please know that my offer stands. If you require any support, Flashpoint stands ready. Our security teams can deploy far quicker than traditional military units."

"I appreciate the offer, Mr. Sanger, but if America goes to war, she'll go to war through Congress. We've had enough back-door conflicts, wouldn't you say?"

A faint smile pulled at the corners of Sanger's mouth, then he started toward the door.

Halfway across the royal-blue carpet, he paused and looked over one shoulder. "William chose well. You'll make a good president."

Maggie said nothing, and Coffman escorted Sanger out. She found her way to the leather-backed chair behind the Resolute Desk and crumpled into it, resting her forehead in her hands and sucking down a deep breath.

The door clicked, and Coffman hurried back in. "I'm so sorry. I should've double-checked—"

"It's fine, Jason. Thanks for getting him out. Who do we have next?"

Coffman consulted the tablet again and grimaced. "The Senate majority leader and the Speaker of the House are waiting for you in the Roosevelt Room."

Maggie ran her fingers through her hair. "Give me five, then show them in."

Coffman slipped out of the room as Maggie slouched into the chair.

It was gonna be a long day.

17

It took only a few hours to scrub the house, removing all traces of their presence from the little shack and packing everything they owned into two suitcases. Banks moved slowly, sweating a lot and stopping from time to time to puke off the back porch.

Reed held her hair and rubbed her back, feeling helpless to ease her discomfort. She looked ready to drop as he slammed the Camaro's trunk and helped her into the passenger seat.

"It's a smooth boat ride, right?" she asked.

Reed started the car, the motor rumbling to life with a dull cough. "Regular cruise ship. Wait 'til you see the Jacuzzi."

It was less than twenty miles from Nacaome to San Lorenzo, the coastal town Reed had selected as their departure point. He could make it in half an hour over the pothole-infested roads, but the freighter he had bartered passage on didn't leave for another eight hours, so he drove slowly, dodging all the worst holes and bumps. Banks held her stomach and watched the rolling landscape drift by, grunting whenever the car jerked through a rut.

Reed rolled his window down and sucked in dusty Honduran air, watching the hills pass on either side without any thought of whether he would miss this place. The freighter was bound across the Pacific, a nine-thousand-mile voyage to Bangkok that would consume the better part of a month. Reed and Banks were traveling off the manifest as "undesignated cargo"—a standard arrangement for black-market passage. The Camaro would slide into a container, and they would stay out of sight until they reached port, at which point, Reed would have to find suitable lodging for an expectant mother.

He'd need money, too. Half of his fifty-thousand-dollar payday from the Diablo job was consumed by his illegal transportation, and the other half wouldn't last long in the bustling Asian city.

But those were bridges Reed would cross when he reached them. Right now, he was only worried about getting Banks safely on the ship and making her as comfortable as possible during the voyage. It was difficult to tell the difference between morning sickness and the affliction of her Lyme disease. The possibility of the two colliding into something worse weighed heavily on him.

San Lorenzo lay on the other side of the Pan American Highway, resting near the Pacific with a population of just over thirty thousand. Reed had driven there on occasion to purchase groceries or under-the-table pharmaceuticals for Banks, but he didn't consider himself familiar with the city. He employed his phone to help navigate through the shopping districts, past the downtown core, and to the port, where long concrete piers jutted out into the water. An expansive delta region obscured his view of the ocean, but a number of large ships lay at anchor against the ports, and an army of longshoremen were busy moving cargo around on forklifts and cranes.

Reed slid the Camaro into a parking spot a half mile from the port and watched through the dusty windshield for a while, acquainting himself with the landscape. The sheer volume of people made him nervous, giving him more possible threats to monitor than he was comfortable with. But then again, the probability of a killer being loose amid that crowd was minimal, and even if there was one, the presence of so many witnesses would inhibit the threat.

Reed rubbed a hand across his chin, brushing beard stubble, then reached for the door. "I'm going to find the ship. You sit tight, okay?"

Banks nodded, still resting both hands on her skinny middle. He wondered if she was thinking about the baby or if she was simply trying not to puke.

The Camaro's door groaned closed, and Reed pulled a jacket over his shoulders, feeling the reassuring grip of his SIG pressed into his belt. Then he left the Camaro and started toward the dock.

In total, Reed had spent only a few months of his chaotic life in Latin America, but he liked it. There was a lot to be said for the gentler pace and calmer approach that Hispanic culture valued. Even in the crowded streets and bustling businesses, Reed felt an overall serenity that he never felt in one of America's surging cities. Maybe it was rose-colored glasses, or maybe it was simply his desperation for a moment's peace, but if he wasn't a man on the run, and Banks wasn't in need of advanced medical care, he might have stayed in Honduras for a lot longer. The people were kind. The food was good.

He just couldn't afford to be caught there.

At the port, Reed moved silently through the crowd, keeping his shoulders loose and blending in the best he could amid the shorter, darker-skinned locals. He knew he stuck out, but if he could at least avoid looking like a killer, he would be left alone.

Reed stopped at a guard shack, waiting in line as a number of longshoremen checked in with plastic IDs and hard hats cradled beneath their arms. He wasn't sure what the protocol would be when he reached the security guard, but his contact had told him to ask for José and say he was looking for work as an underwater welder.

Hopefully, he hadn't just blown twenty-five grand on a total scam.

With two dock workers still ahead of him, Reed saw the American. He knew he was American by the way he stood—stiff-backed and tense. The classic pose of a military or law enforcement veteran. Somebody who was always on guard.

Eighty yards from the guard shack, and back amid the slumped garages and storefronts of San Lorenzo, the guy stuck out like a pile of crap in a field of snow. He wore jeans and a subdued jacket, unzipped and exposing a tight T-shirt stretched over a muscled chest. It was the kind of thing a guy like this wore for two reasons—to show off the fruits of his workout regimen and to leave easy access for his pistol.

Reed disengaged easily from the line, slipping away from the dock and keeping one eye on the man, even as the intruder scanned the port without any effort to disguise his surveillance. He wore large sunglasses and a New Orleans Pelicans baseball hat, shielding his face with shadow, but Reed could tell by the twist of his head and his spring-loaded posture that he was looking for something—or someone.

Reed wouldn't stick around to find out what or who. He melted into a column of longshoremen exiting the port and moving toward the open-air lunch market nearby, conscious of the fact that he stood six inches above the tallest one. He stooped his shoulders, dropping his head and moving toward the first building, which could provide an obstruction between him and the American. But as Reed slipped around the corner, he threw one last glance over his shoulder, and the man no longer stood on the street corner he had occupied only moments before. The American had moved toward the port, slipping amongst locals and making a beeline straight for Reed's position.

Gravel crunched beneath Reed's feet as he hurried down the street, taking two random turns down alleys before slipping back into a muddle of pedestrians amid the market. The air hung thick with the savory odor of roasting meat and fresh vegetables, all melding together with faint traces of sweat and body odor. Reed kept close to the edge of the sidewalk, gradually increasing his pace as he reached the end of the market and looked over his shoulder again.

The man was a hundred yards back, barging through the locals with all the grace of a bulldozer, and plowing straight toward Reed.

Mud splashed across Reed's shin as he hurried through a puddle and turned into an alley. His heart rate quickened, but he didn't panic or reach for his pistol. Not yet. Whoever this man was, he wasn't a trained assassin or a covert operator. No, he was much too blunt and obvious for that. More likely, he was a government agent of some kind, which meant Reed didn't want to kill him, but he definitely wanted to get him as far as possible away from Banks.

At the end of the alley, Reed hung back, stalling until he saw the man cross into the mud puddle Reed had exited fifty yards back. Reed then swerved left onto the next street, slowing his pace enough to allow the man to gain some ground.

The streets here were quieter, with less foot traffic and no cars. Mud puddles the size of small sedans filled the center of gravel paths, forcing Reed to hug the sides of buildings as he moved farther away into the bustle of the market. He made sure the guy saw him take a right into another alley, but as soon as he cleared the turn, Reed broke into a sprint, hurrying to the far end, turning left down the connecting street, then left again down a second alley. In moments he was back where he started, waiting just around a corner and watching as the American crept along a narrow gravel path, one hand held beneath his jacket. Shadows obscured his face, but there was something familiar about his frame. Something distant . . . just out of reach of Reed's tired mind.

It didn't matter. He'd know soon enough.

Reed waited until the American turned down the first alley, then he left the shelter of the second. The SIG cleared his belt without a sound, the safety already disengaged, and Reed's finger resting just above the trigger guard. He hurried across the gravel, moving lightly on his toes, and in mere seconds, he closed the distance behind his clueless target.

The American tensed and started to turn only a split second before Reed grabbed him by the shoulder and jerked, spinning him and slamming him against the block wall of the building butted up against the alley. Reed crashed his knee upward, smashing between the man's thighs the same moment he struck the muzzle of the SIG into the guy's neck and slammed his head against the block.

The guy convulsed, overcome by pain and disabled by the pressure of the gun shoving upward on his chin. He choked but didn't resist, dropping his hands to his sides and rasping for breath.

"Screw you," he wheezed.

The muttered words were oppressed by a heavy, warbling accent. Reed recognized the voice, but he still couldn't place the name. Leaving the SIG jammed into the American's throat, he released the guy's shoulder and knocked both the hat and sunglasses to the dirt.

The guy wheezed again, then spat sideways into the street, his dark eyes glaring pure hatred at Reed.

"O'Dell?" Reed snapped, semi-confusion clouding his tone.

"Hello, Montgomery."

18

Reed shoved the pistol back into O'Dell's neck, driving him against the wall. He tensed his left leg again, but O'Dell clamped his knees together, shielding his crotch.

"Chill out!" the Cajun shouted. "What's wrong with you?"

Reed wrapped his free hand around O'Dell's neck and squeezed just hard enough to make him choke. "Maybe I'm a little angry, O'Dell. Maybe I'm a little pissed off. Wanna take a guess why?"

O'Dell choked and slammed a hand against Reed's ribs, pushing him back. Reed didn't move, but he relaxed his grip. The Cajun coughed, and Reed ran a hand down his side, stripping away a handgun before allowing him to slump to the ground.

"You sleazy SOB," Reed snarled. "Why are you here?"

O'Dell rubbed his neck and glared upward. "Trust me. It's the last place I wanna be."

"Is that right? So, who sent you, then? That backstabbing boss of yours?"

O'Dell kept rubbing his throat. "You watch the news?"

Reed snorted. "What do you think?"

"I think I'm wasting my time talking to your dumb ass, but that wasn't my call."

"*Who sent you?* Trousdale?"

O'Dell slouched against the wall. "The president sent me."

Reed paused, genuinely surprised by the answer. The last time he'd seen O'Dell was when he served as Governor Maggie Trousdale's personal bodyguard. That memory didn't arouse any positive feelings—not for Trousdale or O'Dell.

"The president doesn't send half-assed Cajun donut eaters. Not after me."

"She does when it's off the record," O'Dell said.

"She?"

"Maggie Trousdale is president now."

Reed stood frozen, the SIG still pointed at O'Dell's chest. What he heard made no sense, but he detected no deceit from O'Dell. No games. Just irritation.

"You really *don't* watch the news, do you?" O'Dell said with a dry laugh.

Reed lowered the handgun, letting it hang at his side. "Why should I? America spat me out like bad chewing gum."

"If you ask me, you *are* bad chewing gum. On a good day."

"How flattering, O'Dell. You still haven't answered my question. What the hell are you doing here?"

"Looking for you, obviously."

"Yeah, well, you found me. Nice job."

"Don't you want to know how?"

"I don't really care, but if anything you said is true, I imagine the FBI had a hand in it."

"Smart guy. So, you knew they were tracking you."

"Of course I knew. I wasn't hiding. Just keeping myself far enough out of reach to be left alone. Clearly, not far enough."

O'Dell wiped his lip and twisted his legs to stand. Reed raised the gun again, and O'Dell sat back down.

"What do you want?" Reed demanded.

"Like I said . . . the president sent me. She'd like to fly you to Washington. She needs your help."

"Is that right? You know, the last time I helped your boss, she slid a knife between my ribs like it belonged there."

"That's not true, and you know it. But I'm not here to argue semantics. I'm here to make a deal."

"I'm sure you are. And I'm sure at the end of your deal, I wind up in prison."

"Or with a presidential pardon." O'Dell let the words hang in the air, then gestured to his pocket. "May I?"

Reed's finger dropped onto the SIG's trigger. "Slowly."

O'Dell reached with two fingers into his jacket pocket, producing a simple white envelope. As he held it out, Reed immediately noted the circular blue seal emblazoned on one side. He didn't need to study that seal to recognize it. Any American who graduated fifth grade would recognize that mark—the Seal of the President of the United States.

Reed accepted the envelope and ran his thumb across the embossed surface, but he didn't open it. He looked back to O'Dell. "Speak quickly. I'm short on time."

"Two months ago, the vice president resigned after a scandal. President Brandt nominated Governor Trousdale to be his replacement. She was sworn in three days ago."

"And she offed her boss already? Damn, she's worse than I remember."

O'Dell gritted his teeth but didn't take the bait. "*Air Force One* went down over Turkey early yesterday morning. We've lost all contact with the flight crew. Brandt is presumed dead."

Reed stood very still. A mental image of America's most famous plane crashing to earth in a blast of flames flooded his mind, and for just a moment, he felt something.

Anger. Confusion. Loss.

Then the moment was gone, and his attention returned to O'Dell. "What does that have to do with me?"

O'Dell smirked. "Wow. Heart of stone, huh?"

"Not at all. I just gave up caring about things I can't control. Now, you have ten seconds to give me a reason not to knock your ass out and leave you in this alley."

"We can't get to the crash site. Turkey has sealed off all access, probably due to rising tensions with Iran. President Trousdale needs somebody to recover the flight recorder . . . off the record."

Of course she does.

Reed tore the envelope open with his teeth. He spat expensive stationery over the gravel and then dug out the folded notecard. The presidential seal was embossed on the front again, but only a short message filled the inside.

Reed,
> *I can clean your slate.*
> *Your country needs the Prosecutor.*
> *—M*

The Prosecutor.

The name sent a jolt of lightning shooting down his spine, and he closed the card, running his thumb across the seal again. It was a name he hadn't heard in a long time: *his* name. It was what they used to call him when he was an elite killer, knocking off mob bosses for bigger mob bosses.

The Prosecutor.

Well, the name had fallen off, but the skill set hadn't.

Reed flicked the card at O'Dell and stepped back. "Sorry, dude. I've been around the block with your boss. She doesn't keep promises."

"What happened with the Resilient investigation wasn't her fault. The US attorney backstabbed her as much as he backstabbed you. Things are different now. We're not talking about prosecution immunity. We're talking about a complete presidential pardon. For everything."

"Sounds nice. So, sign the damn thing."

O'Dell scrabbled to his feet, and this time Reed let him. Trousdale's bodyguard folded his arms. "Not before you help us. Nothing is free, Reed."

Again, Reed searched for signs of deception in O'Dell's face. He saw nothing to put him on edge, but if Trousdale were playing games, O'Dell wouldn't know anything about it. He was a henchman, not a captain. He delivered messages; he didn't write them.

Reed slipped the pistol into his holster and pulled the jacket over it. "Sorry. I'm not Captain America. I can't afford to be." He started down the alley.

O'Dell called after him. "Can you afford to let Banks die?"

Reed froze, and his fingers tightened into a fist as he looked over one shoulder. "What?"

"She's sick, right? Lyme disease. Impossible to cure. Just sucks the life out of you, one day at a time."

"You threatening me?"

"No, I'm doing my job. Trust me, asshole. There's nothing I'd like better than to watch you waste away on the run, living out of cars and sleeping with one eye open. God knows you deserve it. But my boss said to get you, and that's what I'm here to do. If you won't do it for yourself, do it for the girl. Or do you not actually love her?"

Reed's jaw twitched. O'Dell's words hit a lot closer to home than the Cajun could know. Reed thought about Banks, nestled in the Camaro, popping second-rate antibiotics and surviving off scrounged-up food.

But not just her. Not anymore. Now their unborn child survived off that same meager nourishment, dependent upon its mother to find a way to be healthy and keep it safe—to find a way to keep it alive. Even if he made it to Bangkok, found a house and a job, and put better food on the table, how long would it last?

O'Dell was right. The running would never cease. He'd been lucky so far with the FBI. They knew where he was, but they didn't have the time or resources to run him down. How long until that changed? How long before they ripped his fragile family apart, right in front of him?

Reed took a step toward O'Dell and raised a shaking fist. "I gave my *life* for my country! I lost *everything*."

"I don't need you to like it," O'Dell said. "I just need you to do it."

Reed imagined the crunch of bone on bone as his knuckles obliterated O'Dell's nose. He could tell by a slight offset that the nose had been broken before—maybe a few times. O'Dell was no stranger to a fight. He was a soldier, just like Reed. He just hadn't been burned yet.

Reed lowered his fist and took a long breath. He bottled the anger up for another time and thought again about Banks. He imagined her in a nice house on a nice American street. A dog in the backyard and a playhouse for the child. A whole room for Banks to fill with guitars and music. All the things she loved best and deserved most.

A peaceful life. A safe, stable life.

Reed relaxed his hand. "Come with me."

19

Reed found the Camaro right where he'd left it. Banks lay curled up in the passenger seat, leaned against one window, sleeping fitfully. As he approached, he spoke softly through the side of his mouth, just loud enough for O'Dell to hear.

"If you touch her, you die. If more of your goons show up, you die. If you make a joke and I don't laugh . . . you die."

O'Dell said nothing as Reed squatted next to the car and tapped gently on the dirty glass. Banks blinked a few times, then sat up, allowing Reed to open the door.

"Find the boat?" she mumbled.

"Not exactly," Reed said. "We need to talk."

Banks stretched and instinctively craned her neck to look out of the car. She saw O'Dell, and confusion clouded her face. "What the—"

She reached for the glovebox, and Reed put a hand on her arm. "Banks, it's okay."

She remained tense, twisting to drop her feet onto the ground. "What's he doing here? Did he bring the FBI?"

"It's just me," O'Dell said. "I promise."

"Cheap words from a cheap man," Banks snapped.

Reed squeezed her arm. "He's alone, Banks. I made sure. Would you climb in back? We're taking a ride."

Banks looked confused, but Reed squeezed her hand and tilted his head toward the back seat. She reluctantly climbed into the cramped rear, piling in next to blankets and a suitcase.

Reed motioned to O'Dell. "Turn and spread."

O'Dell sighed but didn't object. He turned his back to Reed and put both hands behind his head, then spread his legs.

Reed made quick work of patting him down, locating a spare magazine for the pistol he already confiscated, along with a knife and cell phone. Reed passed each item to Banks, then pointed to the passenger seat. "Get in."

O'Dell folded his big frame into the car, and Reed slammed the door. A moment later, they were bumping across another pothole-infested street, turning inland from San Lorenzo. Banks kept O'Dell's Glock pointed at his back, and Reed tilted the rearview mirror until he could make eye contact with her.

"Tell her," Reed said.

O'Dell ran a hand over his mouth and started from the beginning, detailing Trousdale's ascent from unknown governor of the Pelican State to celebrity politician to vice president and now acting president. Maybe actual president, pretty soon.

O'Dell glossed over details of his and Reed's conversation but summarized the offer just as Reed steered off the road at the crest of a hill. Buildings and houses had long ago faded, leaving them surrounded by nothing, save rolling Honduran countryside mixed with light jungle undergrowth.

Reed cut the engine as O'Dell finished his spiel, then jabbed his thumb at the door. "Out."

O'Dell glared at the sprawling countryside. "Seriously?"

"Out," Reed repeated. "Family conference. You're not family."

O'Dell clambered out, slamming the door behind him and retreating twenty yards away before digging a cigarette out of his pocket. Gray smoke swirled around his face, and Reed reached into the Camaro's console to retrieve his phone. What little cell signal he had came from San Lorenzo, now five miles away. It was weak, but enough to generate a couple quick Google searches.

Banks waited while Reed scanned American news headlines, thumbing from one network to the next to read variations of the same stories. He clicked the phone off and dropped it into the console, then stared out his window at nothing in particular. "It's true," he said. "*Air Force One* went down. Trousdale is acting president."

Banks still didn't comment, but Reed didn't press her. She could be a slow thinker, but her thoughts were always worth the wait. "She's a backstabbing liar, Reed. We know that."

Reed ran his finger along the vinyl door liner, brushing away dust and tracing a crack. The car was old, but up until he fled the States, it had been in flawless condition. The bullet holes in the fender and abuse of the interior almost felt like a barometer of the abuse he and Banks were enduring daily.

"Reed?" Banks touched his arm. "You're not actually thinking about this . . ."

"I don't know if we have a choice," Reed said. His voice was dry, and he was surprised by how hard the words were to say.

"What do you mean? Start the car. Let's go back to the boat. Get to Bangkok!"

"And then what, Banks?" Reed's words turned hard as he twisted to face her. "Then we hide in some shack again? Eke out a living sifting through trash? It can't work that way. It's not just us anymore."

Banks's wide blue eyes stared at him with traces of pain, but mostly all he saw was exhaustion.

"We can't run forever," Reed whispered. "If there's even a chance this works out, it may be the best shot we ever get."

"But what if it doesn't? What if you go back to prison, or . . ."

"Or what?" Reed knew what she was thinking. He didn't know why he pressed her.

"Or get killed!" Banks said, a tear slipping down her cheek.

Reed wiped her face with a dirty thumb, leaving a smear of grime. "I'm not that easy to kill," he whispered. Reed pulled her close, resting his cheek against hers. He squeezed her shoulder and breathed in the scent of her tangled hair. Even dirty and battered, she smelled like home. She felt perfect in his arms.

"Do you trust me?" he whispered.

Banks didn't move, nestled into his shoulder, then she nodded once. He gave her another squeeze, then kissed the top of her head and reached for the door handle.

It was muggy outside and smelled of cigarettes. Reed approached O'Dell without a word and held out a hand. The Cajun passed him a fresh cigarette and lit it with the tip of his own. For a while, the two of them smoked in silence, Reed sucking down the nicotine and welcoming the mild relief it brought to his tense body. Then he dropped the smoke and ground it out with his boot. "Where's the damn plane?"

20

The Gulfstream jet touched down in Maryland like a swan gliding into a lake, rolling across the smooth tarmac with barely a sound. It was dark outside, the sun having set a few hours prior, and Reed sat in the tail of the plane next to Banks as she slept. O'Dell sat a few rows away, reading a mystery novel as though he were the only person on board, and Baxter snored at Banks's feet.

Reed suspected that the Gulfstream was a CIA asset, which made this entire scheme both more serious and more covert than he first estimated. The flight lasted right at six hours as the little plane streaked through the sky like a rocket. They ate during the trip, too—reheated food that O'Dell brought with him, washed down with bottled water.

The whole time, Reed was busy second-guessing himself, evaluating whether this entire decision was a catastrophic mistake. In theory, it could be nothing more than an elaborate ruse by the FBI to capture him. But after verifying reports of Brandt's demise and Trousdale's ascension to the White House, Reed didn't think so. Even if Trousdale had nothing to do with this, it seemed unlikely that the FBI had time or interest in bringing him in during the greatest national security crisis since 9/11.

There were bigger fish to fry, which meant O'Dell just might be telling the truth.

The Gulfstream stopped, and O'Dell closed the book. "They're putting Banks up in a safe house. I'll make sure she gets some medical attention and whatever she needs to be comfortable."

Reed looked out his window at the darkened hangar they were parked in. A couple of black Suburbans sat a few yards away, but he didn't see any people.

"Who is *they*?" Reed asked.

"People."

People. Right.

Reed faced O'Dell again. "I don't have to tell you what happens if she's hurt."

"Let me guess. I die."

"Wrong. You live. It's your family who dies."

O'Dell locked eyes with him, blazing pure disgust, then he stood and started to the door. The pilots had clambered out of the cockpit, and the airlock hissed as the door folded outward.

Reed nudged Banks, and she twisted toward the window. "Where are we?"

"America," Reed said, almost as if he weren't American. She sat up and rubbed her eyes, and Reed gripped her hand. "Listen to me," he said. "They're going to take you someplace safe. Baxter will go with you. Your job is to rest up and take care of yourself until I get back."

Sudden fear flashed across Banks's face, and she wrapped her fingers around his arm. "No. No, I don't like that. I should be with you when you talk to her."

"They won't let you, Banks. She's the president now. There's all kinds of security."

"So? I want to know she won't hurt you. I need to *see* her."

The primal instincts spewing from her mouth warmed Reed. He pulled her into a hug and held her close, thinking about how far he would go—and had gone—to protect her. It was understandable she wanted to reciprocate. That was how love worked.

But not this time.

"I'll be safe," he whispered. "I promise."

Standing at the airplane's door, O'Dell cleared his throat, and Reed and Banks wiggled out of the seat. Baxter woke and stood with an irritated snort, blowing saliva and snot all over the expensive carpet. He seemed unfazed by the rapid change in scenery, but by then, he should've been used to it.

Outside, a small army of men in black suits and nondescript street clothes appeared near the SUVs, talking quietly—or simply watching—as Reed helped Banks down the stairs. She felt weak in his arms and frailer than ever.

Two men met them at the bottom of the steps. They might've been Secret Service or CIA, but Reed didn't care. He held Banks close.

"Mr. Montgomery?" one of them asked.

Reed nodded.

"I'm Agent Jenkins with the Secret Service. I'm here to take you to the White House."

Banks clung a little closer, and Reed squeezed her shoulder.

"This is Miss Morccelli?" Jenkins asked.

"Mrs. Montgomery," Banks said.

Jenkins exchanged a glance with O'Dell. The Cajun only shrugged.

"Of course, ma'am. Mr. Smith is going to take you someplace you'll be comfortable." Jenkins gestured to the man next to him—Mr. Smith.

Banks looked up at Reed once more, then wrapped an arm around his neck and kissed him. "Be safe," she whispered.

"Take a shower," he said.

The flicker of a smile flashed across her lips, and she smacked his arm. Then she whistled to Baxter and followed Smith toward one of the waiting SUVs. Only one man climbed into the Suburban with them, leaving Jenkins, O'Dell, and four others waiting alongside the remaining vehicle.

Reed surveyed the small crowd. "Quite the greeting party."

"Your reputation precedes you," Jenkins said without a trace of amusement. "Strip, please."

Reed waited until Banks's Suburban left the hangar, then he stepped away from the plane and pulled his clothes off. He expected some sort of intrusive search upon landing and made no effort to resist. He stood, buck-naked, and waited for them to satisfy themselves that any concealed weapons were confiscated. Then he redressed and followed Jenkins to the Suburban.

They sat him in the middle row, flanked by two men in suits, with O'Dell and another man sitting behind him. Jenkins took the passenger seat, and the driver started the big motor.

"Welcome home," Jenkins muttered.

"Not feeling so welcome, thus far," Reed said.

"Don't take it personally. I give all the president's guests a free colonoscopy."

The Suburban rumbled across the tarmac and took the first gate onto the highway, cruising toward DC without another sound from the cabin. Reed watched the bright lights of the nation's capital flash by and suddenly realized the last time he'd been there was the day he was court-martialed from the Marine Corps.

The memory was as sharp as if it had happened the day before. He could hear the judge's gavel and the sharp *shrick* of the patches being torn off his uniform. At the time, it had been the worst thing that ever happened to him. Now it was just one bad memory in a collage of misfortunes and catastrophes —just more proof that no matter how hard he fought to do the right thing, he'd still wind up in the mud compliments of the corrupt people he threatened.

The SUV stopped at a guardhouse with a steel gate blocking their path, and Jenkins passed the guard his ID after addressing him by name. A moment later, the gate opened, and Reed saw the White House.

He'd never seen it before. Not in person, anyway. Up close, it was much larger than he thought it would be, but just as white. Bright lights glowed from concealed ports in flowerbeds, illuminating the old mansion as quiet sprinklers watered the lawn. He watched the building pass on his left as the Suburban wound around to the South Lawn, then stopped near one corner, where a subdued entrance was guarded by bushes.

Jenkins twisted around the seat. "I'm only going to say this once. My job is to protect the president. If at any point you become a threat, even in my mind, I will kill you. Are we clear?"

Reed grunted, and the doors popped open. He followed Jenkins's men into the White House, stepping into a narrow hallway illuminated by cheap fluorescents. There were scuff marks on the walls, and the carpet was worn. A service hall, he figured, for the Secret Service and support staff. Jenkins led him a few yards inside and through a door into a locker room equipped with showerheads. A fresh change of clothes waited on the counter next to the sink, along with a razor and toothbrush.

"Take your time," Jenkins said. "You should look your best when you meet the president."

Reed detected the sarcasm in the tone but didn't hesitate to strip down again. One of the agents remained in the room while he showered, shaved, and redressed in the provided clothes. They fit well, and he returned to the hall.

"Good?" Jenkins said.

"Good enough."

"Follow me."

The hallways quickly blended together, but Reed wasn't concerned with keeping track of where he was. Jenkins and his army of agents kept close to his shoulders as they eventually marched down a flight of stairs.

"We'll meet her in the Situation Room," Jenkins said. "Maybe you've heard of it."

Reed didn't comment as they stepped out of the stairwell and into a more refined hallway. The air was fragrant, and everything was spotlessly clean.

Jenkins pushed through two more doors, then paused in front of a third. He rested his hand on the handle, then turned back to Reed. "No warnings."

Reed scratched his chin with one thumb and said nothing. The door swung open, and Jenkins and O'Dell pushed ahead, leaving the rest of their men behind as they led Reed into the famed operations center of the president.

A long conference table dominated the center of the room, surrounded by leather chairs. Subdued lights lit the room from recesses near the ceiling, and a screen covered the far wall. But Reed looked past all of that, down the length of the table to where three people sat. Two were men, and he recognized neither but guessed one of them to be a military official by his uniform.

The person his gaze came to rest on sat at the head of the table, dirty-blonde hair pulled back in a ponytail, and simple clothes adorned with no further jewelry than an American flag pin.

Muddy Maggie Trousdale.

She rose as Reed entered, interlacing her hands and watching as O'Dell and Jenkins stepped aside.

For his part, Reed simply jammed his hands into his empty pockets and stared her down, unblinking. Unimpressed.

"Hello, Reed." Maggie unfolded her hands and gestured to the two men standing with her. "This is Jason Coffman, White House chief of staff, and General Yellin, chairman of the Joint Chiefs."

Reed grunted but didn't comment or break eye contact.

The two men shifted in slight discomfort, and O'Dell prodded him in the ribs. "Say something, jerk."

Reed moved to the chair at his end of the table and pulled it back, sitting down and glaring at Maggie the entire time.

She finally looked away, turning to the man called Coffman. "Jason, will you and the general give us a minute?"

Coffman didn't look happy with that. He blustered, but steel crept into Maggie's gaze, and the two men marched toward the door.

"Jenkins, O'Dell . . . if you don't mind."

Reed could feel the discomfort radiating off of the two men, but to his surprise, they vacated the room along with the others, and the door clicked shut.

Reed leaned back in the seat and interlaced his fingers behind his head, enjoying the soft comfort of the premium leather. It felt good on his weary body after so many nights spent sleeping on a castoff mattress.

"Thank you for coming," Maggie said.

Reed's mind traveled back to the last time he saw her—back when she was governor—back when she left him hanging out to dry.

Irritation crept into her voice. "You gonna say something, or what?"

"I'm not sure there's much to say, Madam President. That's the correct title, right? It's not *Miss* President?"

Maggie took her seat, sipping from a water glass before sighing with the laborious weariness of a harried school teacher. "It's acting president, actually. Or vice president. I'm not really sure."

"Big titles. Nice career you've had."

"It's not because of Resilient, if that's what you're thinking."

"It's absolutely because of Resilient, but that's not what I'm thinking."

"So, what are you thinking?"

"I'm thinking I've spent my whole life proving that people never change. Once a snake, always a snake. And yet here I am again, putting my hand out, begging to get bit."

"I didn't bite you before, Reed. And I'm not about to bite you now. If you really believed I was, you wouldn't have brought Banks."

It was a fair statement, but Reed wasn't in the mood to give ground. "What do you want?"

Maggie set the glass down. "O'Dell told you what happened to *Air Force One*?"

"Sure."

"The plane went down in extreme eastern Turkey, pretty close to the Iranian border. Not a very hospitable place, as you can imagine. We could get Pararescue in there, but the Turks are playing hardball. They've locked the whole place down. We can't access the crash site."

"So? Roll over them."

Maggie laughed wryly. "That's always your method, isn't it? Brute force."

"It's my method when small dogs harass big dogs. Absolutely."

"If only it were that simple. Leading up to the crash, we've been managing escalating tension in the Persian Gulf, predominantly with the Iranians. They're spoiling for a fight, which is nothing new, but this crash changes everything. We're in uncharted territory, and if we roll into Turkey with a battalion of Marines, there's no telling when the shooting will end."

Reed grunted. "So, send in the SEALs. Keep it off the record."

Maggie shook her head. "It would be a diplomatic nightmare if the Turks ever found out. Plus, I'd be putting Americans in harm's way."

"That's their job. That's why they joined the Navy."

"Sure. But even then, I don't have the time for bureaucracy. I need a solution now. Something off the record. I need you."

Reed scratched his cheek. It felt odd to be freshly shaven after so long with a grungy beard, but he kind of liked it. It was invigorating. "Let me get this straight . . . You want me to zip into Turkey like a freaking superhero, and then what? Scoop up the bodies?"

Maggie hesitated, then said softly, "There aren't any bodies. We spent the entire day surveying the site with advanced satellite technology. There's . . . really nothing left."

"So, why aren't you president, then?"

Maggie shrugged. "It's just a title. I already have all the power I need as acting president. The people need a moment to grieve before a fresh face is shoved in front of them."

"How diplomatic of you."

"I have to be, Reed. That's the job."

"It's *your* job. Not mine."

"No, you're right. Your job is brute force. And that's why I need you. I *need* that flight recorder."

"The black box?"

"It's orange, actually. But yes, it's all the same thing. *Air Force One* went offline twenty minutes prior to crashing. We have no audio from the cockpit . . . no nothing. The flight recorder is the only way to know what happened."

"You mean the only way to know who to blame."

"Maybe. We . . ." She trailed off and chewed her lip, seeming to evaluate whether she wanted to finish the thought. Then she committed. "We found fuselage debris spread across three miles leading up to the crash site, including an engine cowling. It's very possible the aircraft was hit with some type of heat-seeking missile."

Reed sat still, feeling the weight of Maggie's implication filling the room. He leaned forward. "You're gearing up for war, aren't you?"

"I hope not, Reed. But I can't afford to stick my head in the sand. I need to know the truth before this spills out of control. That's why I need the flight recorder."

Reed weighed the implications of everything being thrust at him. He thought back to Iraq and the wrath of the desert sun. He saw battalions of Marines deploying in Humvees and on foot, moving building to building, blowing things apart and being blown apart themselves. An endless, grinding war. He was a child when it began. He was a man when he joined the fight.

And now we're gonna do it again. All over. Unless I can stop it.

"I want it in writing," Reed said.

"What?"

"Our deal. You're not backstabbing me again."

"I can't put it in writing. This is strictly off the books."

"You mean it's *illegal*. All the more reason to put it on paper. You try to screw me, you get screwed, too. That's the deal."

Maggie started to object again, then her shoulders slumped. "Fine. I'll have them draft something."

"On letterhead. With your signature."

"Fine."

Reed thought about the endless expanse of the Middle East and the hellfire he was sure to face. He didn't mind facing a war on his own—he'd done it before and won—but he also didn't like the idea of trusting something this critical to himself alone. He wasn't invincible.

"Is there anyone who can go with me? I may need backup."

Maggie lifted a phone from the table and hit a button. "O'Dell? Send him in." She hung up, and Reed frowned.

Boots hit the carpet outside, and the door opened.

Reed stood, instinctively placing the chair between himself and the door as a tall man stepped in.

He was broad-shouldered, a little bigger than Reed, with close-cropped hair and the stern face of a born soldier. A crooked grin decorated a face lined with faint scars and the harsh marks of war. It was a face Reed knew like a brother.

"Hello, Jarhead."

21

"I'll give you two a minute," Maggie said. She pushed her chair into place beneath the table, leaving Reed staring at the bulky man standing just inside the door.

To his grandmother, he was Rufus. To the United States Marine Corps, he was Turkman, R. But to his friends, battle buddies, and Reed, he was simply Turk—Reed's oldest and most faithful friend.

As soon as the door clicked shut, Reed pushed the chair aside and wrapped him in a bear hug. Turk returned the gesture with a soft laugh, making Reed feel small as he pounded his back.

"Damn, Montgomery! You look like absolute hell." Turk stepped back, surveying Reed with that same crooked grin. He'd gained some weight since Reed last saw him ten months earlier when he and Banks were married in the mountains of Venezuela. It was Turk who officiated their very unconventional nuptials, but Reed hadn't seen him since.

"What the hell are you doing here?" Reed asked.

Turk shrugged. "Same as you, I imagine. Something to drink around here?"

Reed found a mini-fridge and retrieved two bottles of water. Turk caught one and drained it with a single pull, then settled into a leather-backed chair.

"So. The Situation Room, eh?"

"Hell of a thing, isn't it?" Reed said, resuming his seat. "Who woulda thought the two of us would ever find our way in here?"

"Pretty sure we don't belong."

"Pretty sure you're right. Probably why we're doing this in the middle of the night."

A solemn cloud descended over the room, muting the grins of only a moment before.

Reed sipped his water. "For real. Why are you here?"

The big man shrugged. "She sent a henchman. Told a pretty convincing story. I mean . . . I've been following the news."

"You still living down in Tennessee?"

Turk nodded. "Best I can. Not really sure what to do with myself."

Reed thought he understood. He first met Turk in Iraq when they were both Force Recon Marines, assigned to the same fireteam. Years later, after Turk left the Corps to become an FBI agent and Reed was kicked out, their paths crossed again during the Resilient Pharmaceutical case.

The resulting storm was the end of Turk's FBI career, but Reed wasn't sure he minded. Turk was a soldier, not a cop. He appreciated blunt force far too much to succeed in a more nuanced career.

"So, I guess you're familiar with the situation?" Reed said.

"Yeah. More ass kicking, right?"

"Something like that. She wants me to get the flight recorder from the crash site. It's kind of in a difficult place. I imagine there'll be gunfire."

"Well, I'd certainly hope so."

Reed smiled a little, but the amusement was short-lived.

"I can't ask you to do this, Turk. She offered me a presidential pardon, but there's no win for you here."

"I could play the hero card. Give you the whole spiel about never leaving a man behind and standing with your brothers, but . . ." He crumpled the bottle in his hand. "Truth is, Reed, I haven't been myself since leaving the Corps. They won't take me back now—not after all that business with Resilient. But I wish I'd never left. It's what I do, you know? It's all I know. Protecting my country." Turk looked up. "You couldn't stop me from taking this job with a battalion of jarheads."

Reed grunted. "Turk headed to Turkey . . . Now, there's a hell of a thing."

"Cheesy, right? Might have to start calling me Rufus."

"Rufus? As in, 'Rufus! It's time for supper'? Or 'Rufus! Clean your damn room!'"

"Forget it," Turk said with a laugh. "I take it back!"

Reed finished the water bottle. "Do you trust her?"

"Who? Trousdale? Not for a second."

"But you're here."

"So are you," Turk said.

"I guess we better get started, then."

Reed lifted a phone from the conference table, hitting zero. O'Dell picked up almost immediately. "Can we get some pizzas in here?" Reed said. "And some beer, too. Domestic stuff."

O'Dell snarled a curse and hung up. A moment later, the door opened, and Maggie walked back in, flanked by the general and the man she introduced as the chief of staff. They all looked tired and haggard, but they assumed seats near Turk and Reed without comment.

"Here's the deal," Reed said. "If I do this, we do it my way. Understood? Top to bottom. No questions asked."

Maggie nodded.

"Also," Reed said, "nobody outside this room knows anything about it. Period. The more people who know, the more danger that puts us in."

"Agreed," Maggie said.

"And Turk gets paid fifty grand. Cash. Untaxed." Turk spluttered, but Reed held up his hand, his gaze fixed on Maggie. "We're all patriots. But even patriots have power bills."

Again, Maggie nodded.

Reed turned his attention to the general, sitting up a little and softening his tone. "What's your plan, sir?"

The general cleared his throat. "The crash site is about fifteen miles north of the Iraqi-Turkish border, deep in the mountains. To get you out, we'll have you navigate into Iraq and rendezvous with local Army installments. As far as they're concerned, you're both CIA operatives or unmarked spec ops. They won't ask questions."

"Fifteen miles is a long way to hoof it in the mountains," Reed said.

"I know, but there are some roads, and the area is sparsely populated. I don't expect you to encounter any resistance. As soon as you reach Iraq, we'll have a chopper waiting for you."

"How much does this thing weigh?" Turk asked.

"The flight recorder?" the general asked. "About ten pounds. It should be easy enough to conceal in a big backpack."

"You said 'get us out,'" Reed said. "How do you plan to get us in?"

The general pondered a moment. "I can really only think of one way to get you in quickly without detection."

"Jump," Turk said.

The general nodded.

"HALO jump," Reed corrected. "Get us high enough to avoid radar detection."

"You boys do much jumping?" Yellin asked.

Reed shrugged. "Some, in the Corps. Did a couple HALOs. I wouldn't call myself an expert, but we can get it done."

"The CIA can fly you in on something small and quiet. We'll use a drone to mark the landing site with infrared, and we'll give you goggles to guide you in. If all goes well, nobody will ever know you're there."

"We need weapons," Reed said. "If somebody *does* know we're there, I doubt they'll like it."

"Of course. We'll make sure you're properly outfitted."

"The idea is to *not* start a war," Maggie reminded him.

"Sure," Reed said, "but the whole point of using off-the-books operators is that you get to deny us if we do, right?"

Maggie exchanged a glance with Yellin.

"We'll do everything possible to support you," Yellin said. "We'll put a drone in the air to relay secure radio traffic between us and you, and we'll monitor your location at all times. If something goes sideways, we'll know about it."

And do nothing.

Reed thought it but didn't say it. He'd been hard enough on Maggie for a while.

"When do we leave?" Reed asked.

"Immediately," Maggie said. "It's a twelve-hour flight, and the longer we wait, the worse things get."

Reed exchanged a look with Turk. The big man shrugged.

"Works for me." Reed stood, stretching his muscles. "Where's O'Dell?"

"Outside," Maggie said. "Why?"

"Because I still want pizza."

22

The rest of the campus had long before closed down, but Dr. Wolfgang Pierce's small office was still lit by the soft glow of his computer screen. He sat slouched in a high-backed chair, his good leg propped on the desk, a glass of whiskey cradled in his left hand.

The other leg—the one that was all prosthetic from six inches below the hip—rested against the floor like a lead weight. The pain that radiated from the marriage of metal and flesh never really went away. Wolfgang had invested in a dozen different models and consulted just as many prosthetic experts, but the reality was, you couldn't obliterate your femur and then lie for days in the Colombian jungle, while flesh and bone slowly rotted away, and ever hope to be the same again. Wolfgang could stand, walk, and drive a car, but he couldn't run or even hobble very well. And for the first time in his life, he'd put on weight as a result.

He swirled the whiskey in the glass and stared into the amber depths. He'd never drunk before—not once in his entire brutal life. He'd come close on several occasions, but he always dug down someplace deep and found a way to resist. He thought about his father screaming and throwing furniture inside their shamble of a trailer home while his mother begged for mercy.

That image was always enough for him to refuse even a beer, but lately . . . lately, he wondered. He thirsted for something he'd never tasted. He stopped at a liquor store and purchased a cheap bottle, just because.

Wolfgang lifted the glass and took a long sniff. The smell reminded him of the empty bottles rolling around the floor of his father's pickup. It reminded him of breaking glass and dark bruises, late nights and blood-curdling screams.

Wolfgang threw the glass in the wastebasket and leaned over his desk, running his hands through his hair. He couldn't remember the last time he took a shower or even shaved. He'd need to clean up before the fall semester started. Faculty was forgiving here at the University of Vermont, but they understandably had their limits. He needed this job. He wasn't sure what else to do with himself.

Wolfgang closed out of his email, switching instead to Google and tapping in a quick search. News stories filled his screen, detailing updates on the *Air Force One* story. Not that anyone really *had* any updates. The news was the same: the plane went down, Brandt was presumed dead, and Margaret Trousdale was about to be president.

Trousdale.

Wolfgang cracked open a warm Diet Coke and sipped it as he scanned a CNN article and stopped at a picture of America's first female president.

Some people just failed upward, Wolfgang guessed. He had no problem with a woman as president, and no particular problem with Trousdale, either, but he couldn't help but resent her success—just a little.

Maggie had to be the only member of the Resilient Pharmaceutical team who walked away better for it. That catastrophic six-week investigation cost everybody else in some way.

It left Reed on the run.

It obliterated Turk's FBI career.

It pushed Banks's health to the very edge.

And it cost Wolfgang his leg, his freedom, and in some ways, his entire identity.

Yeah. Screw Trousdale.

Wolfgang hoped she choked on a silver White House spoon.

He closed out of the article and switched the computer off, kicking his drawer closed as he stood. The half-empty bottle of whiskey sloshed as the drawer slammed, and Wolfgang started toward the door.

He stopped as the phone on his desk rang. A sharp trill filled the room and startled him. He almost ignored it, but there was literally nothing else to do besides stumble back to his campus apartment and stare at the wall.

Wolfgang lifted the receiver. "Hello?"

<hr />

Joint Base Andrews

Reed stood on the tarmac outside a hangar, watching as Air Force ground crew fueled another CIA Special Activities Center Gulfstream. The little aircraft appeared identical to the plane Reed and Banks flew in on, but unlike its twin, this Gulfstream was fit with a unique feature—a hydraulically powered door able to be forced open at over thirty thousand feet.

Apparently, this wasn't the CIA's first HALO-jumping rodeo.

Matched with a flight range of over seven thousand nautical miles, the jet would carry them all the way to Turkey with fuel to spare. There was plenty of room inside for all the gear Reed and Turk could dream of, and the two SAC pilots crewing the jet wouldn't ask questions or remember the flight the next day.

Again. Not their first rodeo.

Reed reached into his pocket for a smoke, then stopped himself as his gaze flicked across a wide red sign emblazoned with a bold No Smoking symbol. Jet fuel and sparks—not a good mix.

He ran a hand behind his neck instead, stretching his taut muscles as his mind spun through each stage of the coming mission. It was a good plan, all things considered. Dropping into the mountains was risky, but there weren't a lot of trees in that part of Turkey, and it was rural enough to decrease any chance of detection. Extraction would be a little trickier, but Reed preferred not to overthink it. One thing at a time.

There was something else nagging at the corner of his mind. Something vague but persistent. An intuition, maybe. Or an instinct. A voice warning him to watch his back.

He first heard the voice after arriving at the White House, and it hadn't left him. Reed wasn't usually much on intuition, but when something bothered him long enough, he'd learned to investigate. Once he took to air, he'd be pretty hamstrung in his ability to control anything happening stateside. It wouldn't hurt to have another asset . . . somebody who didn't report directly to the White House.

Reed checked over his shoulder to confirm Turk was still sifting through crates of spec ops equipment, provided off the record, compliments of the CIA, then dug out his cell phone. He sifted through a short list of contacts and selected one near the bottom.

The warm air sweeping across the tarmac tore at his shirt, and Reed stepped behind a storage building to block the noise. The voice that answered was one he hadn't heard in months—almost a year—but it was a voice he'd recognize anywhere on the planet.

"Hello, Wolf."

Wolfgang said nothing for a moment, then laughed dryly. "Why am I not surprised to hear from you, Reed?"

"Maybe because when everything hits the fan I'm usually mixed up in it."

A chair creaked, and Reed winced as Wolfgang let out a pained sigh, but Reed chose not to comment on it. Better to leave old wounds alone.

"Where are you?" Wolfgang said.

"Joint Base Andrews. About to take a little vacation to the Middle East, compliments of the Trousdale administration."

"You never learn, do you?"

"Try not to. I need your help."

Wolfgang didn't answer.

Reed folded his free hand under his elbow and decided to press ahead. "I'm headed to retrieve the flight recorder from the crash site. Trousdale is hoping to get an idea about who's responsible."

"She thinks it was shot down?"

"Possibly. They discovered debris and an engine cowling several miles from the site. Looks like a missile hit."

"Great."

"Yeah. But she can't act without certainty. Turkey is still sealing off the site, so we're going in off the record."

"We?"

"Turk is with me."

"Ha. Turk in Turkey."

"Ironies never cease. The thing is, I've got a feeling about this. I can't quite put my finger on it."

"Let me help you. Trousdale is involved. You're about to get screwed."

Reed rubbed his lip, watching as the ground crew disconnected the fuel hoses from the Gulfstream. "No . . . it's not that. There's something else. Something bigger, I think."

"Okay. So, what do you need?"

"I need you on standby here in the States. Keep your email handy, just in case. I may need somebody to do some digging on this end."

"And of course I've got nothing better to do . . ."

Wolfgang's voice was tinged with sarcasm, but Reed knew the truth. He hadn't kept up with Wolfgang since the end of the Resilient investigation, but he had a pretty good idea what an ex-assassin with one leg would be up to.

Not much.

"Let's say I owe you one," Reed said.

"You already owe me a leg."

"Let's say I bring you one back from Turkey. I'll put it on ice. Keep it real fresh."

Wolfgang laughed for real. "How's the missus?"

"She's good. Happy to be home."

"Let's hope she stays that way. I'll watch my email."

Reed hung up and ran a hand over his face. Turk approached from the crate, gesturing to the ground crew as they loaded a select pile of gear into the Gulfstream.

"We're good to go. It's clean stuff."

Reed checked to make sure the fuel hoses were recovered before lighting up a smoke. Screw the Air Force. They would get over it.

He sucked down two lungsful, then passed the cigarette to Turk.

The big man took a long drag, then cocked his head. "You good?"

Reed stared at the jet, the unease returning to the back of his mind, and he grunted. "Never better. Let's roll."

23

The tanker was Dutch-flagged, but she bore an English name: *Bingham*. Captain Rodrick Turner had commanded the 30,000 deadweight ton vessel for three years, running short routes from Kuwait City, Dammam, and Doha, through the Strait of Hormuz, and into the Arabian Sea, where his liquid cargo was transferred onto ultra-large crude carriers with capacities of over 300,000 deadweight tons. Those mega ships would then churn their way into key ports around the world, delivering a few million barrels of black gold each time.

Bingham was a wheelbarrow, really. Nothing more. Shipping lanes through the Strait of Hormuz were both narrow and strict, making it difficult enough for a seven-hundred-foot vessel to navigate and almost impossible for a fifteen-hundred-foot ultra carrier to squeeze through. Shifting small loads of oil out of the Persian Gulf had become Turner's specialty over the last two decades, but *Bingham* was something special. Turner held a very small stake in the Dutch company who owned her, and even though that stake was far too meager to really call the vessel his own, it still brought him some pride to be her commander.

Maybe one day that stake would grow. The oil business was always on the upswing, it seemed. Maybe one day he'd own a bigger stake and eventually retire off that ownership.

But tonight, all he really wanted to do was make it safely through the strait and offload his cargo—and passengers—onto an ultra carrier. It wasn't altogether unusual for *Bingham* to transport oil workers to and from the ultra carriers. After a few months of working in Kuwait or Qatar, those workers often bartered passage back to their homes via one of the tankers, working as deckhands in exchange for a free ride.

Tonight, *Bingham* transported fourteen such workers, and twelve of them were Americans. That meant the ultra carrier Turner was engaged to transfer his oil to was probably bound for Los Angeles or some other West Coast American city. A long cruise, but still a free ride.

As *Bingham* churned northeast at twelve knots, Turner looked out the window of the bridge toward the distant lights of Dubai, twenty miles off his starboard side. With better than half of his voyages taking place after dark, Turner never got tired of watching the UAE's proudest city glimmer in the Arabian night. The waters of the Gulf were calm, and the lights of Dubai were so crystal clear Turner felt like he could reach out and touch them. He imagined the tallest, brightest light to be the pinnacle of the Burj Khalifa, the world's tallest building, and told himself again that after this trip he really should make time to visit the city as a tourist, not a worker.

He was always telling himself that, but hundred-hour workweeks paid too well to refuse, and really, what was so special about tourist attractions anyway?

Turner checked the ship's heading as Dubai slipped past on his right and *Bingham* churned directly toward Iran, only eighty nautical miles ahead and much closer to their port side. Pretty soon it would be time to begin the turn through the narrowest point of the strait, where the distance between the Iranian coast and the northeastern tip of Oman was less than twenty miles. There were a few islands there and some shallow water, making it the trickiest portion of the voyage.

Two hours slipped by, and *Bingham* closed on the Iranian coast. Turner gave the orders to adjust heading and begin the turn, taking note via the ship's radar that they were the only tanker within ten miles. That was somewhat unusual, but he didn't mind. Less traffic made it easier to clear the strait.

As the coast of UAE gave way to that of Oman, Turner looked out the port side of the bridge toward the murky dark stillness of Iran only ten miles away. He'd passed it a thousand times, but he was always impressed by how desolate it was. Didn't the Iranians have money? Why was their country so dark?

Bingham leaned into the turn, rising a little over a low wave, then the radar chirped. Turner looked down to identify a contact eight miles off their port bow and closing rapidly. It was a small ship—definitely not a tanker—but as he lifted a pair of binoculars, he couldn't see it over the dark surface of the strait.

"Jack, hail that craft," Turner said, addressing his first officer. Jack never got the chance. As he reached for the radio handset, a burst of distorted Farsi tore through the speakers, filling the small room and echoing off the metal walls.

Turner muttered an irritated curse and swept the binoculars over the horizon again. He still couldn't see the boat, but the radar now reported it only six miles distant.

Another blast of Farsi stormed from the speaker, loud and demanding.

Turner snatched the handset off the rack and barked into it. "We can't understand you, dammit! Speak English."

A slight pause, then a new voice came online, heavily accented but speaking broken English. "This is Islamic Republic of Iran naval patrol. Stop your ship and prepare to be boarded!"

Turner muttered another curse and checked the radar. The ship had now closed to just over four miles, and as he swept the binoculars across the horizon one more time, he finally saw it—little more than an outline, running without lights but with a crest of white water surging up from the bow.

An Iranian fast patrol craft—probably a Kaman class, but he couldn't be sure in this light. Turner was something of a hobbyist when it came to naval vessels. He enjoyed spotting them and took pride in identifying various types. The Kaman class was actually just a modified Type 148, originally built for the German Navy by CMN Lurssen, in France. How Iran ended up with Type 148s, Turner had no idea, but they had about a dozen of them, and they were fast and deadly.

Great.

Turner smashed the call button. "Look, buddy. I'm in international waters, legally transporting cargo. You better back off!"

There was more garbled Farsi, then the English speaker returned. "You are in Iranian waters and will be boarded!"

Turner tilted his head toward the nav system. "Jack, double-check the charts."

His first officer stepped to a computer and spent the better part of a minute clicking through two different types of GPS-equipped software. He shook his head. "We're well inside the shipping lane. He's blowing smoke."

Turner hit the call button again. The Kaman was now less than three miles away, clear on the sparkling surface of the Gulf and slowing a little.

"We're right where we're supposed to be, pal," Turner snapped. "Back off."

"Time to begin the turn," Jack reported from the computer.

Turner waved two fingers, giving him the go-ahead, but kept his gaze fixed on the Kaman. At present, *Bingham* was steaming straight toward the Iranian vessel—and Iran, for that matter—but when Jack turned the big tanker to starboard and began their route through the neck of the strait, they would pass the Kaman on their port side.

He better stay there.

Jack moved to the steerage controls and adjusted the heading. Turner monitored the Kaman, waiting to see it slip to his left.

"Halt your engines!" the Iranian demanded.

The Kaman was still dead ahead, *Bingham* now bearing down on it.

"Dammit, Jack. Make the turn," Turner snapped.

"I have! The rudder isn't responding."

Turner lowered the binoculars. His first officer had already disabled the autopilot and was manually attempting to steer the vessel to starboard. *Bingham* didn't respond.

"Halt your engines! You are entering Iranian waters."

"All stop starboard engine," Turner snapped. "All ahead port!"

Jack moved to the throttle controls, killing the right-hand engine and moving to add power to the left. Even with an unresponsive rudder, *Bingham* could still turn. But *Bingham* didn't turn. The vessel churned onward, still not responding to controls.

"Everything's dead!" Jack shouted.

Turner moved to the controls himself, inputting the orders and watching the tachometers for a change in either engine.

Bingham churned on, straight for the Iranian warship.

"Halt your engines! This is your final warning."

Turner hit the emergency stop. The control module built into the panel flashed, and the tachometers dropped to zero as the engines died, but *Bingham* didn't stop on a dime. The vessel plowed onward, pushed ahead by the momentum of 30,000 tons of crude oil crushing through the water at twelve knots.

Turner reached for the radio handset again, smashing down on the button to hail the Kaman, but then he saw the flash. Orange and red exploded from the bow of the warship in a blast of fire, followed by a cloud of smoke.

Even without the aid of binoculars, Turner knew it was a missile. There was just nothing he could do about it. The French-built weapon streaked out of the Kaman at just shy of Mach 1, racing across the space between the two ships in under eight seconds—aimed straight for the bridge.

24

The White House

Maggie spent her second night in the White House sleeping on an air mattress in a small anteroom of the West Wing. There were plenty of guest rooms available in the residence, but Brandt's adult children had traveled to the White House to console their mother, and Maggie wanted to give them as much space as possible. The staff gave her funny looks when she requested the air mattress, but she wasn't in a mood to be argued with. She'd slept on much worse.

As morning dawned over Washington, she rose and showered, then found breakfast waiting for her in the Navy mess—a small restaurant built beneath the Oval Office and operated by the Navy. The food was incredible, and there was plenty of it. By the time she took the stairs to the first floor, she felt better physically than she had in days.

Almost ready to be president.

She met Yellin, Coffman, and Gorman in the Cabinet Room for an expedited morning briefing. None of them looked like they'd slept much, but all wore fresh suits and stood when she entered.

"Good morning, everyone."

"Morning, ma'am."

"Please sit." She took her place at the head of the table, circulating her new mantra through her mind as she did: *Take control.*

If there was one thing that bothered her most about her performance thus far as acting president, it was the chaos that consumed her cabinet interactions. It was time to be the boss. The nation depended on it.

Coffman slid her a thin stack of papers and set a steaming cup of black coffee on her placemat. Maybe it was a lucky guess, but she liked that he knew she drank it black.

"This is your morning briefing, ma'am," Coffman said. "You'll get one every day."

"Hit me with the highlights," Maggie said.

Coffman exchanged a glance with Yellin, and Maggie caught it.

"What happened?" she said.

Yellin took the stage. "A Dutch-flagged oil tanker was sunk last night in the Strait of Hormuz. About a quarter million barrels of oil were spilled, and at least twelve people are dead."

Maggie dropped the briefing. "You said it was *sunk*?"

Yellin nodded. "Seems so, ma'am. We're still collecting intelligence, but our initial assessment is that the vessel was struck by an anti-ship missile. Probably from the Iranians."

Maggie looked to Gorman. "You heard anything?"

Secretary Gorman shook her head. "I've already reached out to Tehran. They're still dodging us. But I was able to connect with the UAE and Oman. Both nations deny any knowledge of the event."

"They didn't do it," Yellin said. "Iran has been bucking for a fight all summer. We knew something like this could happen."

"But we don't *know* they did it," Gorman interjected. "We can't go barging over there making threats without proof."

Maggie could feel things spinning out of control again. She sat forward. "We're not barging anywhere. General, we do need proof. For whoever did it. Please investigate, and then come back with a plan of action."

"Yes, ma'am."

"Jason, what's on my schedule this morning?"

"We've got you online with Chancellor Shultz just before lunch. Should be a quick touch base, but the biggest item this morning is your meeting with the Saudi ambassador. That's in fifteen minutes."

Maggie pivoted to Gorman.

The secretary took the cue. "The Saudis are on edge," Gorman said. "They're worried about moving oil, as ever, but after last night, they may be rattled about national security. I recommend a firm, noncommittal touch. It's important for them to remember who's in charge. They'll push you around if they can get away with it."

"What's at stake?" Maggie asked.

"Nothing, at the moment," Gorman said. "They like to threaten oil reductions and price increases whenever they're trying to push us, but if they're genuinely nervous about Iran, they won't play that card. They need us too much."

"Great." Maggie stood, and the others stood with her. "Please keep me posted on any further developments. I'll see you all this afternoon."

Coffman followed her out, rattling on about protocols and etiquette for meeting an ambassador. Maggie heard about half of it, smoothing wrinkles out of her pantsuit as she reached the Oval Office.

"Remain in control," Coffman said, stopping at the door. "That's the most important thing."

Maggie nodded, her heart already pounding at the thought of another grueling day.

Here goes nothing.

25

Saudi Arabia's ambassador was short, slender, and dressed in a subdued American business suit. He wore round glasses and greeted her with a gentle handshake.

"Madam Acting President, it's an honor to meet with you."

The ambassador spoke flawless English with only a hint of an accent. Maggie made a note of that, chalking it up to probable Western education, then motioned to the opposing couches in the middle of the office.

"Please have a seat, Mr. Ambassador. Can I get you a refreshment?"

The ambassador moved around the couch but waited to sit until Maggie did. "I'm just fine, ma'am. But thank you."

Maggie's throat felt a little dry, and she suddenly wondered about her hair. It was a silly thing to think about at a time like that. She'd left it down, cleanly brushed with just a little hairspray. Was that too casual?

"May I offer my sincerest condolences on the loss of your aircraft," the ambassador said, cupping his hands together over his knees. "Saudi Arabia shares your shock and grief and stands at your side in your hunt for the truth."

"That's very kind of you, Mr. Ambassador. It's been a difficult week, but America is stronger than ever. I'll keep your offer in mind."

He nodded politely, but his countenance darkened a little, like a shadow passing across the room. "His Majesty, King Hashim, asked me to convey our deepest concerns over rising tensions in the Gulf. Our government was proud to work with the Brandt administration on strategies to ease tensions in the region. We hope such activities can continue."

"You mean tensions with Iran?" Maggie might be a politician, but she still hated beating around the bush.

The ambassador smiled tautly. "We don't like to point fingers, ma'am."

"Of course. But I'm a busy woman. I'm sure you appreciate the value of my time."

She left the sentence hanging, and for the first time saw a hint of discomfort in the ambassador's posture. He wasn't sure how to handle her, and she liked that. She didn't want to be handled.

"Tehran has made clear their ambitions for the Gulf," he said. "Our American allies have long understood the importance of stability in the region. To be blunt, ma'am, we are deeply concerned about the security of oil shipments leaving our shores."

"You're concerned about Iranian interference?"

"We would be fools not to be. Or perhaps you are not yet briefed on last night's incident?"

Maggie detected the inference of ignorance and didn't appreciate it. "I'm well aware, Mr. Ambassador. I'm also aware that as of yet, the Iranians have not assumed responsibility."

A coy smile spread across the ambassador's face, a hint of condescension underlying it.

"Madam Acting President, Saudi Arabia is witness to a lengthy history of abuses from our neighbors across the Gulf. Since the seventies, they have made their ambitions of Persian control clear. America may be most concerned about Iranian nuclear programs, but I must advise you, Tehran can strangle the West more quickly with a blockade of the strait than they can ever hope to bomb you out of existence. If the security of the strait is not ensured, His Majesty may feel pressure to take matters into his own hands."

Maggie raised an eyebrow. "Is that a threat, Mr. Ambassador?"

"Not at all, ma'am. Saudi Arabia considers America to be our greatest Western ally. But I would be remiss in my duties as ambassador not to inform you of the imminent threat Iran promises. Especially with international support."

"You mean Russia?"

The ambassador shrugged. "The Kremlin has a strange relationship with Tehran. Not altogether friendly, and certainly not trusting. But as you say in America, the enemy of my enemy is my friend. It is important for both Tehran and Moscow to understand that Saudi Arabia stands in solidarity with America . . . and America with us."

As the ambassador finished the sentence, his tone dropped, and he stared at Maggie, unblinking. She didn't miss the subtext of his message, and she felt a dull tingling in her spine.

"Well, Mr. Ambassador. I appreciate your time." She rose and extended her hand.

The ambassador took it and offered a shallow bow. "It was an honor to meet you, Madam Acting President."

Maggie drew a breath to offer a farewell, but before she could speak, the door blew open and Coffman barged in, breathing hard with sweat trickling down his face.

He ground to a halt when he saw the ambassador, then smoothed his tie and offered an apologetic nod. "My apologies, ma'am. We need you in the Situation Room."

Maggie remained calm. "Will you excuse me, Ambassador? My staff will show you out."

"Of course, ma'am."

He bowed again, and Maggie left him, following Coffman down the corridor to the stairwell. The chief of staff walked briskly, but Maggie didn't ask him for an explanation of his intrusion. Not there.

Within moments she was back inside the Situation Room, plowing in to find General Yellin, along with three other members of the Joint Chiefs, and Secretary Gorman all crowded around the table. Yellin was hanging up a phone, and an aide was adjusting satellite footage over the wall-to-wall screen at the end of the room.

"Talk to me," Maggie said as soon as the door shut.

"Iran is on the move," Yellin said, grabbing a laser pointer and gesturing to the screen. "Our surveillance satellites have detected troop deployments across their Persian coast. At least four battalions of infantry, accompanied by light armor, are moving toward the Iraqi border, with just as many racing south toward the Strait of Hormuz. That force constitutes about half of their standing military."

"They're also deploying naval forces," said someone from the end of the table.

Maggie's head pivoted to identify the speaker, and she recognized Admiral Turley, chief of naval operations.

"They've got seventeen patrol vessels, four frigates, and both of their corvettes putting to sea as we speak. That's enough firepower to lock down the strait, if they want to."

Maggie pushed her chair out of the way and placed both hands on the table. "General, what's your read?"

"I haven't got one, ma'am," Yellin answered. "We're communicating with our intelligence assets to develop an idea about what's going on in Tehran, but in the meantime, we have to consider strategic implications. If Iran moves to close the strait, they could bottle up our Fifth Fleet by midnight."

"Admiral?"

Turley nodded. "The general's right, ma'am. We need to put the entire fleet on full alert and deploy assets to secure the strait. Until we have answers, we have to play it safe."

"Do it." Maggie's attention swung to Gorman. "Secretary, where the hell are we with Tehran?"

"Still no contact, ma'am. They've ghosted us. But we were able to obtain the manifest for *Bingham,* and . . ." Gorman grimaced, then hit a key on her computer. The screen at the end of the room flashed to a black-and-white printed document. "There were twelve Americans on board. Nine of them are dead, and two are seriously injured."

Maggie smacked the table with an open palm. She quickly read through the list of passengers under the "American" column. Twelve people. Nine lost at sea. And she had no better clue who was responsible for that than who shot down *Air Force One.*

"There's something else," Yellin said. He resumed control of the display and projected a zoomed satellite image of barren desert mountains. "This is

Iran's Third Region, constituting six provinces along the Turkish border. If you look here ..."

The general zoomed the image, and Maggie leaned forward. She had to squint at first, but as the picture clarified, she saw a pair of black columns moving along a roadbed, dust rising behind them. The cloud was too dense to make out specifics, but the columns were much too large to be personal vehicles.

"Tanks and troop transports. We're unclear on the exact volume, but I'd estimate at least twenty vehicles and as many as two hundred personnel. All moving to the Turkish border."

"Why?" Maggie asked.

Yellin didn't answer.

Maggie caught him swapping a glance with two of the other Joint Chiefs, and she smacked her hand against the table. "I asked a question, dammit."

"It's just conjecture," Yellin said. "But they may be moving to secure the *Air Force One* crash site."

"Why would they do that? The plane went down in Turkey."

"It went down right on the border. I can't speculate as to their reasons. I can only guess."

"So, guess. That's your job, right? Give me an idea of what I'm looking at."

Yellin folded his arms. "The only logical conclusion is that they want to get there before we do. If they were assisting a rescue operation, Tehran wouldn't have ghosted us, so ..."

"So they're covering something up," Maggie finished.

Again, Yellin didn't answer.

Maggie studied the screen, trying to pick out individual vehicles. She counted at least fourteen, with several more obscured by dust. *A lot* of firepower. Too much firepower for a rescue operation. Too much firepower for a humanitarian mission.

"Put the fleet on full alert, and get me some answers about *Bingham*. And *please*, Secretary, get Tehran on the phone. Whatever it takes!"

Gorman reached for her phone as a dull murmur of voices resumed. Maggie turned back to the door, but Yellin stood.

"A word, ma'am?"

Maggie followed him to the corner of the room, waving Coffman off as he tried to follow.

Yellin spoke in a low whisper, loud enough for only her to hear. "Those troops will reach the crash site well ahead of Montgomery. We may need to reevaluate our plan."

"How so? We need the flight recorder now more than ever."

"Absolutely. But Montgomery is parachuting into a death trap. It was already a risky mission. Now it's damn near suicide."

Maggie looked over her shoulder, back to the screen. She thought about two hundred armed Iranian infantry versus Reed. Montgomery was one hell of a fighter, but nobody could survive those odds. And yet, that changed nothing.

"We need that flight recorder, General," Maggie said, facing him again. "Montgomery knew what he was getting into. The mission proceeds."

26

The Gulfstream turned south over Germany eight hours after departing Joint Base Andrews. It was only another four hours to eastern Turkey, but thanks to a combined time zone shift of plus nine hours, they would reach the drop zone after midnight, local time.

Reed figured that was just about perfect.

As the jet passed over Istanbul and crept closer to the target, Reed sat in the tail of the aircraft reviewing each piece of his equipment for the third time. Dropping out of the sky from an extreme altitude of over thirty thousand feet was a trick he'd only attempted a few times in his life, and he never enjoyed it. He wasn't scared of heights—he wasn't scared of anything. But they made him nervous and sometimes made his stomach flip.

Leaving the plane was the hardest part. Shoving off of solid footing and dropping face-first into a massive expanse of nothingness took all the grit he could muster. After that, things got a little easier. He'd wear thick goggles to protect his vision from windblast, and his teeth would clamp around an oxygen supply to feed his lungs as he free-fell through almost-unbreathable air.

Strapped around his chest would be a plate carrier, equipped on both sides by steel body armor strong enough to deflect a direct hit from a .30 caliber round. Jammed into pouches on top of that armor were five fully loaded magazines to feed the M4A1 rifle also slung over his chest, with a sixth magazine locked into the receiver—one hundred eighty rounds in total. Over the magazine pouches were a series of grenade holsters, each loaded with high-explosive charges to feed the grenade launcher mounted beneath the rifle's barrel.

A Glock 17 loaded with seventeen rounds of 9mm would be secured to his right leg in a drop holster, with three spare mags attached to his belt alongside an LED flashlight and what Reed considered to be the finest fighting knife ever constructed—a Marine KA-BAR.

Nestled in his right cargo pocket was a tool kit to remove the flight recorder, and on his back was a small pack loaded with a medical kit, dry food, and five liters of water. The radio connecting him to the White House via a relay drone snaked through the backpack and fit to his shoulder. Capping it all off was a standard-issue Marine Kevlar helmet. Forty-eight pounds of gear after he ditched the oxygen bottle and parachute upon landing. A lot of freaking weight, but Reed had an uneasy feeling he'd need every round of that ammo.

He completed a communications check with Turk, then grabbed two bottles of water and moved to join his friend near the middle of the fuselage. "How do you feel?" Reed asked.

"Like the world's biggest idiot, if I'm being honest."

"For taking the job or for jumping out of an airplane?"

Turk snorted. "For not demanding a hundred grand."

Reed slapped him on the shoulder and drained the water bottle. "One thing about Washington, Turk. They're big believers in repeat business. You stick around, and you'll make bank."

"Yeah." Turk looked out the window at the empty blackness surging past them. "Assuming I survive, you mean."

Reed followed his gaze. He watched for clouds, but the sky was as clear and empty as a crisp winter night. A good thing, he hoped.

A red light clicked on over the cockpit door, then it rolled back, and the co-pilot stuck his head out. "Ten minutes to drop, sir."

Reed retreated to his gear. "All right. Let's suit up."

Reed stood at the edge of the door as the plane leveled off at 31,000 feet. The aircraft wasn't originally designed to depressurize at any altitude, but the CIA had modified those operational parameters when they fit it with the hydraulic door. Both pilots were already strapping on full-face oxygen masks to keep them breathing until the door could be closed and the cabin re-pressurized.

Reed fit the mouthpiece between his teeth and took a deep breath of mixed air, checking the pressure. It was a little aggressive, but that was okay. Falling at over a hundred miles per hour, he could use a little help getting air into his lungs.

The co-pilot lifted his mask. "Sixty seconds!"

Reed slipped the goggles on and flicked the power switch on the left side. A heads-up display filled his vision, equipped with navigation technology to help him steer toward the crash site. As promised, General Yellin had deployed an Air Force drone to mark the landing zone with an invisible infrared laser. The goggles would guide him and Turk right to the spot, even in pitch blackness.

"Thirty seconds! Door open."

Reed grabbed the overhead railing with one hand, then placed his other on the red lever mounted on the inside of the door. He braced himself, then yanked and twisted. The door hissed, then slowly swung open into the wind, leaving nothing but a roaring black hole on the other side. Reed's head swam, and he could no longer hear the pilot, Turk, or anything except the rush of the wind outside.

Ten ... nine ...

Reed counted down in his mind, advancing to the edge of the door and bracing himself against the frame.

... six ... five ...

He stared into the emptiness and tried not to think about how far he had to fall or what waited for him if the chute never deployed.

... three ... two ...

Screw it.

Reed pushed off into nothingness. The plane vanished from around him as his stomach flew into his throat. He was vaguely aware of stars swirling on all sides as he shook like a leaf. The heads-up display in the goggles flashed, and a number spun, counting down the feet as he rocketed toward the earth like a meteor.

He hit twenty-five thousand feet thirty-four seconds after leaving the plane, and his heart rate leveled out as he spread his arms and curled his legs at the knee. He now fell face-down, staring at nothing but more blackness as the wind surged in his ears. He sucked down air and checked the heading on his display.

Left a little.

He dropped his left shoulder and tilted his head, slicing through the sky like a knife and quickly adjusting his heading. He could see the marker on the ground now—a bright red dot highlighted by the drone, guiding him in.

Fifteen thousand feet.

Reed adjusted his approach and leveled off. The parachute pack vibrated against his back, and he breathed a little slower. An overwhelming rush of adrenaline flooded his veins, clouding out the fear and reminding Reed why he took these kinds of jobs in the first place. They brought him to life like absolutely nothing else could. This moment, only a breath away from death, riding the edge of a knife . . . it was living.

Ten thousand feet.

Reed checked his heading one more time, swerving to the right just a little, then dropped his head to increase speed. A separate green dot on his display marked Turk a hundred yards to his left and about four hundred feet above him, falling at the same speed.

Five thousand feet.

Reed could see mountaintops now. The ridges in the area were rolling, not sharp, moving for miles and miles in every direction. Most of the terrain was obscured by shadow, but at least there were no trees. That was always helpful in a drop like this.

Two thousand feet.

Reed put his hand on the parachute strap but didn't pull. He'd wait until twelve hundred—less than the height of the Empire State Building. The altimeter buzzed through numbers across his display—one hundred and seventy feet per second. He focused on his breathing, remaining relaxed.

Fifteen. Fourteen. Thirteen. Twelve hundred feet.

Reed pulled the cord. The chute deployed and yanked him backward, his feet dropping forward as the wind caught the cloth with a snap and rapidly slowed his descent to under twenty miles per hour.

Impact.

Reed braced himself, lifting his feet to keep from slamming directly onto his heels. He saw rocks and the low scrub brush of a mountainside, and then he was tumbling into a controlled landing. Not a perfect landing, but good enough.

Reed stumbled to a stop and spat the mouthpiece out, inhaling his first breath of Turkish air. It was hot but dry, and a few deep lungsful helped to slow his pounding heart. He peeled the goggles off, then looked up just in time to see Turk make impact fifty yards away, tumbling harder than Reed had and falling to his knees.

Reed tore off the parachute harness, abandoning it on the mountain-side, then broke into a jog across the top of the ridge. The best he could tell, they had landed at the top of one ridge, framed by two others, with sharp ravines in between. The black sky was dotted with stars, looking a lot more still and peaceful than it had only moments before.

Loose rocks crunched under Reed's feet as he approached Turk's landing spot, finding him lying on his side, fighting to untangle his feet from the parachute cord.

Reed drew his KA-BAR and sliced through the rope, tearing it free and helping Turk into a sitting position. "You good?"

Turk grunted and spat out his mouthpiece. "Left ankle."

Reed sheathed the knife and pulled Turk's pant leg up, examining the joint with gentle pressure. Turk winced.

"What do you think?" Reed asked.

"Sprain. Bad landing. I can move."

Reed helped him dump his oxygen tank and parachute harness, then put an arm under his shoulder blades and hauled him up. Turk bit back another grunt, shaking a little as he applied pressure to his left foot. "Sheez . . . Got it pretty good."

"Can you walk?"

"Hell yeah, I can walk."

Reed reached into the cargo pocket of his pants, retrieving a pair of night-vision goggles that locked into the multi-function receiver on his helmet, but he didn't deploy them. For now, he wanted to allow his eyes to adjust to the darkness as much as possible. Natural night vision was always his preference.

"Lock and load," Reed whispered.

He tapped the bottom of the M4's magazine, ensuring it was properly seated, then pulled the charging handle. Turk followed suit, then Reed dug back into his cargo pants and retrieved a navigation hand unit. The device was pre-programmed to communicate with the invisible drone overhead, leading them straight for the crash site.

"Two klicks northeast," Reed whispered. "Ready?"

"Born ready. Bring it on."

27

The day ended no closer to answers about *Air Force One* than when Maggie woke up, but the mystery of *Bingham* was all but solved—the Iranians were responsible. Secretary of State Gorman had finally established contact with Tehran, and while they vehemently denied any involvement in the *Air Force One* crash, they admitted to a patrol vessel engaging with an unknown tanker driving out of the shipping lanes and into their domestic waters.

When pressed about troop movements near Turkey and Iraq, Iranian officials emphasized the necessity of securing their borders and ended the call before Maggie could break in.

"It's a threat," Gorman warned. "Those tankers never leave the shipping lanes. Never. They opened fire on an innocent vessel."

Threat or accident, Maggie didn't care. All she knew was that nine American civilians were dead, and military tensions in the Gulf were spinning out of control. As shadows lengthened into early evening, she secluded herself in the Oval Office and shut the blinds, settling down in Brandt's worn leather chair and staring blankly at a picture on the desk.

The image was of Joshua Simmons, the seventy-two-year-old father of four and grandfather of nine who was killed by the Marine escort chopper during her frantic return to the White House. Simmons was retired after a fifty-year career with the same factory, was an active member of his local church, served every week at his local food bank, and enjoyed aircraft and astronomy—hence his installation of a telescope on the flat roof of his townhome.

It was the telescope that the Marine pilot mistook for a rocket launcher. An honest mistake in the heat of the moment, certainly. But mistakes and honesty would do nothing to assuage the grief of those left behind.

Maggie swallowed hard and reached for the phone on her desk, punching in the number written on the back of the photo and waiting for it to ring. Her throat felt dry, and there was a lead weight in her stomach. She tried to think past the chaos of the day and focus on the task at hand, but on some level, everything felt numb.

"Hello?"

"Mrs. Hickam?"

"Speaking. Who is this?" The woman on the other end of the line sounded exhausted and grief-stricken.

"This is Vice President Maggie Trousdale, ma'am. I'm . . . I'm calling . . ." Maggie searched for the words, and Mrs. Hickam didn't fill the silence. Every moment that ticked by felt like an eternity. "I'm calling to express my grief at the loss of your father and to apologize on behalf of the nation for his tragic loss."

It was a canned line, scrawled on the back of the picture in case she got stuck. She wondered if it sounded as empty as it felt.

Mrs. Hickam still didn't speak. Maggie plowed ahead.

"What happened was a terrible, horrible mistake. I take full responsibility for your father's loss and will personally ensure that your family is taken care of."

"Taken care of?" Mrs. Hickam's voice was flat. "You mean *paid*?"

Maggie hesitated. She had meant paid, of course. How else could she hope to take care of them? But now that the word was spat back at her, it sounded cold and heartless.

"Do you know why my daddy had that telescope, ma'am?"

Maggie fumbled for words. "They tell me he enjoyed astronomy."

"He did. But that's not why."

Mrs. Hickam's words turned sharp. "My daddy volunteered for service during the Vietnam War. He wanted to be a helicopter pilot, more than anything. Like his older brothers. But the Army turned him down because he was dyslexic. He could barely read. He spent the rest of his life collecting little model helicopters, and we gave him that telescope last Christmas so he could watch for them to pass his house. He never let go of that dream. He always wanted to fly . . ." Mrs. Hickam trailed off, a catch in her throat. Then her voice turned hard. "It was one of your *damn* helicopters that killed him. You should be ashamed of yourself. You're not fit to be president!" She hung up.

Maggie sat at the desk, stunned, still staring at the photograph. She knew the words should hit her like a fist in the face, but she felt so numb and disconnected she wasn't sure how to process them. She simply hung up the receiver and picked up the image, staring at the grandfatherly face of Joshua Simmons.

A kind man. A loyal member of the community. An American patriot.

Maggie shoved the photograph into the top drawer of the desk, slamming it shut and placing her face in both hands.

My God . . . My God . . .

A soft knock came from the door, and she sat up, wiping her eyes quickly. "Yes?"

The door glided open, and a little cart rolled through, followed by a tall woman dressed in an impeccable navy blue suit. She was elegant and pretty, maybe in her mid-fifties, a soft smile on her face, and her hair pulled up into a simple bun. "Good evening, ma'am. I have your dinner ready."

Maggie stood up, feeling awkward as the trolley approached. She hadn't ordered any food and felt weird being waited on.

The woman stopped the cart, and her smile broadened. She offered her hand. "Sally Armstrong, ma'am. White House chief usher."

Maggie took her hand, enjoying the gentle grip. "A pleasure," Maggie said. "You'll have to forgive me, Ms. Armstrong. I'm not sure what a chief usher is."

Sally laughed. "It's a funny title, isn't it? Basically, I run the place."

"The White House?"

"Yes, ma'am. The staff, the grounds, the kitchens . . . It's like one big city, and I'm the mayor."

"Must be a challenging job."

"Not at all. It's like coaching the greatest football team on the planet. My people make it look easy."

Sally gestured to the trolley, lifting a silver lid off a tray to expose a steaming bowl of something thick and orange, dotted with chunks of shrimp and chicken. "I took the liberty of selecting your dinner, ma'am. I hope you don't mind. Chicken and shrimp étouffée with white rice and French bread."

Maggie breathed in the rich aroma of her all-time favorite dish. Back in Baton Rouge, she used to order the food on takeout and eat it in her executive office. It was guilty pleasure food. Comfort food.

"How did you know?" Maggie asked.

"Like I said, ma'am. I coach the best football team in the world."

Maggie laughed. "You should send them to LSU. We could use some help."

Sally joined the laugh, then folded her hands. "Well, ma'am, I'll let you eat. If there's anything you need, just hit zero on any phone. We're here twenty-four seven."

Maggie helped herself to a bowl as Sally left the room. She sampled the étouffée with a spoon, and her muscles instantly relaxed to the soothing richness of a Louisiana classic.

This football team can cook.

The food turned a little sour as her mind drifted back to the phone call with Mrs. Hickham, and her fragile appetite evaporated. She replaced the bowl on the trolley and folded her arms, looking across the room to the portrait of George Washington framed over the mantel. The nation's first president. A giant of democracy and freedom.

"You're not fit to be president."

Mrs. Hickham's barb stung her mind again, and Maggie slumped against the desk, dropping her head into her hands. More than ever before, she wished she was back in Baton Rouge, or better yet, back at the lake house drinking beer with her brother, talking about old times.

What am I doing here?

She lifted her head and moved around the desk, tugging the drawer open. The photograph of Joshua Simmons lay bent inside, curling up and caught on something above the drawer. Maggie reached inside to tug it free and felt the hard edge of something jammed into the frame of the desk.

She dropped to her knees and tilted her head to look under, identifying a white envelope with the presidential seal emblazoned on it, just like the card she sent Reed.

Only this wasn't a blank envelope. Beneath the seal, a single letter was marked in black ink—M. Maggie tugged the envelope out and stood by the desk, rotating it in her fingers. It was unsealed, and she could feel a card inside. She ran her thumb under the flap and pulled the card free. Another presidential seal was embossed on the back. She flipped the card over and found a single line written in bold handwriting.

I chose you for this moment. Trust no one. The enemy is within. — W.J.B.

Maggie's blood ran cold, and she looked up quickly, scanning the room to be sure she was alone. Then she flipped the envelope over and checked the marking again. Was it a W? No, it was an M, clearly marked with a faint line scratched beneath it. She stared another moment at the card, reading the line twice more, her mind spinning.

Trust no one. The enemy is within.

What the hell was Brandt talking about? The door swung open, and Maggie started, slamming the card against her chest. Coffman appeared, the dark circles beneath his eyes darker than the last time she'd seen him. His tie was gone, and his coat hung open. She didn't think he'd showered since the crash.

"Ma'am, we—" Coffman broke off, stopping at the far end of the room and hesitating awkwardly. "I'm sorry. I should've knocked."

Maggie clutched the card, and Coffman frowned.

"Are you all right, ma'am?"

Maggie realized her mouth was hanging open. She shut it and nodded quickly, pressing the envelope and the card together and quickly depositing them into the drawer. "Fine, Jason. What was it?"

"Montgomery just deployed, ma'am. The mission has begun."

28

Movement through the mountains was slow and difficult. Shifting rocks covered the windswept tops of each ridge, with occasional vegetation clogging the spaces between bigger boulders.

Turk hobbled slowly, wincing with each step but not making a sound. Reed took point, keeping his right hand on his rifle and maintaining constant surveillance of the ridgelines on either side as he moved. Every few minutes he looked back to check on Turk, but his battle buddy was always there, moving like a relentless force of nature, despite his ankle.

The first kilometer fell away in under twenty minutes, and Reed slowed as they narrowed in on the crash site. It was still dark ahead, with no reflective glimmer on the horizon from spotlights or vehicle headlights—any of the things Reed would expect to see if the Turkish military had established a perimeter around the site.

That was good, but with so many ridges rising so close together, with shallow valleys in between, an entire battalion could hide in the shadows and he wouldn't know it until he was walking down their throats.

"Command, Prosecutor. Comms check, over."

Reed adjusted his earpiece, pulling the mic closer to his mouth.

"Comms loud and clear, Command. Approaching crash site. One klick out."

"Copy that, Prosecutor. Be advised, the location of the crash site is a little farther east than we initially estimated. Adjusting your heading now."

Reed flicked his mic off, raising the handheld navigation unit and waiting as the destination was updated. He breathed a curse.

"What is it?" Turk whispered.

"They lied to us," Reed said. "That plane hit right on the border."

He handed Turk the GPS.

Turk zoomed in the little screen and gritted his teeth. "New plan?"

Reed shook his head. "No. Let's just be sure we stay in Turkey. I hear the Iranians aren't very hospitable."

Turk handed the unit back, and Reed resumed their crawl, swinging east and slogging through beaten grass and sheep excrement.

Just like old times.

As the final ridge loomed up ahead of them, Reed motioned for Turk to slow, then he bent down as he climbed, choosing each step with care to avoid loose rocks. In the distance, he thought he heard a low murmur—the growl of an engine, maybe. Or dull voices. The sounds were so soft and intermittent, he thought he was imagining them, but again, there could've been an orchestra blasting Beethoven a mile away and he might not have heard it. The ridges created sound wave barriers that pushed noise up, not out.

It put him on edge.

"Command, Prosecutor. Be advised, you're approaching the target."

Reed didn't bother to reply. He checked over his shoulder for Turk, then dropped to his knees and crept the final ten yards up the ridge, where he landed on his stomach and army-crawled before he reached the crest. Turk followed, catching up so they both reached the top at the same moment, the valley below spilling out like a lake of shadow.

Reed lifted his eyeline above low shrub brush, his gaze sweeping the valley floor. He couldn't see the crash site in the near-perfect darkness, but he knew it was there, five hundred yards down the mountainside in a shallow stretch of grimy terrain a thousand yards wide and twice as long. The valley opened on its eastern and western ends, and the western end facing inland Turkey was pitch black. But in the east, Reed saw light reflecting across a black sky—a soft glow, like the haze of a small city in the desert. And now he *knew* he heard sounds—the low clamor of men speaking and moving, mixed with the occasional dull thrum of diesel engines.

Not good.

He lifted the handheld and zoomed in on their location, double-checking to be sure, but he already knew what he was looking at. The Turkish/Iranian border ran right along the eastern end of this valley, meaning that whoever or whatever was making that light and noise wasn't Turkish. It was probably the Iranian military—a lot of them—breathing right down his neck.

"Command, Prosecutor. Sitrep, over."

Reed flicked his mic on. "Command, when I've got something to say, you'll freaking hear it. Shut up." He clicked the radio off and glanced at Turk.

"They knew it was here," Turk said.

Reed nodded. "They had to. And they knew about those troops over there, too." Reed deployed the night-vision goggles attached to his helmet. It was time to take a look.

Turk followed suit, and Reed pushed scrub brush aside to open his field of view. The goggles were brand-new and top-of-the-line. In a moment, everything around him was lit up like a football field on Friday night, every corner and extremity misted in green but visible, and almost immediately, Reed found the crash site.

There were no survivors. He knew that the minute he saw the wide trench carved through the valley floor, followed by a shower of debris slung hundreds of yards to every side. Most pieces were no bigger than a sedan, and only some of them were even recognizable. A wheel here, a fragment of a wing there. The entire plane had obliterated on impact, and Reed also saw traces of blackened soot. A jet fuel fire. He grimaced. Nothing was worse than burning alive.

"They hit hard," Turk said.

"Yeah. Hard and fast. Harsh angle, too."

"Where will it be?"

"Tail. They keep the flight recorder beneath the rudder. It's the most likely section to survive a crash."

Reed adjusted the night vision, panning to the right. It didn't take long to find what was left of the tail. The largest remnant of wreckage, the American flag, was still mostly visible, painted on what was left of the rudder. That, paired with one elevator and a fragment of the fuselage, was jammed into the north side of the valley, a few hundred yards from the Iranian border.

Reed focused on the spot and thought about snipers. There was really only one possible reason the Iranians were there in force, and that was to secure the crash site. He had to acknowledge the possibility of precision shooters lined up against the Iranian end of the valley, overlooking the whole basin with infrared or night-vision optics. Moving ahead would've been suicidal. He may as well have put a gun to his head and saved them the trouble.

Reed lifted the goggles, ready to convey his concerns to Turk—even though he knew his battle buddy had already reached the same conclusions—but before he could, a low shudder shook the ground, matched by the distant thump of helicopter blades. Reed pressed himself low to the dirt, sliding under the edge of some scrub brush and tilting his head toward the west, where the sound originated.

The thumping beat grew louder, and Reed was now sure that at least two choppers were bearing down from the west, flying low, obscured by peaks. His suspicions were confirmed only a moment later when two shadows exploded across the ridge, framed black against the night sky, without any nose or taillights.

He deployed the night vision again, adjusting the focus as the two birds swooped in and bore down on the crash site. Attack helicopters—both of them. Reed recognized the profile of American-built AH-1 SuperCobras, but the logos emblazoned on the tails weren't those of any US military branch. It was probably the Turkish Army, but the aircraft swept in too fast to be sure.

The choppers flew close together, swooping near to the ground and pulling up two hundred yards from the start of the crash site. Reed adjusted the focus again, and only a moment too late, he noted the massive spotlights bolted to the noses of both birds. The lights snapped on, flooding his goggles with a nuclear burst of light. He clamped his eyes shut and flipped the goggles up, but not soon enough. His natural night vision was destroyed, and everything turned white.

Reed pressed himself close to the ground, coughing on dust as the choppers split and began slow surveillance sweeps around the perimeter. The pound of the rotors intensified as the right-hand bird swept within fifty yards of his and Turk's position, but the pilot wasn't looking their way.

They both lay still, trusting the dust and shrubs to keep them concealed as the chopper moved slowly to the Iranian end of the valley, quickly turning back a hundred yards short of the border and storming down the length of the crash trench with its sister flying right next to it.

As both aircraft surged back toward Turkey, Reed propped himself up on his elbows. He instinctively looked back toward Iran, deploying his goggles again. The brush and shallow concealment at that end of the valley was completely disrupted, leaving clouds of dust hanging in the air. Gentle wind from the west pushed those clouds toward Iran in a mini dust storm, clogging his view. For now.

"Turkish army?" Turk asked.

Reed nodded. "And they'll be back. It's time to move." He clambered to his knees and double-checked his rifle. "Move east along this ridge. Get within two hundred yards of the border and find some cover. I'm gonna enter the valley here and move to the crash site. If one of those Iranians opens fire, you let 'em have it."

Turk followed Reed's gesture to a point of overwatch short of the border, and he nodded. They exchanged a fist bump, then both men scrambled to their feet.

Turk hobbled out while Reed held out one arm for balance and dashed down the mountainside, skidding amid brush and dodging boulders. He blinked to keep his eyes clear amid the continuing dust storm, wishing he'd kept the goggles from the jump. He hadn't anticipated this much dust, but he was grateful for it. If there *were* any snipers embedded along the east ridge, they wouldn't be able to see him for at least a few minutes, not even with night-vision optics.

He made it halfway down the ridge and accelerated as the terrain leveled out. The gear on his back dragged his shoulders down, and the plate carrier slapped his chest with each step, but Reed didn't feel the pressure. He kept charging until he reached the start of the crash trench, then turned to move along it.

In the distance, he could still hear the choppers. He wasn't sure if they were headed back his way or simply hovering out of sight. The ridges distorted everything.

He suddenly remembered that his radio was off and flicked it back on to an immediate storm of chatter from the White House.

"—inbound! Repeat. Turkish Armed Forces *inbound* from the west. Do you copy?"

"I copy, dammit. How many, and how far?"

"At least fifty. Half a mile, moving on foot. Accompanied by two attack helicopters."

Great.

Reed broke from a jog and back into a run, scanning the ditch with his night vision as he passed. Fragments of insulation, sheet metal, and leather upholstery littered the trench, mixed with the occasional odd item like a can of tomato sauce or a lone shoe. Reed saw at least one body, half buried by debris, with only the legs sticking out. A little farther on, a disembodied arm lay by itself, still wearing a sleeve.

"Prosecutor, are there any survivors?"

"Negative. It's total carnage here."

The pound of the helicopters beat from the western end of the valley, and now Reed was sure they were headed his way—slower than before, probably escorting the ground troops. That meant the initial sweep had been a surveillance pass. Next, the ground troops would secure the perimeter, locking anybody and everybody out.

Then they would take the valley.

Wrong place, wrong time. Screw me.

Fifty yards ahead, rammed into the side of the mountain with the American flag coated in a thick layer of dust, *Air Force One*'s tail lay waiting for him. From his angle, he could see that the left elevator was torn away and missing, leaving a gaping hole inside. The rest of the tail still appeared to be intact.

"Prosecutor, be advised, we're increasing altitude on the drone to avoid detection by those choppers. We—"

The feed on the radio crackled out, and Reed impulsively looked up. Nothing but black sky. Wherever the drone was, it was well out of sight to the naked eye, but if those SuperCobras were equipped with appropriate radar, they might just pick it up.

" . . . hear . . . contact . . ."

"Come again, Command?"

No answer.

Reed jogged to the edge of the trench and flipped his radio to shortwave. "Turk! Do you have Command?"

"Negative. They just dropped out."

"They pulled the drone. Watch my six. I've almost reached the tail."

"Copy that, Prosecutor."

Reed let the M4A1 rest against its sling, and he broke into a run along the final fifty yards to the tail. The closer he drew, the larger the wreckage loomed out of the hillside, towering over his head like the face of a building. The scratched and flame-seared face of Old Glory stared down at him, sending a strange chill shooting up his spine.

Reed had fought in a lot of places and experienced more than his share of war zones, but something about seeing such a familiar American symbol torn and battered this far from home hit a little harder. He ducked his head as he approached the gaping hole left by the torn-away elevator. His night vision illuminated the interior, driving back the shadows and exposing jagged edges of metal. He twisted to slip inside the tail, rolling onto his stomach and lifting his head toward the rear extremity of the fuselage.

And there it was. The flight recorder hung undamaged, bolted to the rear of the aircraft, right where it should've been. Soot soiled one side, but orange paint still gleamed through. Reed's heart thumped, and he rose to his knees, reaching into his cargo pants for the tool kit.

It was at that moment that Turk's anxious voice burst through the headset like a storm. "Montgomery! Turkish troops entering the valley, headed straight at you. One thousand yards and closing!"

29

Reed's fingers numbed as he stripped the tool kit out and stood beneath the flight recorder. Even standing, the unit hung a full foot over his head, leaving him craning his neck to locate each of the bolts holding it in place.

The White House intel was good, though. The flight recorder was secured in place with six fifteen-millimeter bolts. Reed slapped the appropriate socket onto his ratchet, then went to work cranking the bolts free. The flight recorder was a lot larger than advertised, and it looked heavier, too. There was no way he was fitting it into his backpack, but maybe he could strap it on his back like a sleeping bag.

The first bolt fell free as the pound of the SuperCobras returned. Reed felt the shattered fuselage beneath his feet shudder as both aircraft tore overhead like twin hurricanes. Through the gaping hole to his right, he saw bright light splash across the hillside, but for the moment, he was sheltered from view.

"Sitrep," Reed said, keeping his voice calm as the second bolt dropped out and he moved to the third.

"Seven hundred yards. Fifty infantry, still headed straight for you."

Coming for the damn flight recorder.

The third bolt jammed, and Reed cranked down on it, then yanked it free with brute force. The flight recorder sagged a little, and he moved to the next. "You know, I really hate this job," Reed muttered.

"Stop whining, Montgomery. You're having the time of your life."

Reed moved to the last bolt. He twisted on the ratchet, and as it slipped off, his knuckles slammed against the steel housing of the flight recorder. He bit back a curse and returned to the bolt, supporting the unit with one hand while cranking down on the bolt with the other. It twisted slowly, still providing resistance as his shoulder muscles began to cramp.

"Four hundred yards," Turk radioed. "Choppers coming back."

Reed didn't need to be told. He felt the shudder in the fuselage as at least one SuperCobra hovered directly overhead, beating right down on him. Dust filled the interior of the tail, obscuring his vision. He coughed and yanked on the ratchet, completing two more turns. The bolt dropped free, and he caught the flight recorder as it fell.

It was definitely heavier than ten pounds. Twenty, at least. He dropped to his knees and laid it on the ground, stripping his backpack off and withdrawing a small bundle of military-grade parachute cord from inside. He sneezed on more dust as the roar overhead continued. The chopper made no indication of leaving.

"Is that bird gonna move?" Reed called.

"Doesn't look like it," Turk said. "It's spotlighting a path for the infantry."

Of course it is.

Reed ran multiple lengths of the cord around the flight recorder, lashing it to the outside of his backpack like a chunk of firewood. He tested the weight, then cursed and tore the pack open, dumping food and excess gear across the floor of the shattered tail. He couldn't run with all this weight—not fast enough, anyway.

He zipped the pack closed again, then reached over his shoulder and tore the back side of his plate carrier open, lifting the rear plate out and tossing it to the floor. If anybody shot him from behind, he'd just have to die. Or maybe flight recorders were bulletproof. Reed wrestled the backpack over his shoulders and latched the front strap, then grabbed his rifle and smacked the underside of the magazine, just to be sure it was seated.

The chopper still hadn't moved.

"Turk, you got a clear shot on that light?"

"Copy that."

"Take 'em out. Both of them."

"Hold one . . ."

Reed braced himself at the edge of the gaping hole, standing just inside the shadow. He never heard Turk's shot, but a moment later, the light outside simply vanished, leaving only the dull glow of the second chopper's spotlight, someplace farther away. An instant later, that too was extinguished, and Reed launched himself out of the tail.

The flight recorder jerked at his shoulders, sliding back and forth as Reed turned right and hurtled eastward at a breakneck pace. Dust and wind swirled around him, filling his throat as he jumped over aircraft debris and stumbled through shallow depressions. Overhead the helicopters churned, turning in slow circles as their blown-out spotlights stared down at him.

Behind him, faint shouts filled the air, but Reed didn't have time to wonder how close the Turkish infantry were, or if they were equipped with night-vision optics. He hurled himself ahead, clearing the end of the crash site and turning south, back toward Turk.

Then the first SuperCobra opened fire. A roar of machine gunfire filled the valley, and an explosion of dirt erupted into the air twenty yards to his right. Reed hurled himself to the ground, sheltering behind another fragment of the fuselage as the aircraft dumped lead into the valley at random, stitching ruts up and down the base of the mountain in an aimless search for a target.

"Draw fire! Draw fire!" Reed shouted.

He didn't hear Turk's shots, but he saw muzzle flash from the ridge and looked up to see the SuperCobra twitch, rolling to one side to dodge the incoming rounds. The aircraft gained altitude rapidly, then its heavy gun unloaded on Turk's general position.

Reed flicked his rifle to full auto and unleashed a quick hail on the chopper, then he dashed ahead without waiting to see if his panicked shots did anything to relieve Turk. He wasn't sure if the Turkish pilots were using any manner of infrared optics, but regardless, he had to get the hell out of the valley. And with a small army of Turkish infantry at his back, there was only one place to go—straight into Iran.

The flight recorder beat against his shoulders as he swerved boulders and hit the valley wall. He scrambled up and to the left, fighting for purchase wherever he could find it. Behind him, the two SuperCobras churned up and down the valley, firing quick bursts at random into the hillside.

"Turk! You still with me?"

"Copy that. Pinned down on the ridge."

"Stay put. I'm gonna swing east and circle in from behind."

"Wait . . . East?"

"Copy that!"

Reed's breath came in short waves as he reached the top of the valley mouth and began to slow. Beyond the darkness, directly ahead, an entire Iranian force waited in silence, observing the Turkish operations from a distance. The soft haze Reed had seen before from their truck lights was long gone, leaving the edge of Iran pitch black. But Reed wasn't fooled. They were there, and he was exposed.

He moved for cover behind a boulder, dropping to his knees and keeping the rifle at the ready. To his right, the mouth of the valley ran like a line to the south, where the bulk of the next peak towered high above. Turk lay on the west side of that peak, but in order to reach him, Reed would need to swing east as he moved south, circling around the ridge to avoid exposure to the choppers.

And that would bring him deeper into Iran.

I hate this job.

He jerked the hose of his water bladder free of his backpack strap and sucked down a few deep gulps, then ran his index finger across the face of his night vision to clear it. The image was still hazy, but he could now scope out a path along the back side of the valley opening, moving down amid more scrub brush and short trees. He couldn't see any Iranian soldiers hidden along that path, and he didn't see why they would be concealed farther back.

If he were in their shoes, he'd want some distance from whatever storm was exploding in the valley below. That gave him a precious opening.

Reed hustled to his feet and hurried down the slope, dropping out of sight as the SuperCobras continued to orbit and fire randomly into potential cover. Those gunshots grew muted as he dropped a hundred yards down, then turned right and jogged south. The stillness was disconcerting after the chaos of only moments before. Even with the roar of the choppers not far away, a strange emptiness surrounded him, mixed with the unsettling sensation that he wasn't alone. Reed kept his head low, navigating by the green illumination of the night vision, and keeping his footfalls soft.

Yards fell away beneath his feet, and Reed breathed easily. The backpack dragged down on his shoulders, and the incessant slamming of the unsecured flight recorder bruised his back, but he kept moving, both hands on his rifle.

He had no idea where the border was exactly, but he knew he had to be on the Iranian side of it. The continued stillness made him increasingly uneasy, but he reached the southern side of the valley and circled east, moving around the base of Turk's peak. The ground there was firm, but the brush and trees thinned, leaving him more exposed to anyone on his left.

Reed slowed, creeping from one concealment to the next. Each step was calculated, moving only on the balls of his feet. He stopped every few yards and remained still, sweeping the territory around him for any sign of hidden soldiers.

There was nothing.

He moved another few dozen paces, holding the rifle into his shoulder as he approached a bulge in the bottom of the peak. He would need to move a little farther east to circle around it.

Reed froze when the crunch of a boot ground against the rocks on the far side of the bulge. He was caught between concealments, still ten yards from the next tree and unable to retreat without stumbling blindly backwards. Another footfall mixed with dull voices. He didn't recognize the language, but it sounded similar to Arabic. Farsi? Iranians, then.

Reed moved right, breathing low. Two more yards lay between him and the next tree, but the sounds of boots were now joined by the glint of a flashlight reflecting around the corner. He shoved his night vision up to avoid being blinded and then moved quickly to the tree. He dove behind it just as four figures dressed in combat gear stormed around the bend, all carrying AKM assault rifles. The lead man wielded a flashlight, blasting light onto the path ahead, but ground to a halt and held up a fist as he completed the turn. The three others stopped, sweat trickling down their faces. Reed could hear their individual breaths as they stood only feet away from his inadequate concealment behind the tree.

The soldier with the flashlight muttered something in Farsi, then lifted the light and scanned the path. The beam came to rest on one of Reed's broad footprints, and the guy traced the trail straight toward the tree. Long before it reached him, Reed was already raising his rifle, flipping from automatic to semi-auto and aligning the red dot of his optic with the lead soldier's forehead.

The light reached him, and Reed opened fire.

30

The White House Situation Room

"What happened?"

Maggie stood at the end of the table, pointing at a blank screen. Blurry visual feeds of the crash site were replaced with empty blackness, and all audio from Reed had been lost.

"It's the drone, ma'am," Yellin said, lifting a phone. "I'm working on it."

Maggie pressed one hand over her mouth, staring at the screen as though sheer willpower might bring it back to life. Only Coffman and a military aide joined her and Yellin in the Situation Room. This off-the-books mission was too sensitive to share with anyone. Well, anyone except the flight crew, the ground crew at Andrews, the CIA SAC unit who shared the plane and the weaponry, and whoever was flying this drone.

Yellin hung up the phone. "It's the Turkish helicopters, ma'am. They're equipped with Longbow-style targeting radar—"

"English."

"They can see the drone!" Yellin said, his face flushing. "The Air Force had to take it up to stay out of sight."

Maggie rubbed her mouth, thinking about that flood of Turkish infantry surging into the valley. She thought about the much larger Iranian force camped just a few hundred yards on the other side of the border. She thought about Reed, sandwiched in between.

The Prosecutor was on his own.

31

Three of the Iranian soldiers took bullets to the head before the fourth could react, and even then, all he managed was a random burst of gunfire before Reed took him out with two quick shots.

"Contact!" Reed snapped into the radio. "Move south!"

The quick pops of Reed's rifle were muted by the perpetual blast of the SuperCobras, but on this side of the mountain, there was nothing to stop the sound waves from carrying straight into the Iranian camp.

Reed stormed out from behind the tree and leapt over the bodies, breaking into a run as shouts echoed from farther down the ridge to his left. Guns clinked, and then a spotlight flashed on. Reed just ran. Now that the element of surprise was gone, the best he could hope for was speed and violence of action.

The pop of an AK snapped to his left, and Reed swerved to the right, flicking the M4 to full auto and firing in the direction of the muzzle flash. A man screamed, and the AK went silent. Reed cleared a shallow ditch and flipped the night vision back down. Ahead, his path disappeared into an avalanche of loose stones and boulders, and beyond that, he saw the curve of the ridge blocked by taller trees and scrub brush. Turk still lay around the bend, on the Turkish side, overlooking the crash site from the south.

Reed was on his own. Behind him, the pound of boots mixed with shouts in Farsi, and Reed caught himself on the edge of a boulder to keep from free-falling. The bottom of the valley was still a hundred yards down, and now that he looked, he saw half a dozen Iranian troops moving in.

Outstanding.

AKs popped, and a bullet zinged off the boulder next to his hand. Reed flung himself behind the boulder as those first shots were joined by a storm. From the valley floor below him, more gunshots snapped, and a shard of rock ricocheted off his knee.

Reed deployed the grenade sight on the front of his rifle and wrapped his hand around the launcher's grip. A hundred-yard shot was child's play, even in the dark. Time to hit back. He pivoted to the left, risking exposure long enough to identify his target. The cluster of muzzle flashes at the bottom of the ridge made it all too easy.

The grenade launcher popped, and almost instantly, the weapon made impact, detonating with an ear-clapping blast. The rifles went silent as Reed pumped the launcher open and fit a new grenade in from his chest rig.

Pop!

Another high-explosive charge tore through the ranks of soldiers lining the path behind him, and more wretched screams filled the air. Reed followed up the blast by dumping the remainder of his magazine into the darkness, just for good measure. Some of the rounds hit home, marked by further cries.

Reed dropped the magazine and slammed home a new one, then left cover and slogged through the loose dirt and stone. The worst thing about avalanches was that they might resume at any moment. A displaced rock or an air pocket might be all it took to send him tumbling deeper into Iran amid a storm of debris.

"Sitrep," Turk radioed.

"East side of your ridge, trying to circle around." Reed's reply came clouded with heavy breathing, but his voice remained perfectly calm. The screams behind him were now joined by more shouts, and then the spot-light returned, flashing almost directly over his shoulder.

Reed hit the ground automatically, and just in time. Heavy bullets whis-tled overhead like hornets, and he slid to the left, half-falling ten feet down the slope to take cover behind another boulder. This one was smaller than the first, and not quite wide enough to shelter his entire body. Reed pulled his legs in and wormed to the top edge of the rock, pressing his face just far enough around the edge to return fire. The rifle snarled half a magazine worth of 5.56 rounds toward the muzzle flash, and at least one AK fell silent. Then Reed was forced to jerk back behind cover as the full focus of Iranian fire bore down on his boulder.

The small-arms fire came like a storm now. Reed curled into a ball to protect his extremities, but there was now no doubt he couldn't move. The hail was ceaseless—so loud he clamped one hand over his most exposed ear. A stray round grazed his helmet, and Reed pulled himself farther behind the boulder. From the bottom of the ridge, another spotlight swept the darkness as a new detachment of infantry clambered over the bodies of their grenade-blasted comrades to approach him from his exposed side.

Reed fit another grenade into the launcher, smacking it closed and spreading his knees to allow room for the rifle to slide between them and point toward the bottom of the slope. It was impossible to properly aim from this distorted position, but he'd be damned if he let some Iranian thug shoot him up the ass.

The grenade arced down the slope and smacked the ground at the edge of the Iranian detachment. It detonated with a thunderclap, and bodies hurtled to the ground. But this time, there were survivors, and they imme-diately directed fire up the hillside. Bullets sliced through the air at random as they searched for a target, but with each sweeping pass, those swaths came closer, and still, the hellfire from the soldiers on the ridge persisted.

The game was almost up. Reed could leave cover and take his chances with the troops on the ridge, or he could lie there and wait for the gunmen in the valley to get lucky.

Either way, he was screwed.

The snap of fresh gunfire rang from the south, and Reed instinctively pivoted the M4 to cover his exposed side. But the muzzle flash lighting up the blackness from two hundred yards away was singular—not a fireteam, a lone shooter. And the bullets snapping overhead weren't directed at Reed.

Screams flooded from the detachment on the ridge, and Reed's radio chirped.

"Follow the pretty light, Montgomery. And run like hell!"

Reed rolled to his feet and dashed straight toward the lone muzzle flash, keeping his head and shoulders low as he cascaded down the slope. Turk's shots zipped overhead like threads through a needle, finding their marks in the Iranian entrenchment. The harder Reed ran, the more shots whistled in both directions, but most of the gunmen were forced to take cover as Turk's dead eye picked them off like rabbits.

"Change mag!" Turk shouted.

Reed slid to the ground, pivoting around and dumping a full magazine into the darkness as Turk reloaded. Then he was on his feet again, running the last fifty yards as Turk's cover fire resumed.

Reed found his battle buddy dug in behind a slight rise, lying on his stomach with his rifle pressed against the ground. A field of gleaming brass lay around him like fallen confetti, but as Reed slid into the cover, they were both forced to duck beneath a fresh storm of lead. The air itself seemed to explode with fire and fury, and all Reed could smell was gun smoke.

Turk tore his magazine out and slammed a fresh one in place. "I'm almost dry," he shouted.

Reed stole a glance over the rise, noting the entrenchment of Iranian infantry firing on their position from just under three hundred yards away. Meanwhile, the soldiers at the bottom of the hill had dispersed and were working their way up, moving to join their comrades and take ground.

Reed reflexively reached for another grenade, but his fourth and last charge was gone—blasted from its retainer strap by a stray round. He slumped down. "We gotta move south. Can you run?"

Turk grimaced. "I can try."

Reed flicked the night vision down and checked the path around the back side of the ridge—the path Turk had followed to get there. It was almost twenty miles back to Iraq, and even if Turk could force a mad dash out of this firestorm, there was no way he could make it that far.

They'd need a truck and a road, which brought more exposure and risk. But first things first. They had to get the hell out of Iran.

"When I say *go*," Reed said, "we're gonna make like a bat out of hell. Hoorah?" The battle cry of the Marine Corps slipped out of his mouth before he could think about it, and he slapped Turk on the shoulder.

Turk nodded and rolled onto his knees, ready to launch himself onto his feet, but before he could, Reed heard another sound—something far deadlier than the ceaseless snarl of small-arms fire. This sound was deeper and more menacing.

Helicopter.

"Down! Down!"

Reed pushed Turk back onto the ground as the thunder of the approaching choppers grew louder. The two SuperCobras burst over the mouth of the valley, banking right and lighting up the night with a tidal wave of automatic gunfire. The choppers screamed along the ridge, then the hiss of a rocket was followed by a plume of white smoke.

"Go! Go!" Reed shouted.

He grabbed Turk by his chest rig and hauled him up. They burst down the side of the ridge as the rocket detonated in the entrenchment of Iranian soldiers. This time there were no screams following the blast—just a ringing in Reed's ears hallmarking the total devastation.

"Move!" Reed shouted, pushing Turk from behind as his friend struggled on his busted ankle. The choppers beat the air, and for a moment, the guns fell silent, but if either of the pilots identified the two men running south, back into Turkey, it would all be over.

Reed heard a shriek, quiet at first, but growing rapidly louder. He looked over his shoulder just in time to see the first SuperCobra go up in flames as the missile detonated, obliterating the aircraft in a split second while illuminating the sky as bright as day. He ground to a stop as he saw another missile leave the ground a mile away, deep inside Iran, and race toward the second bird.

The Turkish pilot was good. He was probably the best his country had to offer—an elite combat pilot trained for special operations missions anywhere in the region, with years of experience behind the stick and thousands upon thousands of flight hours.

But he never stood a chance. The surface-to-air missile racing toward him was much too large to be built for helicopters. This weapon was designed for much bigger aircraft. When it hit, there was simply nothing left. Just a flash of light, and the SuperCobra vanished as if it never existed.

Reed and Turk stood in stunned shock, gasping for air as the light slowly faded from the sky. Sweat streamed down Reed's face, and his body felt numb from the successive shockwaves of heavy explosives. As the last of the glow died away, he looked quickly to his right and saw the full expanse of the valley below. It was packed with Iranian troops—at least a thousand of them. And not just infantry. There were tanks, armored assault vehicles, and a full row of truck-mounted surface-to-air missiles.

He saw it all in the last light of the blast, and then everything went dark and still again. Reed dragged the back of his hand across his face, swabbing away sweat, then shoved an arm beneath Turk's shoulders.

"Come on. We've got to move."

32

"What was that?" Maggie demanded.

The satellite feed over the Turkish/Iranian border lagged and was spotty at best, but without the drone, it was the best they could manage. Maggie saw the twin flashes of golden fire only seconds apart, lighting up the ridgeline that ran along the border in a blurry blast of orange and yellow.

Then nothing . . . Just darkness again.

Yellin lifted a phone, punching in numbers without answering Maggie's question. He growled something into it, then slammed it down.

"What happened?" Maggie said.

"We had to recall the drone," Yellin said. "It was running low on fuel."

"What about the blasts? Were those bombs?"

Yellin shot Coffman an angry glare.

The president's chief of staff cleared his throat. "Ma'am, you need to call in the cabinet. This just became a lot more than a recovery op."

Maggie stared at the blank screen, trying to visualize the blasts again—trying to remember what else she saw. More infantry? Were those tanks? "Do it," she said.

Coffman started making phone calls, and Yellin slid closer to Maggie, keeping his voice low. "Those were surface-to-air missiles. Somebody just shot down both Turkish choppers."

"Iran?"

"Seems so, ma'am."

"What are you thinking, General?"

"I'm thinking we're running short on options. We can drag our asses waiting for Montgomery to turn up, or we can call it what it is." He stopped short.

"What? *What* is it?"

Yellin spoke through his teeth. "The simplest answer is almost always the right one. *Air Force One* went down within spitting distance of Iran, and here we find them at the border . . . with surface-to-air missiles."

Maggie looked away. She'd been avoiding this conversation from the moment the crash site was identified so close to Iran. It was why she wanted the flight recorder so quickly. It was the only way to justify what she knew came next.

"Ma'am," Yellin pressed. "We have to confront this."

Maggie stalled, looking to Coffman as he hung up the phone.

"Ten minutes," he said.

"Assemble the Joint Chiefs." Maggie pivoted to Yellin. "And don't breathe a *word* of this to anyone. If we're going to war, we're doing it on solid intel, not speculation. Facts. You hear me?"

Yellin bristled and didn't acknowledge her comment as he stomped off, dialing a cell phone.

Maggie didn't care. All she could think about was the smoldering wreckage of three aircraft lying on the border with Iran, and the obvious implication behind them. Things were spinning out of control, and unless she found a way to put on the brakes, it was about to get a lot worse.

33

Coffman assembled the cabinet in record time. Gorman looked as she always looked—more tired, but still fully dressed and put together. Everybody else was in various stages of "just rolled out of bed." Even the Joint Chiefs showed up in partial uniform, packing in around the table as Coffman updated everybody on the developments near *Air Force One*'s crash site, conveniently skirting Montgomery or anything about his mission.

The chief of staff for the Air Force, General Albert Porter, was the first to speak. "What aircraft were shot down?"

Maggie thought he looked like he hadn't slept in a week. There was a hunch in his shoulders she'd never seen in any service member, let alone a general.

The Air Force took it personally when *Air Force One* was lost.

"We're not sure on that," Coffman said. "It appears a couple of Turkish helicopters were brought down. Possibly SuperCobra attack aircraft."

"What were they doing there?" Porter asked.

Yellin broke in. "Damn good question. Our best guess is that they were deployed to secure the crash site. Do we have any better satellite imagery?"

Yellin addressed the last question to an aide in the corner.

The man with bloodshot eyes was hunched over a computer. "We're working on it, sir."

"Secretary Gorman, I need Tehran on the phone," Maggie said.

Gorman looked up from her computer. "I can try, ma'am, but it's like three a.m. over there."

"Let me rephrase. If they'd like to have a chat before they kick off World War Three, they should pick up the damn phone!"

Gorman flinched. "Yes, ma'am. I'll get them on the line."

"Get that Turkish idiot out of bed, too."

"President Polat?"

"That's the one. Wake him up!"

The buzz of activity filling the small room reminded Maggie of the disorientation she felt after a long night of drinking in a college bar—vague but persistent.

"General!" A military aide, dressed in an Army uniform, looked up from a laptop. He hurried around the table and pressed the computer in front of Yellin.

Yellin squinted at the screen. "How old is this?"

"Twenty minutes, sir."

Yellin's cheeks flushed, and he pivoted the laptop toward Maggie. "Ma'am, you should have—"

Phones rang, and Maggie could barely hear the man sitting next to her. She leaned forward and called for him to repeat himself. His cheeks flushed a darker crimson, and then something smacked the table next to her.

"Silence!" Coffman shouted across the room, bringing it to a grinding halt almost instantly.

Everybody sat frozen, phones hanging in midair as Coffman's shaking hand trembled against the table.

"This chaos is unacceptable," he snapped. "Keep calm, or get the hell out."

Yellin scooped a secure data cable off the floor and jammed it into the side of the laptop. "You should see this on the screen, ma'am."

The massive screen at the end of the room blinked, then a dark gray map of the Middle East filled it, marked in places by red and yellow dots.

The map came into focus, then Yellin lifted his laser pointer. "Each of these dots represent heat signatures recorded at various Iranian military bases across their western border and interior. It's too dark for our cameras to take clear pictures, but using infrared technology, we're able to monitor equipment movements, even at night." He clicked a key on the laptop and zoomed in on a larger red dot in southwestern Iran. "This is one of Iran's chief mechanized military depots. Tanks and armored assault vehicles."

He hit the key again, and the red dot fragmented into dozens of small orange signatures, each moving in a line, headed southwest. Yellin tapped through a few more keys and slipped from one slide to the next, calling out the names of various land, air, and sea bases as he moved. At each one, he used the laser pointer to mark aircraft idling on runways, tanks churning down highways, and ships warming up to put out to sea.

As he concluded, Marine Commandant General Tucker leaned back in his seat and ran a hand through his hair. "God save us," he whispered. "They're deploying their entire military."

"How many?" Maggie said.

"A quarter million infantry," Yellin said. "Twenty-five hundred tanks. Six thousand assault vehicles. A couple hundred aircraft."

"Where are they going?"

"It's impossible to say, ma'am, but . . ." He clicked another key on the laptop, and the slide flicked back to the original map, only this time, yellow lines were traced to connect the trajectory of each deployed force, capping off in bold arrows pointing to the extreme northwestern and southwestern corners of the country. Those arrows pointed clearly at only two places: Kuwait and the Strait of Hormuz.

"They're gonna lock down the Gulf," Tucker snapped. He spun in his chair to face Maggie. "Ma'am, we need to place our installations in Iraq on full alert and put reinforcements in the air, *now*."

"He's right, ma'am." Admiral Dan Turley, chief of naval operations, leaned over the table a few chairs down. "I can have the Fifth Fleet fully deployed in four hours. But with your permission, I'll move the Sixth Fleet out of Naples and toward the Suez Canal. We'll show them overwhelming force and shut this thing down before it spins out of control."

"Too late for that," Yellin said. "The Sixth Fleet has its own problems to deal with."

He smashed a key on the laptop again. This time, the map displayed a large body of water surrounded on all sides by land, like a massive lake. Maggie recognized Turkey on the bottom half of the screen, which meant the north half must be . . . Russia.

More red marks littered the Russian coast, with a cluster around a spot labeled "Sevastopol" on the Crimean peninsula.

"Moscow is deploying its Black Sea Fleet," Yellin said. "Their Thirtieth Surface Ship Division is putting to sea as we speak, led by the guided missile cruiser, *Moskva*. Their Fourth Independent Submarine Brigade is also housed in the region, with four out of seven attack subs currently unaccounted for. Best guess, they're already steaming into the Mediterranean. Your Sixth Fleet has its hands full, Admiral."

"How are the freaking *Russians* involved?" Coffman said.

Gorman broke in. "Tehran maintains diplomatic alliance with Moscow. They wouldn't plan any type of mass military action without the Kremlin being clued in on it."

"Would Moscow support an Iranian war?" Maggie said.

Gorman grimaced. "Moscow has signaled support for Iranian interests for some time. Iran sells them a lot of oil, but it's impossible to say if Moscow would take an active part in a conflict. If I had to guess, I'd say the Russians are posturing. Pushing us while we're down."

Yellin gritted his teeth. "The Russians don't posture. With that much firepower, they could strike multiple naval or ground targets anywhere in the region, and we'd have almost no warning. We need to shift naval assets into the Mediterranean, immediately, and deploy ground forces into Iraq to secure the region. With your permission, I'd like to take us to DEFCON Three."

A heavy hush fell across the room, and everybody looked to Maggie. She just stared at the map of Russian naval deployments, imagining missiles rocketing out of the Black Sea, pointed toward the west. "What does that mean?" she asked.

"It means we increase force readiness and put the Air Force on standby," Yellin said. "At DEFCON Three, they can deploy in fifteen minutes, and the rest of the DOD is on standby to take offensive action."

Maggie glanced quickly across the lineup of Joint Chiefs, down to Gorman. Nobody was ready for this. "Do it," she said. "Bring us to

DEFCON Three and shift your naval assets, but I'm not deploying troops into Iraq. Not without congressional approval. We fought too hard to get out of there to run right back in."

"Ma'am," Yellin started.

Maggie smacked the table. "Not a debate, General. You want boots on the ground, you call Congress. Do what you can with the Navy."

"Yes, ma'am."

The buzz of activity resumed as phones began to ring.

Coffman pressed close to Maggie's arm, keeping his voice low. "It's time to think about next steps. You need to take the oath."

Maggie spun on him, her stomach in knots. Coffman faced her with sad but steady eyes, projecting strength she knew he didn't feel. He was being a rock, even in the face of devastating loss and imminent war. He was doing his job.

"Not yet," Maggie said. "Not yet."

"Ma'am?" Gorman stood at the end of the table, holding up a phone. "I have President Polat on the phone."

"Hang up," Maggie snapped. "He can't help us now. Ring up the Russian ambassador. I need Moscow on the line, ASAP."

34

Reed and Turk fought their way around the bottom of the ridge, plowing ahead by the guidance of their helmet-mounted night vision. The fading clamor of Iranian military units was joined by the dull rattle of mechanized transport, but the farther they moved south, the safer Reed felt.

At least for now.

When they lost contact with Washington's drone, they lost all pinpointed navigation. The plan had been to follow guidance transmitted from the drone as it led them into Iraq and to the military rendezvous point that waited for them there. But without the drone, finding that rendezvous would be like finding a needle in a haystack, and Turk would never make it that far anyway. Not on a busted ankle. It was already all he could do to stagger along, one arm hooked around Reed's shoulders and his right leg scraping along the ground. The ankle was now swollen to roughly twice its normal size, and Reed suspected it to be broken, not just sprained.

They needed a truck, and that truck needed a road. They would find both nearer to civilization, but this deep in the mountains, with the sky blocked out by towering peaks, Reed had no clue where to look. All he could do was stick to the goat paths and keep moving south.

After a solid hour, Turk shook Reed's shoulder and nodded at a clean patch of dirt sheltered by a boulder. Reed was only too happy to set him down, the muscles in his back and shoulders a tight mess of burning aches as he staggered to a seat. Every part of him hurt, and his ears still rang from the firefight in Iran, but it felt good to take a load off.

He sucked water from the bladder in his backpack, flipped his night vision up, and squinted at the sky. He had no idea what time it was but estimated sunrise to be about an hour or two away. The grayish murk of predawn had replaced the perfect black of midnight, and the air felt a little warmer. Or maybe he was just warmer.

"Where are we?" Turk whispered.

Reed swabbed sweat from his face. "No idea. Turkey, I hope. Could be Iran."

"Sure it's not Iraq? Looks like Iraq to me."

They shared a quiet laugh, and Reed checked his radio. All satellite connection was gone, leaving them with nothing but shortwave communication. He also checked the nav unit, but the device wasn't equipped with a GPS—just a location beacon designed to lead him along behind the drone.

"How you fixed on ammo?" Reed asked.

"Mag and a half. And a pistol."

A quick survey of his chest rig confirmed that Reed was similarly equipped. He hadn't realized at the time just how many rounds he was dumping at the entrenched Iranians on the ridgeline. It was like an action movie—everybody just unloading on everything like ammo was limitless.

"What's the play?" Turk asked.

"We gotta find a vehicle. You'll never make it twenty miles on that busted hoof of yours."

Turk rolled his leg and grimaced. "What's wrong with my hoof? I could hoof it to Australia."

Reed sucked down a little more water. He could've easily drained the bladder, but he was conscious of how limited their supply was. They might have to make it for a while—days, maybe—on what remained.

"All the same," Reed said. "We'll both feel a lot better taking a truck back to Iraq. Hopefully we can hook up with some jarheads at the border and make this easy."

Turk gestured to the flight recorder still dangling from Reed's backpack. "That thing heavy?"

"Not bad."

Turk sipped water, then winced as he sat upright. "What do you think's on it?"

Reed glanced over his shoulder at the bulky orange device. There was a sizable scar on it from a stray Iranian bullet. For all he knew, that bullet could've killed him.

"Nothing I really want to hear," Reed said quietly.

"Some things never change."

"Like what?"

"Like this place," Turk said. "Like these wars. For millennia, empires have risen and fallen, and this place just stays at war. No matter what."

"Where the hell did you learn a word like *millennia*?"

Turk tossed a rock at him. "Screw off, Montgomery."

Reed brushed dirt off his sleeve where the rock hit and thought about cigarettes. He could've killed a pack right then. And a six-pack of beers, too.

Turk said, "I do wonder, though . . ."

"Wonder what?"

"Well, I know it's classified or whatever, but I always kinda assumed *Air Force One* had anti-missile technology. I mean . . . it seems pretty obvious."

Reed had thought the same thing. Whatever the nature of *AF1*'s highly secretive capabilities, he presumed them to include such basic abilities as missile defense. How had a truck-mounted weapon circumvented the most technically advanced aircraft in the world?

"Nothing's invincible," Reed said. "And don't forget the mountains. If the plane was flying low enough, it may not have detected the weapon until it was too close. Maybe somebody got lucky."

"Why would it be flying low?"

Reed shrugged. "How would I know? That's why they want the flight recorder."

He dismissed the train of thought. It wasn't his job to unpack the mystery. Once he landed back at Andrews, he was dropping the hunk of steel in Maggie's lap, collecting his pardon, then getting back to Banks. Even in the storm of gunfire and the endless adrenaline rush of the past several hours, she hung in the back of his mind like a ghost—just out of reach, but always with him.

"I can go now," Turk grunted.

Reed held up a finger. "Shh."

Turk froze, and Reed lifted the edge of his helmet to fully expose his ear. Then he listened. He heard it again, faint on the mountain wind but persistent. The low rumbling rattle of mechanized movement. Trucks? Or tanks, maybe. Coming from the east.

"Stay here," Reed whispered.

"Yeah, screw that."

Turk hauled himself to his feet, wincing but stable. They moved quietly through the scrub brush and stacks of rocks before ascending the next ridge. It was a two-hundred-yard scramble to the top, using boulders and short trees for leverage. Turk fought his way up without assistance, using his rifle at times as a brace before they dropped to their stomachs and army-crawled the final twenty yards.

Long before they reached the ridge, the noise from the next valley had tripled in volume. Reed could now pick out the familiar rumble of heavy trucks mixed with the clinking rattle of a couple tanks, but he saw nothing in the murky gray of predawn light. The convoy of vehicles on the roadbed three hundred yards away moved without headlights, but he could smell their dust on the air, and a quick deployment of the night-vision goggles exposed the entire column to his view.

"My God . . ." Turk whispered.

Two dozen trucks moved from right to left across their field of view, crawling northward through the Iranian mountain range. They were led and trailed by a tank, and infantry clung to the sides of the heavy vehicles with assault rifles slung over their backs. But what caught Reed's attention wasn't the infantry, the trucks, or even the tanks. It was what was mounted *on* the trucks.

Surface-to-air missiles. Dozens of them, shrouded by tarps but obvious to a trained eye. There was enough firepower to bring down a hundred aircraft.

"Maybe they got lucky," Turk said. "Or maybe they just unleashed sixty of those suckers and set the sky on fire."

35

It was after ten p.m. in Washington, but the West Wing ran at full throttle. A steady stream of aides and military officials scurried in and out of the Situation Room while Maggie remained glued to her chair, fielding the information as it surged at her like a fire hydrant.

Immediately after reaching DEFCON 3, everything changed. She could feel it in the tone of the people around her. The aides were on edge, while the military officials seemed zoned in—like hunters about to take a shot—not stressed or afraid, but very ready.

Gorman fielded calls from London, Paris, Tel Aviv, and Berlin. The US wasn't the only nation carefully monitoring Middle Eastern developments, and the Israelis in particular were ready to fight.

Maggie refused every call, directing Gorman to pacify Israel while placing Germany, France, and the United Kingdom on full alert. She could deal with their allies in the morning. Right now, she needed Moscow on the phone.

The Russian Embassy still hadn't made contact with the Kremlin—or at least, they claimed they hadn't—but Gorman had one of her aides calling the embassy every ten minutes to check. If something didn't break loose soon, Maggie would put somebody on a plane to fly over there and kick down a door.

"Ma'am, we've got an update on troop movement," General Yellin said, tracing an oversized tablet with a stylus. The imagery displayed was still murky gray but much more visible than only hours before as the Persian Gulf approached sunrise.

"The Iranians are concentrating forces in two places. Here, in the south, they're building up just east of the Strait of Hormuz. We're also seeing Iranian naval assets shift in that direction, but it's too soon to determine their intentions. Iranian ground forces are also massing farther north at a city called Abadan."

Yellin marked the spot, and Maggie leaned in. "How far is that from the Kuwaiti border?"

"Just over twenty miles."

"Do they have any vehicles?"

"Tanks and troop transports. If they decided to deploy, they could storm the border in under an hour."

"Is the Kuwaiti military on standby?"

"Absolutely, but they're helpless against this level of force. They're counting on us to bridge the gap."

Of course they are.

Maggie hit zero on her phone and waited for the White House operator. "Yes, ma'am?"

"Get me CIA Director O'Brien."

"One moment, please."

Maggie blocked out the noise around her. O'Brien didn't keep her waiting.

"Director O'Brien."

"Director, it's Vice President Trousdale. I need a moment of your time."

"Of course, ma'am."

"I presume your people are monitoring the situation?"

O'Brien sounded mildly offended. "Yes, ma'am."

"I'm standing over a toolbox full of drastic measures, Director. I need to know *exactly* what Iran is up to."

"We're monitoring troop deployments across the region," he said. "I don't advise drastic measures, but it does seem military action is imminent. Unless they're just posturing."

"If they were posturing, they'd be answering the phone. You don't make threats without making demands."

"It's possible they want to rattle us with protracted silence and aggressive military deployment. The Iranians have played this game before."

"They've never shot down *Air Force One*, have they? I don't need speculation, Director. I need *intel*."

O'Brien said nothing, and Maggie gave him time to think.

"Our sources in Tehran are unreliable," he said at last. "But . . ."

"But?"

"We do have one report indicating a possible Iranian attempt to seize the Gulf."

"What does that mean?"

"It means they'd cross the strait and take control of the Omani peninsula while storming Kuwait from the north. With a three-quarter grip on the region, they would be incredibly difficult to displace. And . . ."

"And?"

"And our assets in Moscow are reporting full alert inside the Kremlin. We've tracked increased communication between Moscow and Tehran for a few months now. It seems logical to conclude that whatever the Iranians are plotting, the Russians are in on it."

Maggie thought about the bulk of Russian naval assets deploying into the Mediterranean. Iran she could deal with. The prospect of a world war was something else entirely.

"Thank you, Director. Please keep me posted."

Maggie hung up and drained her water glass. "Nick? Where's Nick West?"

The national security advisor stuck his head out from a crowd of military aides at the end of the room. "Here, ma'am."

Gordon held up a phone. "I've got Russian President Nikitin on the line!"

Maggie waved her off. "Put him on hold. Nick, get over here."

The national security advisor hurried down the length of the table, shoving past a mess of chairs.

"Ma'am!" Gorman objected.

"*Hold*, Lisa."

Nick reached the corner of the table next to her.

When Maggie spoke, she kept her voice low enough so only he could hear. "What would be the implications of full Iranian control of the Gulf?"

Nick flinched. "The Persian Gulf?"

"Obviously."

He looked off to one side and wiped his nose with the back of one thumb. "Economic chaos," he said. "Twenty-one percent of the world's oil flows out of the Gulf. If they controlled it, they could throttle the supply, inflate prices, restrict access . . . whatever they wanted."

"What would that do to *us*?"

Nick hesitated, then shook his head. "I really don't know, ma'am. Fuel prices would skyrocket. Supply chain would choke. Inflation would kick in. It's a worst-case scenario, short of nuclear war. And it might take a nuclear war to retake the Gulf."

"Ma'am!" Gorman called again. "I can't keep him waiting."

Maggie snapped her fingers. "Quiet! All of you! Put him through."

The room fell still, and Maggie waited as Gorman introduced her as the acting president, then hit a button and nodded.

Maggie lifted her receiver. "Good morning, Mr. President." Maggie wasn't sure if she expected Nikitin to use a translator, but the smooth, educated voice of Russia's leader answered her directly, in accented but fluent English.

"Good evening, Madam Acting President. May I express my sincerest condolences on the loss of your aircraft. President Brandt was a strong leader and a good friend."

Nikitin spoke softly and slowly, but the casualness in his tone negated any sincerity he might've been angling for.

"Thank you, Mr. President. I didn't realize you knew President Brandt so well."

"Well," Nikitin said, "how well can you really know the self-proclaimed leader of the Free World? Washington is a mire of illusions. But I don't have to tell you that, do I? I'm curious . . . Had you ever visited your nation's capital before? It must be such a change."

Maggie flushed a little. It was time to take control. "Mr. President, I don't have time for banter. I'm calling to find out why you're deploying naval assets into the Mediterranean."

Gorman stood up, but Maggie didn't care. She'd always valued a direct approach, especially when dealing with smug bullies, and thus far, Nikitin felt firmly situated in that category.

"I'm not sure I enjoy your tone, Madam *Acting* President. Russian naval assets move at our discretion. We do not require American approval."

"Maybe not. But you'd be well advised to make your intentions clear before plowing straight toward my Sixth Fleet with the bulk of your guided missile frigates."

"Guided missile?"

Maggie didn't believe Nikitin's feigned confusion for a second.

"You must mean our Black Sea Fleet!" he said. "Yes, I was advised this morning of a training exercise. A typical thing, I assure you. Nothing to be concerned about."

"Oh, I'm very concerned, Mr. President. I'm concerned because your *training* exercise coincides precisely with massive Iranian military deployments along the Persian Gulf. Or maybe you didn't know?"

Gorman's eyes pleaded as she motioned downward with one hand. "Gentle," she mouthed.

Nikitin took his time replying. "What the Iranians do is of no matter to us," he said at last. "But as you say in America, for the record, we support any nation's right to protect its own borders."

"Don't pretend you aren't aware of what's happening in Iran, Mr. President. If Iran were concerned with self-defense, they might be communicating with us. Let me be perfectly clear. We *will* defend ourselves, whatever the cost. Don't make the mistake of aligning yourself with an unstable and ruthless regime."

"Madam Acting President, I do not wish to become political. But since you feel no need to guard your words with any pretense of respect, I will be just as bold. American aggression in the Middle East has long overstayed its welcome. While the wreckage of your aircraft still smolders so close to Iran's border, Tehran could be forgiven for fearing a rash and uninformed reprisal, especially when recent oil negotiations have so harshly discounted

Iranian interests. I would strongly advise you that *any* American military action in the region may be interpreted as a further overstep of Western imperialism . . . and be confronted as such."

Maggie kept her words calm. "Is that a threat, Mr. President?"

"Of course not. It is merely . . . an observation. Iranian interests and Russian interests sometimes coincide. And when they do, well . . . This is what we train for. Good evening, Madam Acting President."

The phone clicked, and a White House aide came on the line to inform her that Nikitin had left the call. Maggie simply hung up.

Gorman leaned across the table. "What did he say?"

"A lot of things," Maggie said. "But the bottom line is . . . Moscow stands behind Iran."

36

The sky brightened over Iran as Reed and Turk retreated to the valley floor and spread a map across the dirt. Reed had packed it as a precaution—a lesson he learned the hard way after relying too heavily on faulty navigation tech during the Iraqi civil war. Once again, his over-preparation proved invaluable as he laid a compass on the map and then looked up to scope out the ridges around them.

"The best I can tell we're about twenty-two miles north of Iraq, just west of the Iranian boarder. There's a village about three miles southwest of us. Not much to look at, but there should be a vehicle we can take. From there, it's a short drive to the border, then we can contact Washington."

Turk traced the path with one finger. "Good plan."

"Good plan, except for the three-mile part. Can you make it?"

Turk looked down at his wounded ankle. It was propped up on a rock to reduce blood pressure, but it was still swollen to the size of a small cantaloupe. "Don't think I have a choice," he said.

Reed checked the sky. The first rays of an Iranian sunrise were cresting the nearest ridge. In just a few hours, the whole region would become oppressively, suffocatingly hot. So hot that the dusty floor of each valley felt like a cookie sheet in an oven, slowly roasting them alive. If it was hard for Turk to move now, it would be impossible then. They had to hurry.

He helped Turk to his feet, using the compass to take a bearing before setting off. In addition to the promise of insufferable heat, the sunrise would kill most of their cover. It was crucial to get away from the Iranian border before then.

Dry air sucked the moisture from Reed's lips as he slogged along at no better than one mile per hour. Turk gritted his teeth and kept quiet as they fought their way up a ridge, scrambling through rocks and more scraggly scrub brush, but Reed could see the agony in his face. Tear stains mixed with sweat trails, and Turk fell more than a few times. But somehow, he always found a way to dig a little deeper and keep going.

The flight recorder now felt like fifty pounds on Reed's shoulders, dragging him down with each step. Every few yards, it would rotate, and a new edge dug into his back through the backpack and the empty plate carrier. He shrugged his shoulders to shift it again, and he pressed on. If Turk could overcome a busted ankle, he could deal with a little weight.

The sun crested the top of the mountains and superheated the air in mere minutes. Reed set Turk down under the mediocre shade of a dehydrated tree, then took a few sips of precious water, which was hot now, like everything else.

"How much farther?" Turk croaked.

Reed looked to the ridges and checked the compass again. In truth, he had no idea. It was impossible to measure distance in a place so uniform in appearance. Ridges blended together, and valleys merged into an endless grind of dirt and heat.

"Not far," he said.

Turk laughed, spitting hot water onto the ground. "That's what you said two hours ago."

"More Tylenol?" Reed asked. Turk had already consumed four pills.

"It ain't doing much good. Let's keep moving."

Reed hoisted him up again and then started up the next ridge. It was a steeper climb than the last several, with no clear goat path to follow. Reed had to chart a course amid thinning trees, with nothing but dry grass to claw their way over as sandy soil often gave way beneath their feet.

With each step, Turk bit back a grunt, sweat streaming down his face. Reed thought he was close to giving out as they finally crested the last ridge. Sunlight glared down, and Reed tore his helmet off, running a dirty hand through his hair as he peered into the next valley. At first glance, it looked just as empty as the last, but when he squinted, Reed saw sunlight reflecting off metal roofs a thousand yards away, nestled at the bottom of two ridges with a narrow dirt road running right through the middle.

Reed smacked Turk on the back. "See? Told you."

Turk grunted a dry laugh, and they started down the slope. In the back of his mind, Reed was vaguely uncomfortable with walking in the open like this, but there was almost nothing in the way of cover for a few hundred yards on either side, and they were deep enough inside Turkey now to give him a little peace of mind.

At the bottom of the ridge, they avoided the road, instead cutting through goat pastures that ran along the eastern half of the valley. The little village was invisible now, but Reed knew it lay on the other side of a slight rise directly ahead.

"Just a little farther."

Turk stumbled on, and they cleared the rise and stared down into the village two hundred yards away. Turk slid to his knees, and Reed followed, cradling his rifle and lifting a pair of binoculars from his pocket.

"Check the map," Reed said.

Breathing hard, Turk unfolded the map across the dry grass. He traced it with his index finger, then looked to the surrounding ridges for a landmark. "Got it."

"How far to Iraq?"

"Not too far. There are roads the whole way, but I doubt they're paved. We should find a four-wheel-drive."

Reed swept the binoculars across the village. It was mostly quiet, with about a dozen houses clustered along the road, a couple larger community buildings, and a single service station with a lone fuel pump. Stuck amid the houses, he identified a couple of dusty SUVs, but most of the parking places appeared empty. He guessed there must be some sort of industry nearby. Something that pulled the majority of residents away during the day. That was good, except it left few vehicle options.

Reed settled on a battered Nissan Xterra so covered in dirt he couldn't identify the color. It sat high off the ground, with a stance indicating off-road capabilities.

Good enough.

"Got it," he said. "Nissan SUV, three houses from the right."

"I see it," Turk said. "Keys in the house?"

"We'll hot-wire it. We can't risk the attention."

"Copy that. Ready when you are."

Reed helped Turk up again, but this time he didn't support him. Instead, he took point, both hands on his rifle as he slouched low and fast-walked toward the village. Turk kept up the best he could, grunting a lot but not complaining.

Reed reached the Nissan fifty yards ahead of Turk and quickly cleared the area around it. The houses on either side of it were small, dusty, and perfectly still, and their empty parking spots were marred by fresh tire tracks, leaving Reed to wonder if the Nissan was disabled.

He checked the door and found it unlocked, then peered around the SUV's rear. Turk had staggered to a stop, swaying on his feet and slouching against his rifle. His face had drained of color, and he looked ready to drop.

"Turk! Let's roll," Reed hissed.

Turk nodded and took a staggering step forward, then collapsed at the same moment a rifle shot cracked like a bullwhip. Reed instinctively snatched his rifle to his shoulder as the air filled with dust from bullet strikes only yards ahead of Turk.

"Cover! Cover!" Reed shouted, sweeping the ridgelines behind Turk in a frantic search for the shooter.

As the next shot split the air, Turk rolled onto his stomach and scrambled for the porch of the nearest house. Reed saw the bullet find its mark in Turk's right leg, but he focused instead on the brief glint of muzzle flash marking the shooter's location on the eastern ridge. Sunlight obscured his vision as he switched the rifle to semi-auto and squeezed off three quick shots.

Dirt exploded along the ridge where his rounds made impact four hundred yards away. Reed didn't wait for another shot from the sniper. He left cover and hurtled toward Turk like a charging bear. His friend lay on his stomach, halfway onto the porch, blood pooling around his hip.

Reed grabbed him by his plate carrier and jerked him across the floorboards, then he rammed his left shoulder into the front door as the sniper's third shot tore through one of the porch's posts, sending splinters of wood flying like a shotgun blast.

Turk hit the interior hardwood floor with a grunt, and Reed slammed the door shut. Another sniper round snapped through a front window, blasting glass over a sagging couch before obliterating a small television set.

Reed hit the deck and pulled Turk behind the couch, leaving a trail of blood across the floorboards. "Where you hit?"

"Thigh," Turk grunted. "Clean exit."

Reed drew the KA-BAR and sliced into Turk's saturated pant leg, ripping it back to expose the wound. The bullet had entered from behind, about six inches below his buttocks, and had indeed passed all the way through, leaving a messy exit wound on the front side.

Great.

"Who gave you permission to get shot?" Reed tore into his left cargo pocket as another bullet ripped overhead. He unpacked a wad of combat gauze and quickly crammed one end of it into the face of Turk's wound, then wrapped the gauze around his leg and wrenched it tight.

Turk gritted his teeth, and Reed repeated the procedure, wrapping round after round over the wound and cinching it each time.

"You're a real piece of work, Turk. Next time you get shot, have the decency to take it up the ass and crap it back out."

"Copy that." Turk attempted a laugh, but the pain playing across his face was too real.

The next round from the sniper burst through the bottom half of the window and whizzed by Reed's right cheek. He snarled a curse and knotted off the bandage, then snatched up his rifle.

Enough, asshole.

Reed scrambled to the bottom of the window frame and cautiously raised his head. He immediately ducked again as a bullet tore through the woodwork. The next round came directly after, slamming into the back of the couch. "Anybody in the house?" Reed shouted.

There was no answer from the darkened interior beyond the living room.

Reed scrambled back to check Turk's wound. Much of the gauze had turned red, but the bleeding seemed to be under control. He pulled on the knots to be sure they were secure, then stole a glance through the window. "Here's the deal," he said, dropping his mag to check the load.

About fifteen rounds remained, plus the last full mag in his chest rig.

"That guy saw two people run in here, and if he gets the idea one of us moved, he'll follow suit, and we'll never get out."

Reed shoved Turk's rifle next to him, then laid his own on top of it. "You stay here and fire both guns through the window. I'll leave through the back and circle around behind him. Hoorah?"

"You've got to be kidding me," Turk muttered.

"About which part?"

"The part where I lay here like a sitting duck and draw fire!"

Reed grinned and smacked him on the shoulder. "Don't get shot next time. See you in twenty."

Reed moved on his knees into the kitchen, then stood and checked his pistol. It was fully loaded with seventeen rounds in the mag and one in the pipe, plus the two spare mags and the knife. Hopefully, it wouldn't come to the knife.

He ditched the backpack and the twenty-pound flight recorder it held. The relief on his shoulders was immediate, and he shot Turk a thumbs-up. His wounded friend lay against the wall, the two M4A1s propped up on his thighs like freaking Scarface.

Reed rushed to the back door and kicked it open as the sniper fire resumed from the ridge.

37

The yard behind the house was little better than an oversized sandbox, littered with toys and surrounded by a low fence to keep the family dog in. That dog lay in a puddle of blood in the middle of the yard, a gaping hole torn through his torso.

Asshole.

Reed kept the house between himself and the sniper and leapt the fence. He heard Turk scrabbling inside, then twin snarls filled the valley as both rifles opened up.

The sniper returned fire immediately, and Reed located his muzzle flash on a ledge four hundred yards distant from the house, about two hundred yards up the far ridge. To get there without exposing himself, Reed would need to move down the valley to the south, then take the goat trails onto the ridge and slowly work his way up and behind the sniper.

Only he couldn't move slowly. He had to move *now*. Every second that dripped by increased the likelihood that the sniper would relocate, completely changing Reed's battlefield math. He kept behind the row of houses and sprinted. A few stray chickens and a small dog marked his progress with disgruntled clucks and barks, but he still saw no people. At the end of the row, he waited at the last house and leaned out to check the road. It was empty and quiet, with Turk's position five or six houses to his left, but he couldn't risk exposing himself until Turk drew fire.

As if on cue, both rifles opened up again and were answered by a barrage of quick shots from the heavy rifle on the ridge. Reed dashed across the street and slid behind the next house like a runner onto home base. Dirt exploded around him, but the sniper kept firing at Turk.

Scrambling back to his feet, Reed started immediately up the ridge, identifying a goat track and hurtling up it. His heart thundered, and the thin air of increased elevation burned in his lungs, but he kept moving.

This plan of his was great in theory, but in addition to the risk of the sniper relocating, there was also the risk of Turk being shot. Again.

Reed's foot slipped on loose dirt, and he hit his knees, almost tumbling sideways. The incline here was much worse than what he'd traversed previously, forcing him to grab on to small brush and trees wherever he found them, just to keep from falling. Another hundred yards, and his head began to swim. Behind him, the snarl of the M4s was more sporadic, and he wondered how many rounds Turk had left. He also didn't hear the sniper returning fire.

Not good.

The top of the ridge fell beneath his feet, and he turned north, launching forward. A single crack from the sniper filled the valley below, helping him to refine his approach toward the shooter. Turk's rifles didn't answer.

The last stretch burned in Reed's legs and chest. He slowed as he approached the sniper's position from behind and above, then drew the pistol. Each step was calculated now, finding solid bits of dirt without any rocks or debris to send showering downward and expose his position.

As Reed closed the last fifty yards, he thought he heard the sniper. The familiar snap of a magazine was followed by the smack of a bolt closing. Reed lowered his shoulders and held up the Glock, creeping around a short scrub tree and looking down.

The ledge the sniper lay on jutted out of the ridge, about twenty feet down. Reed saw the muzzle of the rifle stabbing out over the empty valley, pointed toward the house, but he couldn't see the sniper. The man was dug into a shallow cave, shielding himself from Reed's view.

Reed crept to the left, moving closer to the drop-off. The ridgeline here steepened so much as to become a cliff directly beneath the sniper's cave. The only direct access to that ledge was from the north—a winding path that would expose Reed to the sniper's peripheral vision long before he obtained a clean shot with the pistol.

Smart. *Damn* smart. Whoever this guy was, he wasn't an amateur. This was precisely the sort of position Reed would've selected himself if he were shooting alone without a spotter. If he had a grenade, Reed would've simply chucked it over the ledge and blown the guy into bloody pieces, but without one, there was really only one option.

Reed dropped to his stomach and wormed over the ground, approaching the cave from the top. Dry grass and shrubs tore at his arms and legs, but his movements were obscured by another two blasts of the rifle. As he approached the edge, he slowed, then drew the pistol and moved to his elbows, inching his way the final five feet.

He saw the muzzle of the rifle first, jutting out over the cliff, still pointed at the house. Then he made out a gloved hand wrapped around the weapon's grip, slowly squeezing off shots. Behind the hand was a black sleeve, then the crest of a floppy hat blocking out the sun from the top edge of the scope.

Reed crept forward another foot, fully exposing the head. He slowly extended the Glock ahead of him, then twisted his head to get a better view of the sniper. From this angle, Reed couldn't aim, but he didn't need to. Five or six 9mm rounds blasted on instinct toward the shooter's head was more than enough to get the job done.

Just a little farther . . .

Reed pushed himself forward, wrapping his arm around the lip. Then the ledge gave way without warning, collapsing beneath him like a false floor. Reed crashed down, feet flailing as he fell twenty feet and landed in a pile of earth with a choking thud. He thought he heard the sniper shout, but everything was lost in the cloud of dust that consumed the little cave.

Reed choked and yanked at the pistol. It was wrapped beneath him, buried under a large rock. He looked quickly to his left, where he knew the sniper should be. The man was already clawing his way out of the dirt, abandoning his buried rifle and moving to his hip for a pistol.

Reed deserted the Glock and rolled to his left, landing on his feet and charging the guy as his pistol cleared the holster. Reed sent his right foot smashing into the sniper's wrist like a sledgehammer, knocking the gun across the cave floor, then he grabbed the man by the chest rig and reached for his throat.

The sniper reacted just as quickly, rolling to the right and sweeping at Reed's legs with both of his own. Reed saw the move coming in time to dance back, but he had to release his hold of the sniper's chest rig. The guy stumbled to his feet, and Reed swept the KA-BAR from his belt.

Knives. Why does it always have to be knives?

The guy reached for his own blade, but Reed didn't give him the chance. He lunged forward and rammed his right boot in between the guy's knees, knocking him off balance the same moment Reed swept the KA-BAR toward his face.

The sniper raised his arm instinctively to shield himself, and the blade sliced deep into his forearm. He screamed and twisted, stumbling backward toward the ledge. Reed followed, ducking a wild right hook and delivering a quick slash across the guy's left thigh.

Another scream, but Reed didn't let up. He followed the slash with a left hook straight onto the guy's chin. The sniper's head snapped back, and he flailed with both arms as he approached the ledge.

Reed swept with the KA-BAR, slicing into his exposed neck and ripping through his windpipe as if it were butter. Blood gushed out, and the guy just stood there on the edge of the cliff, choking and staring wide-eyed at Reed.

He wasn't Turkish or Iranian. This guy was white with bold features and blue eyes. Was he . . . American? Reed didn't have time to care. He wiped his nose with the back of his knife hand, then took one step forward and pushed the guy with his left fist. The sniper tumbled backward into open air and free-fell like a rock. The body landed with a thud, leaving Reed standing on the ridge, Turkish wind rippling across his face, and the knife dripping with blood in one hand. He wiped the blade over his thigh, then slipped it back into its sheath.

Best knife ever built.

Reed staggered back to the cave and sat on the ground, dropping his head as he fought to catch his breath. His heart still pounded like a drum, but the exhilaration of being alive after another brush with death was undeniable. He sifted through the dirt but couldn't find his pistol. He took the sniper's SIG P226 instead, noting the clean chamber and flawlessly maintained bluing.

Who was this guy?

He kicked through the soil, exposing enough of the rifle to confirm what he already knew: the weapon was an AR-10, American-built and equipped with a match-grade trigger and quality optic. Reed recovered a shell casing, rolling it across his palm, then rotating it to expose the base— 7.62x51mm NATO, match-grade ammunition. He fingered the shell casing as he calculated all the possible angles of this new development. Almost none of them made sense.

His radio chirped, and Turk's ragged voice rasped through. "You good, man?"

Reed pocketed the shell casing and stood up. "Copy that. Sniper bit the dust. Headed back."

38

Maggie finally went to bed a little after midnight, returning to the air mattress in the West Wing and instructing Coffman to wake her if there were any new developments. Despite the feeling that everything was spinning out of control, there wasn't much for her to do at this point. They would work to get Tehran on the phone the next day, leaning on diplomatic solutions to de-escalate, while also preparing for the eventuality of a possible invasion of Oman and Kuwait. She'd do anything to forestall it, but if Iran invaded either country, America would be forced to respond.

Another endless war in the making.

Maggie awoke to a gentle tapping on her door. She sat up and brushed hair out of her face. "Yes?"

"It's me, ma'am," Coffman said. "I have breakfast for you."

Maggie checked her phone. Seven a.m.

Coffman was a good man. He knew to give her as much sleep as possible without allowing her to oversleep. God only knew what panic would overtake the country if word slipped out of a lazy commander in chief.

"I'll be right out," she said.

Five minutes in front of the mirror wasn't nearly sufficient to clean the exhaustion from her face, but it helped. She straightened her hair, changed into a fresh pantsuit, and washed her face. Makeup could wait.

Outside the bedroom, Coffman waited in the hall. She doubted if he'd slept, but he was dressed in a fresh suit and stood tall as she stepped out.

"Good morning, ma'am. Get much sleep?"

She laughed dryly. "What do you think?"

"Extra coffee, then. The Navy serves the best."

He escorted her down the hall but turned past the Navy mess, which was half-full of presidential aides and military officials. He led her to the Oval Office, where breakfast waited on the coffee table. Pancakes, bacon, a fruit bowl, and . . . shrimp and grits?

Oh, these people are *good.*

Maggie fixed a plate and took it to the Resolute Desk, settling into Brandt's chair and chowing down without shame. Coffman fixed her coffee and poured himself a cup, then stood next to a window and stared out over the Rose Garden.

Maggie gulped down black coffee to wash away her grits and watched him over her mug. Coffman was clean and wore a fresh suit, but he couldn't hide the hunch in his shoulders. Weary eyes and sagging cheeks hall-marked his sleeplessness and the strain that tore at his mind. The chief of staff looked like a Marine, fresh off the beaches of Normandy.

Maggie lowered the mug and leaned back in her chair. She felt like he looked. "You knew him well?" she asked softly.

Coffman didn't look away from the window. A small smile tugged at his lips. "I worked for President Brandt since he was a congressman. I followed him to the Senate, managed his campaign for the presidency . . . all the way to the top." He glanced sideways at her. "I was supposed to be his secretary of commerce, you know. Gonna kick-start my own career."

"What happened?" Maggie asked.

Coffman shrugged, looking away. "I was too good at my job, I guess. Too good at being chief of staff." He was quiet a long moment, then he grunted softly. "Yes, ma'am. I knew him well. Better than anyone."

"I'm sorry." Maggie wasn't sure what else to say, but she hoped the sincerity in her words meant something to him.

Sometime the day before, she'd blocked out her own emotions, sliding deep into a rut of Teflon leadership. Unbreakable. Unbendable. It was what the country needed, but she could only imagine that as the reality of Brandt's death sank over the White House, the staff must've been coming apart inside.

Coffman looked over his shoulder. "You're president now. I don't want you to doubt that you can depend on me. As long as I'm here, I serve the country."

There was no bravado in Coffman's words—just confidence.

Maggie pivoted her chair to join in his survey of the Rose Garden. It was beautiful in mid-summer, lush with red, white, and pink roses. She could easily see how such a small patch of dirt had become so famous. "What do you think?" she said.

"Ma'am?"

"What do *you* think?"

"About . . . what?"

"All of it. Any of it. You've worked in this place years longer than I have. You know these people better than almost anyone. Am I playing chicken with Iran right now? Should I hit them with a sledgehammer?"

Coffman took his time answering, and Maggie thought of Larry and men who measured their words. She liked that.

"Iran isn't the problem," Coffman said. "Russia is. Without Moscow, Tehran will fold like a cheap jackknife. But together, they're a real issue."

"So, should we hit Russia with the sledgehammer?"

"Not unless you're ready for World War Three. I still think there's hope for finesse. Or at least to keep the conflict contained to the Gulf."

"How?"

Coffman scratched his cheek. "I think you're right to rely on Secretary Gorman. If she can connect with Tehran, there's hope to de-escalate this. But in the event things spill into conflict, we need to think about the American nationals trapped in Oman and Kuwait. These aren't just our allies Iran is messing with. Our own people are over there. Thousands of them."

Maggie's shoulders sagged. "I know."

She'd strained over that most of the previous night. Tens of thousands of innocent civilians, many of them Americans, trapped in oil-rich nations, defenseless against invasion. A massacre waiting to happen.

"You should deploy troops, ma'am," Coffman said. "I'm not a military strategist, but it seems obvious that having boots on the ground to secure Kuwait and the strait prior to an invasion is optimal."

"I won't deploy ground troops without congressional authorization," Maggie said. "Not unless national security is at stake. We've seen that movie before, and it never ends well."

Coffman stared into his coffee, again taking his time. "President Brandt felt the same. But if you're asking me to speak honestly, allowing this thing to boil over before it's addressed is a mistake." He faced her as he finished the sentence.

Well, I asked him to be honest.

"What do you propose?" Maggie asked.

Coffman stepped around the nearest couch and leaned against its end, cupping his mug. He shrugged. "There are other options besides deploying Marines. If you're uncomfortable with the idea of signing off on American troops, we could consider a third-party option."

"Third party? As in . . . mercenaries?"

Coffman pursed his lips. "In Washington, we prefer the term *private security contractors*. But yes, ma'am. That's the idea."

Maggie chewed her cheek. She thought about her meeting with Lance Sanger the previous day. Sanger made a similar comment when she used the word *mercenary*. At the time, it put her on edge. But didn't everything about this place put her on edge? It felt like living in a house full of invisible, human-sized mousetraps.

"What do you know about Lance Sanger?"

Coffman squinted. "The guy who was here yesterday?"

"Right."

"President Brandt knew him. I've only shaken his hand. I wouldn't say I know much about him."

"He offered his support in the Gulf. His company is called Flashpoint—private security contractors, as you say."

"Well, I don't know how many men he can spare, but if he's ready to help, it may not be a bad option. We can deploy his people under executive order and sidestep the necessity of congressional approval. It's a bold option, but you won't see any backlash if American lives are in jeopardy."

Maggie picked at a thumbnail, once again feeling overwhelmed and uncertain.

"I chose you for this moment."

Brandt's message echoed in her mind, adding to her confusion and unease.

What did he mean by that? "I chose you." Chose for what? The presidency? Did Brandt . . . expect to die?

No. Surely not.

"Jason," Maggie said. "Did Brandt ever . . . talk about death?"

"Death?" Coffman frowned. "What do you mean?"

"Did he . . ." Maggie hesitated, weighing her words and searching for the right combination to get her question across without sounding crazy.

The phone on her desk rang sharply, jarring her out of her thoughts and saving her from indecision. She scooped it up and answered automatically. "Governor Trous— I mean, this is—"

"Ma'am, this is General Yellin. We need you in the Situation Room. We have Montgomery on the phone."

39

Northeast of Mosul, in the sheep and goat mountains of Iraq's Erbil Governorate, the Kurds lived separate from the rest of the country. A proud and culturally distinct people, they spoke Kurdish, not Arabic, and despite carrying Iraqi passports, they maintained their independence as a completely separate ethnic population.

In Reed's experience, Kurds were fine people. They were excellent soldiers and loyal friends, and he fought alongside many of them during the Iraqi civil war. He appreciated their dedication to their heritage, even if the rest of the region never would. When things hit the fan before, he could always count on the Kurds, so it made sense now to seek them out in a time of need. It didn't hurt that Turk spoke a little Kurdish.

As soon as they hot-wired the Nissan and made it across the border, Reed was quick to find a lone goat shepherd's cottage deep in the mountains. He knocked on the door, bloody shirt and all. Kurds were no strangers to violence and had more than their fair share of experience dealing with battlefield wounds.

The man who answered was old and stooped, but he didn't ask questions when he saw the bandage wrapped around Turk's thigh or the pallor of his cheeks. Within minutes, Turk was on his back, lying across the shepherd's table as the old man's wife bustled around, heating water and unpacking fresh bandages. While the shepherd worked, Turk lay still, grimacing from time to time but grunting soft words of grateful Kurdish.

"I need a phone," Reed said.

Turk translated through gritted teeth.

The shepherd struggled to understand at first, then walked into the kitchen, returning a moment later with a battered satellite phone.

Reed nodded his thanks and powered the phone on as he walked outside. He dialed the number Yellin gave him from memory and waited as the phone slowly connected. It took a minute to reach somebody on the other side of the world, but the audio was surprisingly clear when an aide answered. In under five minutes, he had the general, the White House chief of staff, and the acting president herself on the line.

"Reed, are you all right?" Maggie said.

"You sound surprised," Reed said. "Guess you knew about that hornet's nest of Iranians, huh?"

Dead silence.

"Don't worry," Reed said. "I've found it in my heart to forgive. But next time there's an army breathing down my neck and you don't tell me about it, we're gonna have problems."

"I'm sorry, Reed. We had trouble with the drone. Those choppers—"

"Save the excuses. That's not why I called. Turk is banged up and needs immediate medical. Trace this call and send a chopper, ASAP."

"No problem. We're putting a medevac in the air right now. How bad is he?"

"Broken ankle and gunshot to the leg. Plenty of blood loss, but he's hanging in there. Tell those medevac guys to step on it."

"Reed, this is General Yellin. The chopper is in the air. You have my word. What can you tell us about the crash site? Did you recover the flight recorder?"

Reed scrubbed sweat from his face. "The crash site was a wreck. I found no survivors. I think it's safe to say the aircraft decimated on impact, and then it burned. I didn't find his body, but I wouldn't hold your breath on Brandt."

Maggie spoke again. "And the flight recorder?"

Reed hesitated, chewing his lip and watching a slow column of goats—just dots on the horizon—moving across a ridgeline. "Gone," he said. "I got inside the tail, but the recorder was blown away sometime during the fight. Could be anywhere between here and Istanbul."

Reed heard muttered curses, but he just waited.

"Okay," Maggie said at last. "Thank you for looking. The chopper will be there shortly."

She hung up, and Reed stood for a while, tapping the phone against his open palm and thinking about the crash site and the missiles—thinking about that 7.62 casing he recovered from the sniper.

He walked to the back of the Nissan and threw the hatch open. The flight recorder lay just inside, banged up and dirty, but still intact. He hoisted it out and walked into the house, setting the heavy device on the table next to Turk.

"Ask them for a computer," Reed said. "It's time we figure out who's lying."

40

The White House Situation Room

Maggie hung up the phone but didn't say anything. She took the call on speaker, and both Yellin and Coffman heard the entire thing. There wasn't much to say.

Of all the things I dreamed of being as president, this wasn't it.

Yellin cleared his throat. "Ma'am, we have to make some decisions now."

Maggie felt a little emotionally disoriented, as if she didn't know how to process what she should be feeling, but the analytical side of her mind was sharper than ever. Yellin was right. It was time to act.

"What's your recommendation, General?"

"We need boots on the ground in the Gulf. Regardless of who brought down *Air Force One*, we can't ignore Iran any longer. Tehran doesn't want to talk. They want war."

Coffman nodded his agreement. "The general is right, ma'am. Fuel prices rose another eight percent on average today. The country is panicking. If we don't take decisive action now, we risk losing a lot more than just the Gulf. And like we discussed before . . . there are Americans over there. Thousands of them."

Thousands of Americans.

Maggie thought about Joshua Simmons—the old man and his telescope. An innocent civilian caught in the crossfire. Whatever happened next, she wouldn't allow further civilians to be gunned down. Not on her watch. "What options do we have with existing forces in the region?"

Yellin took that one. "We're limited, ma'am. With the Fifth Fleet, we can launch air-to-ground assaults and provide some security in the strait, but we can't do much about an actual invasion of Kuwait. I need ground troops for that."

"How long would it take you to deploy them?"

"Scale-downs in Iraq have limited our ground presence in the region. I'd need some time to position them. But with your permission, I could put first-strike forces in the air now and have them in Baghdad by midnight."

"Do it. But they don't leave Iraq without my authorization."

"Understood, ma'am."

"Jason, reach out to Mr. Sanger. Ask him what assets he can deploy directly into Kuwait City for the protection of our citizens there. As many as he can spare. I'll sign an executive order to authorize it."

"Yes, ma'am."

The room was quiet, and Maggie knew they were all thinking the same thing, but she had to be the one to say it. She had to be the one to step up to the plate.

"Schedule another press conference," she said at last. "It's time I took the oath."

41

There was a shrieking hiss, and Lt. Laura Hutchins's head slammed against her helmet. No matter how many times she did this—no matter how hard she pressed herself against the back of her seat—she still felt the jolt as the steam-powered catapults hurled her sixteen-ton F/A-18E Super Hornet from zero to 165 miles per hour in under two seconds.

The jet left the end of the carrier and dropped straight toward the ocean. Just a split second of plummeting before the engines caught, and she raced skyward like a bullet, heart pounding, blood surging.

There was no roller coaster on Earth like it—no thrill that matched the rush she felt each time she was launched off the *Ronald Reagan*'s flight deck like a pebble leaving a slingshot. It was what she lived for and what she'd dedicated her entire life to experiencing.

Laura knew she needed the rush since she was six years old. Other girls liked dolls and Hannah Montana. She liked air shows and absolutely anything *fast*. The faster, the better.

Sports cars were a start, initiated by midnight races outside her hometown when she was only fifteen. Laura attended a private school full of rich kids with expensive European cars. She wasn't rich. Her parents worked four jobs between them to give her the opportunity to have "a better education," but once she developed a reputation as a speed demon, the other kids were happy to toss her the keys and stand back.

Pretty soon, the sports cars were too slow. Too controlled. That was when she discovered Japanese sports bikes . . . the next level of mania. A boyfriend with a Kawasaki opened the door, and she never looked back—not until her exceptional prowess at science-based academia attracted the notice of a Navy recruiter . . . and a new thrill was promised.

Only, to unlock this thrill, she'd need to do a lot more than make out with a skinny kid behind the high school gymnasium. The recruiter said her chances of becoming a Navy fighter pilot were slimmer than those of becoming a superstar celebrity. First she'd need to attend the Naval Academy, where only one out of a thousand applicants were accepted. Then, assuming she made it that far, she'd need to make it into flight school—a chance of one out of ten thousand.

And even if she made it into flight school, her chances of earning her wings as one of the most elite fighter pilots in the world were barely fifteen percent. Laura liked those odds. Overnight, her whole world orbited around a dream of hurtling through the air at up to twelve hundred miles per hour, carrying death under her wings and nothing but smoke in her rearview. This was the *ultimate* rush, the opportunity she'd sacrificed her early twenties to earn, and no matter what happened the rest of her life, nothing would compare to finally achieving it.

Laura leveled the Super Hornet off at fifteen thousand feet and looked through the canopy at the sprawling mass of the Persian Gulf far below. The water was perfectly blue—sparkling in the midday sun. USS *Ronald Reagan* already looked like a spec on that blue expanse, miles away as she gently circled, then charted a course for the Strait of Hormuz.

She was flying support on this sortie, serving as wingman for a captain piloting an identical F/A-18E five hundred feet to her ten o'clock. The mission was simple—blaze into the strait and rattle any Iranian vessels in the area. Maybe light them up on targeting radar or take it to the deck and blaze past them like bats out of hell.

Laura was well aware of the evolving situation in the region and the recent demise of *Bingham*. She knew Americans died on that tanker, and she was only too eager to strike back. If it were up to her, they'd skip the intimidation factor and move straight to weapons hot.

"You awake, Hutch?" Captain Rollins spoke calmly over the radio, no hint of nerves in his voice. This was just another exercise—another routine flight for the best pilots in the world.

"You better believe it," Laura said.

"Stay loose back there, and watch my six. No hero ball today."

Laura grinned. After arriving at the Gulf, she'd become known for executing aggressive maneuvers and pushing her flight protocols to the very extremes of their limits. Her commanders back on the *Reagan* hated her for it, lecturing her about "playing hero ball" with a fifty-million-dollar aircraft.

But Laura never technically broke the rules, and she managed the more advanced maneuvers with ease, so what the flight commanders interpreted as "reckless," her fellow pilots viewed as ballsy.

She was okay with that.

The miles faded beneath the two aircraft, and the next thing Laura knew, they were dropping to three thousand feet and screaming into the strait. From this altitude, the narrow stretch of water looked little wider than a river, with a smattering of shipping vessels hugging the Omani coast as they slipped through. Word of *Bingham*'s sinking had rippled through the region, and nobody was edging one foot closer to Iran than necessary.

"Iranian patrol boat, ten o'clock," Rollins said.

"I see him."

"Let's wake him up."

Rollins rolled left, and Laura followed, pushing the jet into a screeching dive straight for the tiny naval vessel. She saw men scrambling across the deck like ants, pointing at the sky and gesturing to each other. A rush of adrenaline charged her blood as the digital altimeter spun like a clock on crack. A thousand feet. Eight hundred.

"Pull off," Rollins said.

Laura banked right and lifted the nose, engaging the afterburner and hurtling skyward again. No sooner was her nose pointed toward a cloudless

blue sky than a red light flashed on her flight panel. Her ears flooded with a
buzzing alert, and the adrenaline of only moments before was instantly
replaced by edging nerves as she reflexively looked over her right shoulder.
She couldn't see anything, and her heart began to thunder.

Rollins's voice remained icy cool. "Stay loose. Iranian F-Fives on your
six, four miles."

Laura didn't need to be told. The continued alert of an enemy-targeting
system locked on her tail flooded her headset as she banked hard right,
circling to follow Rollins. It was the afterburner that did it. The Iranian F-5
locked onto the heat signature, providing a clear targeting formula, even at
that distance.

Laura rolled into position behind Rollins, and the buzzing finally quit.
Ahead she saw the two F-5s racing toward her as little black specs growing
rapidly larger. Her dash flashed again as attempted targeting pulsated from
the F-5s, but Rollins's calm voice resumed.

"You take right, I'll take left. Keep 'em off your ass, and and stay loose.
They're just playing chicken."

"Copy that."

Laura waited until her F-5 was barely a quarter-mile distant, then she
dove. Blue sky turned to blue waves, and she raced downward, watching
her scope to help track the enemy aircraft. As she expected, the Iranian
turned clumsily to the left and also dove, trying to keep up.

But the dated F-5 was no match for the sleek and agile Super Hornet.
Laura pulled up five hundred feet off the waves and circled left, adding
more afterburner for boost and quickly arcing through a half circle. The
Iranian was a mile away, still diving for the waves in a frantic effort to keep
up. In another thirty seconds, Laura would be right on his tail, half a mile
back.

A perfect shot.

The flight panel illuminated bright red, and the buzzing resumed.
Alerts on her dash notified her of a missile lock, followed almost immediately by a weapon launch. Laura impulsively started to look over her
shoulder again. This time she caught herself, returning to the flight panel
to identify the source.

Surface to air.

"SAM!" Laura shouted. She couldn't see the missile, but based on their proximity to the coastline, it could equally be coming from Iran or one of their ships.

Either way, this changed everything. These guys weren't playing games anymore. They wanted to kill.

"Weapons hot," Rollins said. "Clear to engage."

Laura was way ahead of him, activating the four AIM-120 and two AIM-9 Sidewinder missiles hung beneath the jet's wings. Within seconds, she could deploy enough firepower to knock absolutely anything out of the sky, but that wouldn't deal with the SAM.

Finally, she saw it. The display inside her helmet shield caught the missile rocketing in from the Iranian coast, soaring straight toward Rollins.

"Seven o'clock, missile—"

"I see it!" Rollins snapped. "Stay on your bogey."

Laura hesitated, looking between the incoming weapon and Rollins, three miles away. He was just swinging into targeting position behind his F-5 and had yet to do anything about deflecting the incoming SAM.

"Laura. Do your job!"

Her head snapped out of the fog, and she searched for the F-5 again. Three seconds of indecision had offered the Iranian time to identify her tactics and swerve into a roll again, almost slipping out of her grasp.

Lose sight, lose the fight.

The adage from her flight instructor echoed in her mind, and Laura's trained instincts clicked into gear.

Not today, dude.

She rolled hard left and pulled the Super Hornet into an aggressive turn to follow the F-5. G-force tore at her body, and her vision narrowed as she screamed in behind him, but Laura didn't pull out. She knew her limits, and how far she could push them. This was no different than dog-fighting school back in Nevada. No different, except she was about to kill this guy.

The F-5 swiveled into her line of sight, and Laura pulled out of the turn just as she felt herself losing control. The Super Hornet leveled out, leaving the Iranian's tail fully exposed, half a mile away.

Weapons hot.

Weapons lock.

Fire.

The AIM-9 dropped from her right wing and screamed forward at Mach 2.5. She knew it was going to be a hit the moment she pressed the trigger, but she didn't have time to celebrate. Again her display was illuminated with SAM warnings, but this time there wasn't just one missile—or even two.

Five separate weapons hurtled skyward, only miles away. Laura rolled right as the Iranian F-5 detonated like a piñata to her left. She was vaguely aware of Rollins's bogey also bursting into flames, but now the surface radar from the Iranian coast was all over them, and when she checked the scope, she saw another wing of four F-5s racing toward them from inland Iran.

They were screwed.

42

"Repeat after me. I, Margaret Louise Trousdale, do solemnly swear ..."

Maggie's fingers rested on a leather-bound Bible, her right hand raised as she faced the chief justice of the United States Supreme Court. To her right, the Rose Garden was filled with reporters, all waiting in reverent silence while she performed the oath of office in front of a virtual nation.

" ... that I will faithfully execute the office of president of the United States."

Maggie's lips moved, but the words sounded like they were coming from a different person, as though she were just a ghost observing from across the room. She compensated for the surrealness by keeping her head high and shoulders squared. The picture of a strong leader. The picture America needed to see.

" ... and will, to the best of my ability, preserve, protect, and defend the constitution of the United States."

"So help you, God?"

"So help me, God."

"Congratulations, Madam President."

A chill rippled down her spine, despite the thick August heat. Cameras flashed, and the justice shook her hand. Maggie faced the cameras, allowing them to snap a few more pictures before she lifted a hand and started toward the Oval Office.

"Madam President, where are you headed?" someone shouted.

"Back to work," she said with a brief nod.

The door closed behind her, and Maggie leaned against the wall, grateful for the blinds that blocked away the reporters. Sometime soon she'd need to address them, but right now, she just needed to breathe. The world still spun around her, and she felt like a load of bricks weighed against her chest.

I'm president now. It's up to me.

The door to the corridor opened, and Coffman stepped in. He hesitated just inside, glancing awkwardly around as Maggie rested her head against the wall.

"Come in," she said, straightening and walking to Brandt's desk.

No. *Her* desk.

"Do you need a minute, ma'am?"

"We don't have a minute. Where's Yellin?"

"Still in the Situation Room."

"Any updates on those jets?"

"He's on the phone now. Should have something soon."

"Well, get him in here. And get Gorman, too. I'm tired of being in the Situation Room. Feels like I'm in a hole."

Coffman hurried out. Just prior to the inauguration ceremony, Yellin had received word from the Fifth Fleet about two Super Hornet fighters shot down near the Strait of Hormuz. Details were slowly developing, but the summary wasn't good. Maggie could feel things spinning out of control, and no matter how hard she crammed her feet against the floor, she couldn't seem to slow the spiral.

Coffman returned with Yellin and Secretary Gorman only minutes later. All three looked grim, but Gorman offered a hand and congratulated Maggie on the inauguration.

"Thank you," Maggie said. "Please have a seat."

The three of them clustered around her desk, and Maggie gulped down water. "What happened?"

Yellin spoke first. "We deployed some fighters to the strait as a show of force. They were under standing orders not to fire unless fired upon."

"And?"

"And they were ambushed. Both aircraft shot down. Only one pilot survived. She managed to eject in time."

Yellin slid a file folder across the table, and Maggie flipped through it. Mug shots of Navy pilots Captain Alan Rollins and Lieutenant Laura Hutchins headlined each page.

"Did we get her back?"

"Yes, ma'am. She dropped into the Gulf, and we got a chopper there before the Iranians found her."

"Good. What's the situation now?"

"Quiet again. We put about thirty aircraft in the air, and they backed down. But it's only temporary. They were testing us here, and they're emboldened now."

Yellin trailed off, and Maggie looked up from the mug shots, both eyebrows raised.

"Ma'am, this isn't going to get better. I've got ground troops in the air, but I don't need them in Baghdad. I need them in Kuwait and the UAE."

Maggie shook her head. "No. We've been over this. Park them in Baghdad, and give me time to de-escalate. Lisa, do—"

Gorman held up a hand, her gaze fixed on her cell phone. Without comment, she hurried away from the desk and held a hand over her ear, speaking into the phone. Then she rushed back. "Ma'am, we've got Iranian President Asadi on the line."

Maggie sat up. "Finally. Send it to my desk."

Gorman snapped instructions through her cell, and almost immediately, the phone on Maggie's desk flashed a red incoming-call light. Maggie reached for the speaker button, but Gorman spoke first. "If he's calling, he's worried. We've been trying to make contact for two days and have heard nothing. Why would he call now? It must be the fighters. Whatever he says, we need to keep communication open while also remaining in charge."

"Anything else?"

Gorman hesitated. "He's a sexist, ma'am. He may not want to speak to you."

Maggie sneered. "Well, I've got all kinds of experience with sexists."

She smashed the speaker button and sat back, folding her arms. "President Asadi?"

An accented voice spoke in English. "To whom do I speak?"

"You're speaking to President Margaret Trousdale. I'm glad you called."

There was a long pause, punctuated by angry breathing. "Is there not a *man* I can speak to?"

"You're talking to *the* man, Mr. President. The one with her pen on Iran's death warrant if you attack more of my aircraft."

Gorman made a calming motion with both hands. Maggie ignored her and stared at the phone.

"They said you were sultry, Madam President. In my country, we cut out the tongues of insolent women."

"Well, in my country, we promote them. Now, why haven't we been able to reach you? Our presidential aircraft was brought down within spitting distance of your border, and you've deployed troops all up and down the Gulf. You might try answering the phone—"

"Do not accuse me of this!" Asadi snapped. "Iran had *nothing* to do with the death of your president. Do you think we'd kill a man and let a woman take his place?"

"I think you'll do almost anything to advance your agenda. I also think you're moving a lot of troops, and it's making my people nervous. What are you up to, Mr. President?"

"What are we *up* to? You insult me! Iran is not a midnight thief, sulking into your home after dark. We must protect our borders from the threat of Western imperialism!"

Western imperialism.

Maggie had heard that phrase before, quite recently, but not from Iran.

"What part of protecting your borders involves attacking our aircraft?"

"Your aircraft violated Iranian airspace, Madam President. We will shoot down as many such aircraft as it takes to protect our sovereignty. The Gulf will bleed red before we are done if you do not withdraw your forces."

Maggie looked to Yellin. He shook his head, confirming what she already knew. Those Navy pilots wouldn't have invaded Iranian airspace. Not yet. But pressing the point with Asadi wouldn't fix anything now.

"It would behoove you not to make threats, Mr. President. My people are edgy. I'd say they have a right to be. We have reason to believe you're lying to us about—"

"Let me tell you what to believe, you American *whore*. Believe that Iran will do whatever is necessary to protect itself, even if our protection requires an act of war. That is all."

Asadi hung up, leaving the Oval Office buzzing with a dial tone.

Maggie smashed the button to end the call. "Well, he's delightful."

"I'm sorry, ma'am," Gorman said. "Asadi has never been easy to deal with."

"He doesn't *want* to be dealt with," Yellin said. "He wants a fight, and if we back down now, we'll never recover the initiative. Please, ma'am. Ask Congress for a declaration of war."

Gorman broke in. "A declaration of war? Against *whom*?"

"Iran!" Yellin almost shouted.

Gorman objected. "We don't have proof they hit *Air Force One*!"

"Does that even matter anymore?" Coffman said. "No matter who brought that plane down, Iran wants a fight. If we don't secure the Gulf, fuel prices will double by next week. Have you been outside? You can *feel* the fear in the air. You could cut it with a knife."

Maggie looked back to Gorman.

She shook her head. "It's not just Iran, ma'am. We know that. If we declare war now, where will it end? How far will Russia go?"

"Well, we agree on that," Yellin said. "It's *not* just Iran, which is why it's so important to shut them down now. Russia is testing us using Iran as a tool. If we can't handle Iran, how could we handle Russia? The world is watching. We can't fumble this."

Gorman opened her mouth again, but Maggie held up a hand. "I've heard you both. General, how many men have you deployed to Baghdad?"

"Six thousand Marines, and light armor."

"Double that. Do we have any naval assets we can move into the Arabian Sea to support the Fifth Fleet?"

Yellin didn't hesitate. "The Seventh Fleet could spare a carrier and a few frigates. But it'll take time to move them."

"Then get going on it." She turned to Gorman. "Secretary, how long would it take to call an emergency meeting of the United Nations Security Council?"

Gorman frowned. "Maybe . . . tomorrow. I'd have to make some calls."

"Do it. Get it scheduled as soon as possible. Jason, make my travel arrangements. I'll attend myself."

Everyone looked confused.

"I don't understand," Coffman said. "What's the play here?"

Maggie rested her head against the chair. The tall back made her feel stable and confident. "The play is to confront Russia. You said we don't know how far they'll go, Secretary. I'm going to find out."

43

The apartment was small and smelled of mold. Other than the bed, a table with a single chair, and a computer desk, it was empty. Nothing hung on the walls, and there was no food in the fridge. Empty takeout cartons littered one corner next to an overflowing trash can. The whole place needed a solid scrubbing and a couple cans of paint.

Wolfgang owned a sizable home outside of Buffalo, fully equipped with a gourmet kitchen and an underground research laboratory. He bought the property years before, back when he was in love and dreamed of things like a quiet family life.

Those dreams shattered when his fiancée was gunned down while working an anti-terrorist op, but he kept the property and built the house. For a time, he used the gourmet kitchen and enjoyed home-cooked meals. As the years passed, he found himself doing less of that and spending more time downstairs, slaving in the laboratory. Dreaming. Hoping. Searching for a cure to his baby sister's incurable genetic disease. He funded that research with contract killing and filled the gaps in between with collegiate study—eventually earning a doctorate.

After losing his leg and his illicit career with it, he was forced to take a job at the university, and it was too far to Buffalo to make the drive daily. So, he rented this dingy little apartment and ordered takeout and tried to pretend the mess around him wasn't a mirror of his mental state. It wasn't long before that he would've never tolerated living conditions like this. He wore expensive suits and had his hair cut once a week. A spotless Mercedes coupe and polished shoes completed the look of a man who would do absolutely anything to never return to his poverty-stricken roots.

But now . . .

Wolfgang sat at the little table, a bag of McDonald's carryout untouched next to him. The food smelled old and greasy, making him nauseous. Through the grimy window of his apartment, he looked out over a small park in downtown Burlington. It was poorly maintained, a reflection of the ghetto around it, but he couldn't deny the bright glow of summer green. Today was a hiking day—a swimming, biking, mountain-climbing day. At least it was if you had ten toes.

Wolfgang swallowed cold black coffee and sagged into the chair. He thought about the drawer next to his bed and the Glock 10mm lying inside. He thought about the smooth *shlick* of the slide ramming a round into the chamber and the five pounds of pressure required to press the trigger.

One pull. One quick blast.

The gun was the only clean thing in the apartment—unused, but not forgotten.

For years he'd clung to life in the name of finding a cure for Collins. For years he'd failed. Hadn't he earned the right to be selfish?

Wolfgang's gaze drifted to the bedside table, lingering over the drawer handle. How many men had died at the muzzle of that same pistol? They all deserved it. Didn't he?

A dull chime rang from the laptop resting on the desk, drawing Wolfgang's attention away from the pistol. He hauled himself up and hobbled across the room, kicking the chair back and hitting the space bar to wake up the computer. The machine blinked to life slowly, and he navigated to his email server—the source of the noise. It was probably an email from a student complaining about a deadline, or another lecture from administration complaining about his "temperament."

But no . . . The message in the box was headed by a single letter "R." No name.

Wolfgang clicked it. There was no message inside—only a digital file. An audio recording. Wolfgang slipped his headphones on and played the file.

Immediately, he knew what it was. The abstract hum of avionics punctuated by the mechanical snap of pilots repeating orders to each other was a sound he'd heard before. He listened as the first officer rattled off protocols and the captain confirmed as he implemented each one. Their voices were perfectly controlled, but he detected a faint undertone of panic.

The file ground on like a train wreck, grating to listen to but impossible to ignore. Wolfgang leaned forward as the last ten seconds churned by in a rapid succession of building disaster. The pilots remained calm and professional, but right before the end, the first officer breathed a panicked prayer, and the mic caught it. Then the audio simply stopped.

Wolfgang hit replay, focusing on each individual sound, listening for something in particular, and not hearing it. He played the file twice more, studying the beeps of the flight controls and the ambient noises outside the cabin. Still, he heard nothing. And perhaps more importantly, the pilots *said* nothing.

Wolfgang hit reply on the email and shot back a quick note.

THIS ISN'T RIGHT.

He stroked his chin, replaying the chaos in his mind—placing himself in that cockpit and filling in the gaps of data with his imagination.

What did he see?

The laptop chimed again. Another message from Reed.

I KNOW. INVESTIGATING. NEED HELP.

Wolfgang shot back a reply without hesitation.

HOW?

Reed's next note was just as immediate and just as simple.

FOLLOW THE MONEY.

44

Maggie had never flown in anything quite like the brand-new *Air Force One* —an identical sister jet of Brandt's recently demised plane. Altogether unlike the interior of the previous presidential aircraft she'd seen in pictures, the new jet was modern in every possible way, with plush leather chairs and the most cutting-edge technology.

It was quiet, too—the quietest aircraft she'd ever flown in, leaving her feeling like she was floating more than rocketing through the sky. She sat next to a window in the small presidential conference room and looked out across a sea of clouds. The sun turned their top edges gold, and the sky beyond was so perfectly blue, it looked like a painting.

It was probably the most beautiful thing she'd ever seen, but she lacked the ability to appreciate it. The knots in her stomach twisted a little harder, and the strain at the back of her mind tugged downward perpetually. But she sat straight-backed in the pivoting chair nearest the window and kept her hands folded in her lap.

Calm. Ready. The picture of a president.

Coffman was the only other person in the room. He sat a few feet away at the table, working on a laptop and looking ready to drop, but she had yet to see him embrace the exhaustion. Coffman was like an old Johnson outboard hanging off the back of a fishing boat . . . He simply kept churning.

Maggie looked to her lap where an iPad lay, news stories curated from an assortment of national networks displayed across the screen. She used one finger to scroll down, quickly scanning headlines as she moved.

"GAS PRICES IN SAN JOSE TOP $5.00 PER GALLON"

"GOVERNORS OF SIXTEEN STATES CALLING ON PRESIDENT TROUSDALE TO DECLARE STATE OF EMERGENCY"

"FUEL SHORTAGES SPILL INTO VIOLENCE AT CHICAGO PUMPS: TWO DEAD"

"OPINION: WHY HASN'T TROUSDALE DECLARED WAR?"

Maggie selected the last article and quickly scanned the piece. It wasn't long and didn't waste time beating about the bush. The columnist—some Harvard grad she'd never heard of—drove right to the point.

...as tensions spill out of control in the Gulf and panic overtakes the land of the free, we're all left wondering . . . Where is our fearless leader? Who is this woman standing behind the nuclear button? And why is she asleep at the helm as the country spins into chaos?

Maggie read those last lines twice more, letting them sink in. If the twenty-something-year-old Harvard grad who penned them were sitting here now, how would she answer?

"Flashpoint has deployed troops," Coffman said, spinning around in his chair. "I just got a note from Mr. Sanger. Thirty-five hundred riflemen, two hundred armored vehicles, and fifteen security helicopters will land in Kuwait City by nightfall. He's working to assemble more."

Thirty-five hundred. Was that enough to stop the flood of an Iranian invasion?

"Have they begun an evacuation?" Maggie asked.

Coffman rubbed his eyes, dropping his glasses on the table. "They're trying, ma'am. It's hard to get people to leave."

"What?"

Coffman shrugged. "Think about hurricanes or wildfires. Some people won't leave, no matter how strong the threat. They just don't believe it's real."

Maggie studied the passing clouds. She imagined a horde of invaders just off the coast of New Orleans, ready to storm her swampy home at a moment's notice. Would she leave? Hell no. She'd load up a shotgun and meet them on the front porch.

Maybe it was time to let Yellin shift forces into Kuwait. The building army in Baghdad was imposing, but it was hours away from saving the tiny nation if Iran moved ahead. Should she meet the threat head-on? Declare war?

"Trust no one."

Brandt's penned warning returned to her mind out of nowhere. She thought back to the scratched note, and uncertainty returned, numbing her mind with pointless strain. No matter how long she pondered over that subject, she couldn't make sense of the note. It only added to her existing paralysis of analysis.

Maggie chose to push the thought away, deliberately switching her mind to a safer subject. "Why do they call me *Saint*?"

"Ma'am?" Coffman stared at her, bleary eyed.

"When they rushed me into the bunker the other day, I heard the Secret Service call me *Saint*."

"Oh." He scratched behind his head. "I guess . . . because you're from Louisiana. Like, the New Orleans Saints, maybe? The Secret Service gives a call sign to everyone they protect."

Maggie nodded softly, watching as Coffman's eyelids drooped in spite of himself. He looked ready to drop dead, and she wondered how many days it had been since he got a full night's rest. This man was like a freaking Marine—a relentless force of stability in the midst of the storm. She wished she had a dozen like him.

"When we land, you should stay on the plane," she said. "Get some sleep."

Coffman just stared at her, as if he were unpacking what she said, his mind slogging through a quagmire. Then his shoulders dropped. "I'd like to refuse, but I think you're right."

The seatbelt light clicked on overhead, followed by the calm voice of the Air Force captain in the cockpit. "We're making our final approach, Madam President. Please fasten your seatbelt."

Maggie locked the belt in place as the giant plane arced gracefully down through the clouds. In the distance, the majestic skyline of New York City filled the horizon, rising like a monument to all things empire. *Air Force One* circled once, then glided to a smooth landing at John F. Kennedy International Airport in Queens.

Marine One waited on the tarmac a short walk away, and within minutes, Maggie was in the air again, rocketing westward toward Manhattan. A decoy *Marine One* flew just ahead of them, along with two Marine Viper helicopters on either flank. Those three aircraft landed first before Maggie's chopper settled like a feather onto the Wall Street heliport.

"The Beast"—one of the massive, presidential limousines—waited to cart Maggie to the United Nations Headquarters in Midtown. She settled into the back seat and watched the buildings roll by as Jenkins and O'Dell rode silently ahead of her, both wearing dark sunglasses.

Maggie had insisted that O'Dell join her on this trip, and Jenkins hadn't argued much. Her Cajun bodyguard seemed to be earning respect amid the established Secret Service officers and had even been granted a sidearm after clearing some manner of extensive background check.

"When we arrive, I'll place two agents at your side, along with Officer O'Dell," Jenkins said. "There may be tourists or protestors present at the entrance. I'd ask you to ignore them and let us get you inside as quickly as possible."

Maggie simply nodded.

"We'll escort you to the entrance of the Security Council and wait just outside."

"Thank you, Jenkins."

Up ahead, Maggie saw the United Nations Secretariat building shooting skyward—a simple rectangular tower dressed in glass. The flags of every member nation waved in the breeze outside, and beneath them, a swarm of people waited behind barricades, chanting and waving signs. Maggie could hear them as The Beast pulled into the circular driveway and turned toward the headquarters building. Their voices were a confused muddle of conflicting demands, but the signs were easy enough to read.

Make love, not war!

Leave Persia to the Persians!

Nuke those jerks!

Maggie read them, then looked away, waiting for the car to stop. An army of Secret Service agents spilled out of two Suburbans, quickly surrounding her car before somebody approached her door.

"Remember, ma'am . . ." Jenkins said. "Straight inside."

Maggie nodded and took a deep breath, then they were outside. The muted voices of only a moment before now assaulted her like a tidal wave, and she ducked her head as agents propelled her toward the door.

"Ignorant whore!" someone shouted.

"You're destroying this country!"

The agents pushed from behind, and Maggie broke into a jog. The voices faded and were then blocked out entirely as the glass doors of the headquarters building closed behind her. Maggie was conscious of O'Dell walking right at her elbow, but the other agents quickly fanned out, leaving her room to breathe.

Secretary Gorman appeared out of nowhere, offering her hand. "Welcome to the United Nations, ma'am. Have you met Ambassador Carrie?"

Gorman gestured toward a tall, slender woman with a tight smile. She looked a lot like Gorman, but perhaps a little warmer.

"Tracy Carrie, ambassador to the United Nations. It's an honor to meet you, Madam President."

Maggie clasped her hand, then hurried to follow as Gorman led her down hallways and up a set of stairs to the Security Council chamber.

"Everyone is assembled," Gorman said. "Ambassador Carrie wanted to walk you through a few things before you enter."

Carrie spoke quickly, articulating each word with the easy precision of a person accustomed to operating under pressure. "All the permanent members are present, ma'am. You'll be invited to speak first and may address the chamber in English. Everybody is equipped with earpiece translators, if necessary. Russian Ambassador Belov speaks fluent English but may choose to use Russian to throw you off. The French insist on speaking French."

Carrie made an apologetic shrug, but Maggie wasn't perturbed. "Will you be in the chamber, Ambassador?"

"That's up to you, ma'am."

"Join me. You too, Lisa."

Gorman nodded, then they all stopped at the entrance of the chamber. A uniformed United Nations officer reached for the door as the Secret Service agents fell back.

To Maggie's surprise, O'Dell shot her a quick wink. The gesture, however small, brought her courage. She squared her shoulders, then plowed ahead.

45

The chamber was large and square, with a three-quarter circle wooden desk filling the center. Soft blue chairs lined the outside edge of that desk, with nameplates and microphones laid out in front of them.

A marble slab adorned with ornate paintings of ancient warriors and council members was at the far end of the room beneath recessed lighting, and the remainder of the chamber was filled by red chairs for observers and media.

Only there were no observers that day, and no media. Most of the table was occupied by men and women in business suits, with a smattering of support staff seated behind them.

Carrie led the way around half of the table, smiling and nodding at a few individuals before gesturing to an open chair near the middle. "We're late," she whispered as Maggie passed.

Maggie settled into her chair and noted the glass of water waiting for her. She sipped it and quickly scanned the nameplates resting around the inside of the circle.

They weren't nameplates, actually. Or at least they didn't feature names

—only countries. United Kingdom sat to her left, followed by France, then Russia, Albania, Brazil, Gabon, and Mexico. To her right, she was joined by China, followed by Ghana, India, Ireland, Kenya, Norway, and the United Arab Emirates. Each plate was framed by a serious man or woman sitting behind it, staring at her, unblinking.

Quite the welcome.

Ambassador Carrie passed Maggie a small plastic earpiece linked to a wire. "Translator," she whispered.

The room grew suddenly still as everybody took their seats, then the gray-haired man sitting behind the United Kingdom plate cleared his throat. A secondary plate resting next to his national identity read "President."

"The eight thousand, eight hundred and thirty-seventh meeting of the United Nations Security Council is called to order." He smacked a small gavel against his desk, sending a thunderclap through the large room. Then he consulted his notes.

"The provisional agenda for this meeting is the situation in the Persian Gulf." He paused and glanced around the room, waiting for objections. Nobody spoke, and he tapped the gavel again. "So adopted. This emergency meeting of the United Nations Security Council was called at the request of President Margaret Trousdale of the United States. As a courtesy of her emergency request, I would like to give her the floor. Madam President, you have the floor."

All eyes turned to Maggie. She adjusted the microphone, quickly consulting her notes about how she should address the chamber. "Your Excellency, Mr. President. Excellencies, Ladies and Gentlemen. I appreciate your consideration in rearranging your schedules to meet with me today. As you are aware, the situation in the Persian Gulf is rapidly deteriorating. Following the crash of our aircraft carrying President Brandt, escalations in the Gulf region have spilled out of control. While Turkey has denied us access to the crash site to conduct a full investigation, Iranian armed forces have deployed along the Turkish border near Kuwait and across the Strait of Hormuz from Oman. Our intelligence assets have identified significant portions of Iran's primary military forces postured in a state of aggression against Kuwait and the strait, and our attempts of diplomatic outreach to the Islamic Republic of Iran have been met with hostility or altogether ignored."

Maggie paused to scan her notes again. The remainder of her address was typed in clean font, waiting to be read. But a voice in the back of her mind nagged at her, warning that nobody was paying attention. She scanned the room and noted a mix of bored, alarmed, or impassive faces. Her gaze settled on Ambassador Belov, where he sat behind a bold plate labeled "Russia." His hands were folded in his lap, the vague hint of a smirk toying at his mouth.

She pushed her notes to one side. It was time to go off script.

"There's been a great deal of chaos in American news media over the last few days, as you can imagine. I've been hesitant to make any statements of aggression while our investigations—as hamstrung by Turkish obstinance as they are—proceed. But inside the confines of this chamber, allow me to be blunt. America stands on the brink of war. The crash of our aircraft and the death of President Brandt are tragedies that demand answers, and we will do whatever is necessary to uncover the truth. Iranian aggression in the Gulf region during this unstable period is extremely ill-advised and could easily be interpreted as the preemption of war. I'm here today to ask the United Nations to pass a resolution condemning Iranian military action and demanding that they withdraw all forces from sensitive borders—or face immediate sanctions."

Belov's smirk faded.

Maggie stared right at him. "America doesn't want a war. Nobody wants to see more of our young men and women gunned down, or more of our limited global resources wasted on bullets when so many are starving. But we will do whatever is necessary to protect ourselves. I'm asking this Security Council to take action in helping us to prevent armed conflict . . . before it's too late."

Maggie nodded at the president, and he spoke into the mic.

"I thank the president of the United States for her statement. I will now give the floor to those members of the council who wish to make statements."

The ambassador for the UAE raised a hand almost immediately. He spoke in calm, confident Arabic, and Maggie heard her earpiece click on as the translator went to work.

"The United Arabic Emirates share the grave concerns of our American allies. For many months, we have warned this council of increased tensions with Iran, but our pleas have fallen on deaf ears. President Bakir has asked me to implore this council to stand with us against this imminent threat, before it is too late."

President Bakir.

Maggie remembered the name of the Emirates' so-called hotheaded president. Lately, his prophecies of war didn't seem so hotheaded.

The mic passed around the room, and one member after another expressed support for the resolution. Only China skipped their turn, and Maggie watched the Chinese ambassador exchange a glance with Belov.

The president asked if any other members wished to make a statement. Belov sat back in his seat, gently spinning a pen on his desk mat. He waited until the president drew a breath to speak again, then he leaned toward his mic. "The Russian Federation congratulates President Trousdale on her unexpected and meteoric rise to the White House." He spoke in English, not Russian, with that hint of a smile playing at the corner of his mouth again. "Moscow has asked me to convey our deepest sympathies to the United States for the unexpected, and *unexplained*, loss of your aircraft. President Brandt was a friend of peace and global security, and the strength of his leadership is sorely missed during this unstable time."

Maggie felt the sting of his backhanded insult but didn't show it. She leaned toward the mic and spoke bluntly. "Does that mean you support my resolution, Mr. Ambassador?"

"Ma'am, no . . ." Gorman whispered.

Maggie ignored her and watched Belov's smirk turn closer to a sneer.

"No. It does not. The proudest traditions of this Security Council promise every nation the right of self-defense, including the Islamic Republic of Iran. Moscow is deeply concerned by the eagerness of Washington to assign blame for this tragedy, and it is sympathetic to Tehran's desire to proactively protect themselves. This council speaks with great trepidation of Iranian soldiers gathered *within* Iran's own borders, while ignoring the mass of American forces congregating in Baghdad and the Gulf. As you say in Louisiana, Madam President, we have a chicken-and-egg situation. Moscow has instructed me to invoke Russia's right of veto as a permanent member of this council against any resolution unfairly targeting Iran's right of self-defense. Such is my duty."

Belov's faint sneer faded into mock concern. "May I propose, Excellencies, that in place of the discriminating measure being discussed, this council deliberate on a joint investigatory delegation to assist America with uncovering the truth of this crash? After all"—his gaze shifted back to Maggie—"with a global superpower standing on the brink of war, accountability should be paramount."

Maggie's jaw locked, and she reached for the mic.

Gorman placed a hand on her arm and leaned close. "Ma'am, please. This isn't the place."

Maggie looked to Carrie, and she shook her head softly.

"President Trousdale?" the president said.

Maggie returned to the mic. "I ask this council's forgiveness for my early departure. Ambassador Carrie will take my place for the duration of this meeting. Pressing national security concerns demand my attention." She stood and turned for the door without another word, Gorman hurrying to follow her. Conversation resumed behind her, but Maggie wasn't paying attention. Her blood boiled.

This was a waste of time.

She plowed through the door and found O'Dell waiting in a row of chairs, along with Jenkins and the security detail. They all moved quickly to their feet, taken off guard but falling in around her like a well-oiled machine.

"Ma'am, please. I *need* to speak to you," Gorman said.

"Speak," Maggie snapped, marching toward the door.

Gorman struggled to keep up. "Leaving this way sends all the wrong signals. Russia is playing games like they always do, but we can't beat them by abandoning ship."

"That's exactly how we're going to beat them," Maggie said. "We're not getting pushed around here. Instruct Ambassador Carrie to veto any measure for a joint investigation of the crash site. We don't need our hand held."

"Ma'am." Gorman put her hand on the door, temporarily blocking Maggie's path. "I'm telling you, as your secretary of state, this is a mistake. I understand your desire to confront Iran, but sometimes to control Russia, you have to play ball with Russia. A joint investigation of the crash site—"

". . . would give Moscow access to classified details of that aircraft. Or do you really think they care about *accountability*?"

Realization dawned behind Gorman's gray eyes, and her hand slipped from the door handle.

Maggie pushed ahead. "Instruct Ambassador Carrie . . . America will veto *every* resolution until Iran is confronted. No exceptions."

The Beast waited at the curb, surrounded by an army of Secret Service agents. The driver looked into his rearview mirror, a question on his face as Maggie slid inside.

"Back to the chopper," she said. "Get me to the White House."

As soon as the limo was pointed back toward the heliport, Maggie used the secure phone nestled in her armrest to dial Coffman's cell.

He answered on the second ring. "Ma'am?"

"I'm headed back."

"Uh . . . okay. Did they not pass the resolution?"

"Russia vetoed it. They're standing behind Iran, and I'm done screwing around. It's time to make a statement."

"Okay . . ." He sounded disoriented and maybe a little rattled. "What do you need, ma'am?"

"I need you to get the Speaker of the House and the Senate majority leader on the phone. I'm ready to take military action."

46

Reed stepped off the dusty Air Force C-5 Galaxy, a battered laptop under one arm. A military ambulance waited near the back of the giant aircraft, its lights flashing slowly as Turk was carried out on a stretcher. Navy Corpsmen assigned to a Marine battalion in Baghdad had stabilized Turk, sealing his wounds and splinting his ankle, but he still needed fluids and would remain under intensive medical care for the next few days.

After the chopper arrived in northern Iraq, Reed and Turk quickly found themselves in Baghdad, where a full-scale military buildup was underway. Rows of C-5 Galaxies sat on the hot asphalt, offloading thousands of Marines alongside dozens of Humvees and Bradley Assault Vehicles. It was a show of force Reed hadn't seen since the Iraqi civil war, and it brought to mind all kinds of bad memories.

It didn't take much convincing for Reed to catch a ride back to Andrews on one of the empty C-5s. The plane took off at noon, local time, meaning that after fourteen hours of flight time and nine time zones crossed, they landed at just after five p.m., Washington time.

Reed felt like he'd been run through a car wash fifty times. He needed a shower, a case of beer, and a whole pack of cigarettes, followed by a long night snuggled into bed next to Banks. But all of that would have to wait. America was about to go to war with all the wrong intelligence.

Reed bummed a cigarette off an Air Force private, then used his cell to dial Wolfgang.

Wolfgang answered immediately. "You back?"

"Just landed. What've you got?"

Wolfgang spoke in a steady stream, barely stopping to breathe. Reed stood in the shade of a utility shed, five hundred yards from the tarmac, and sucked on the cigarette, staring at the C-5 but not really watching it. When Wolfgang finally stopped, the smoke was almost gone.

"Can you prove it?" Reed asked.

"I can prove the financials. Everything else is just circumstantial. These people aren't idiots, Reed. They don't leave tracks."

"No, but if they squealed loud enough, we wouldn't need tracks."

"What are you thinking?"

Reed watched as fuel trucks surrounded the C-5, flooding its fifty-thousand-gallon tanks with fresh jet fuel. Across the tarmac were columns of Marine infantry—maybe three hundred of them, mostly kids not old enough to drink—waiting patiently to board, already outfitted in desert-tan uniforms.

"I'm thinking I've got a war to stop," Reed said. "Email me those financials. Should be enough."

"Why do I get the feeling you're about to go Rambo?"

Reed flicked the cigarette butt away. "Probably because I'm about to go Rambo." He hung up, then dialed O'Dell. Maggie's bodyguard didn't answer the first time, bumping him to voicemail. Reed called again. On the third attempt, O'Dell finally answered.

"Who is this?" O'Dell barked.

"I need your help," Reed said.

"Montgomery? Screw off. I'm busy."

"Don't hang up," Reed snapped. "This is about your boss."

Reed heard a rustling sound, then a door closed.

O'Dell spoke in a low whisper. "What about her?"

"She's about to make a mistake she can't recover from. More importantly, she's about to get a whole lot of good Marines killed."

"What are you talking about?"

"I'm talking about *Air Force One*. I'm talking about World War Three. You wanna stop it?"

Teeth ground. "Listen, jackass. If you know something, you should call Homeland Security. We're busy here."

"Homeland can't save your boss. Only you can do that." Reed snapped his fingers at the private, and the little guy scurried to pass him another cigarette.

"All right, asshole. I'm listening."

It took only a minute for Reed to convey everything O'Dell needed to know. The president's bodyguard listened without question, but Reed wasn't sure if he was sold. When he got to the part about what he needed, he knew he was walking on thin ice.

"That's all?" O'Dell asked at last.

"That's all. I'll do the rest."

"Why those two?"

"Because one of them is lying. Maybe both of them. I plan to find out."

The phone went quiet for a while, and Reed got the feeling O'Dell was still riding the fence. He decided to push his luck. "Do you know what I'm looking at, O'Dell? I'm looking at three hundred Marines about to board a plane to fly halfway around the world and shoot at people they don't even know. Nine out of ten of them won't be alive next week if you don't listen to me, and you can take that to the bank. Once the genie is out of the bottle, you can't put it back. It's all up to you, O'Dell. If you love that swamp hole you call a home, you'll protect it."

"Okay," O'Dell said at last. "I'll do it. But if you're wrong, this is gonna get messy."

"If I'm wrong, this is gonna be war. The kind of war nobody survives."

47

The White House

The two politicians sitting across from Maggie were the picture of everything wrong with Washington. The first was a tall, spindly man with white hair and a crystal smile so fake it made her cringe. Senate Majority Leader Harvey Whitaker of Maryland.

The second was a short, overweight man without a hair on his head. Triple chins jiggled over his collar, and sweat beaded up on his scalp, regardless of the temperature. Speaker of the House Richard Holland of Arkansas.

The men represented opposite parties, but as far as Maggie was concerned, they were both slimeballs. She could smell the political corruption and entitlement wafting off of them like bad aftershave. It flooded the Oval Office and left her feeling defiled, as though she needed a long shower in bleach.

"I appreciate you both for making time to see me on such short notice." Maggie sat across from them, shoulders back, the picture of authority in the room. No matter what happened next, it was critical for her to control this meeting. If either one of these snakes interpreted what she said next as a requested favor, they'd expect to cash in later.

"Of course, Madam President," Whitaker said. "I know the Speaker and I share your concerns about the security of our country. I think I can speak for us both when I say we're prepared to do whatever is necessary to keep our people safe."

Holland shot Whitaker a sideways look but didn't object. He only smiled. A wide, fatty expression mired by a trickle of sweat running down one cheek.

Maggie tried not to puke. "I'm glad to hear it, gentlemen, because your country needs you to shelve partisan differences and work together."

Another snakelike glance from Holland. He still didn't say anything, and Maggie thought she knew why. Whitaker and Brandt had shared a party. Maggie was still an Independent, which made her something of an unknown quantity. Holland probably wanted Whitaker to do the probing and find out whether Maggie would pick a side. Predictable, but no less detestable.

Maggie turned to Holland. "Speaker, tonight I'll be addressing the nation. During that address, I plan to call on Congress to pass legislation empowering me to deploy troops throughout the Persian Gulf. Can I count on you to make that happen?"

There you go. Choke on that.

Holland swabbed his head, shifting uncomfortably. His suit jacket was unbuttoned, but it still looked ready to burst as it bulged around his considerable gut. "You're asking for a declaration of war, Madam President?"

His Arkansas accent was about fifty percent contrived. Maggie knew Holland grew up predominantly in Pennsylvania, only moving to Arkansas a few years prior to running for Congress.

"No," Maggie said. "I'm asking for legislation authorizing me to deploy a defense force to protect our allies in the region. Something similar to the Authorization for Use of Military Force Act signed into law after 9/11."

Maggie let Holland marinate in the awkwardness and uncomfortable silence. She expected this reaction and was ready for it.

"Ma'am . . ." Holland hesitated. "I'm not sure I understand what you're asking."

"*I'm* not asking, Mr. Speaker. The country is asking. If Iran is allowed to run roughshod over the region much longer, our economy will spiral. I doubt you fill your own tank, but fuel prices are skyrocketing. If Iran invades Kuwait and we're forced to counter-invade, thousands of American lives will be lost. We need boots on the ground long before then."

"That seems like something you could do with an executive order," Whitaker said. Maggie saw the gleam of discernment in his eyes and knew he was the smarter of the two—probably by far. A true master of the political game.

"Possibly," Maggie said. "It's a gray area, frankly, and the Trousdale administration would like to avoid those wherever possible. For the sake of the nation, this needs to come from Congress. It needs to come from *you*."

Whitaker made a show of sipping his coffee. Holland twiddled his thumbs.

Are you freaking kidding me?

Maggie hadn't expected enthusiasm, but blatant stonewalling hadn't entered her mind either. She knew this was probably the point in the conversation where she was expected to offer a trade—some kind of pork, probably, to add to the bill—but that wasn't happening. She wouldn't begin her administration by groveling to the establishment.

"I really hope we can get these fuel costs under control soon," Maggie said, lifting her own coffee cup. "Frankly, if prices rise much farther, I may be forced to open the strategic reserves."

Neither man commented. They couldn't see the invisible fist flying at them like a freight train.

"Obviously, our priorities will be the military. We may have to relocate existing fuel supplies and shipments to cover those needs. Some states may see increased prices . . . but we're all in this together, right? I'm sure those states will understand." She held the coffee cup midair, locking eyes with each of them. She saw the shift in their countenance. Holland flushed red, while Whitaker turned cold.

"Realignment of the fuel supply—" Whitaker said.

"Falls under the jurisdiction of an executive order," Maggie finished. "And that's *not* a gray area." She set the cup down.

Whitaker leaned back and offered a wry smile—a live-to-fight-another-day smile. "Madam President, of course you have my support. If Speaker

Holland will get a bill through the House, I'll get it through the Senate."
Whitaker turned to Holland.

The rotund speaker pursed his lips, but there was no place for him to
turn. It would be political suicide to refuse now. "I'll assemble a bipartisan
coalition to draft the bill, ma'am. We'll use this as an opportunity to reach
across party lines."

Maggie rose and offered her hand, suppressing a cringe as Holland
shook it.

The three of them stepped to the door, but at the last moment,
Whitaker stopped. "I'll catch you on the Hill, Rich," he said.

Holland flushed again, but there was no eloquent way for him to
remain in the room.

Whitaker shut the door behind him. "Brave of you, Madam President.
Blackmailing Congress on your first bill."

"Brave of you to come in here with your hand out while our country is
in jeopardy."

Whitaker pocketed his hands. The condescension radiating off him
made Maggie nauseous.

"How about a nickel's worth of free advice?" Whitaker said.

"I'll pass, thank you."

Whitaker grunted. "Well, here it comes anyway. I'm sure you think
you're hot stuff, jumping from law school to governor to the White House at
the drop of a hat. But you've got a lot to learn about Washington, Madam
President. I'll help you this time, because believe it or not, I care about my
country. But do yourself a favor and pick a team. When you ride the fence,
you just get pissed on by both sides."

Maggie held her chin up, taking the tirade in silence. Everything in her
wanted to jack-slap him like a Mississippi redneck in a Louisiana bar, but
she just waited until his condescending smirk returned, then gestured to
the door. "I'm sure you understand, Majority Leader. I've got a busy day
ahead."

He offered a shallow bow. "Of course, ma'am. I look forward to our next
conversation."

Whitaker reached for the knob as Maggie turned for her desk. Halfway
there, she stopped, calling over her shoulder. "Majority Leader?"

Whitaker looked back.

"You were right about one thing. I am hot stuff. Be careful I don't burn you."

Whitaker left the door open and vanished into the corridor outside, leaving the reek of corruption wafting in his wake.

48

"On in five, Madam President."

The press secretary stuck his head into the makeup room, making eye contact with Maggie in the mirror. She puckered her lips to tighten her cheeks as a makeup artist applied foundation.

"You have a lovely complexion," the artist said. "With a little care, we could really capitalize on that skin tone."

"Are you telling me I don't take care of myself?"

The artist turned red and pulled her hand back. "No, ma'am! I didn't—"

"Relax," Maggie laughed. "You'd be right. I never was much of a makeup girl."

She pivoted the chair to look at herself in the mirror. The artist was good, no doubt about it. She used a subtle touch to highlight Maggie's cheekbones and minimize the circles under her eyes without making her look plastic. If she wasn't a simple swamp girl, Maggie might be impressed enough to want to learn how.

"That'll do," Maggie said, pulling the napkin from her neckline. The artist hurried off, leaving Maggie to herself for the first time in hours. She rested her hands against the armrests of the chair and inhaled, long and slow.

A president at war.

Dammit, she wasn't cut out for this. Her mind slid back to that fateful meeting with Brandt at Camp David, and she shamelessly cursed her predecessor.

"I chose you for this moment."

Brandt set her up. He shoved her into this corner like a square peg in a round hole.

And he was wrong. I'm not the right person for this.

"Ma'am? We're ready for you."

It was the press secretary again. Maggie couldn't remember his name, but right then, it didn't matter. It was time to face the nation. She rose from the chair and stood tall, the simple black dress she wore hanging elegantly just above her knees. She looked good in it, and that gave her some confidence.

The press secretary rattled on about network coverage and other things she didn't care about as he led her down the hallway of the West Wing toward the briefing room. O'Dell fell in beside her along the way, and Maggie walked slowly, measuring her steps and reviewing in her mind what she would say.

A word she never dreamed of saying. A word she never dreamed of hearing.

War.

The press secretary pushed the door open, and Maggie stopped cold. Coffman stood behind the podium, framed on either side by American flags. That she expected, but joining him was Lance Sanger, CEO of Flashpoint Defense.

"What's he doing here?" Maggie directed the question at O'Dell.

"Coffman called for him, ma'am. Something about a show of unity."

O'Dell looked away as he spoke, his gaze flicking toward the floor.

He's lying, Maggie thought. But she didn't have time to discern why. She'd get to the bottom of this afterward.

"On in ten, Madam President," somebody said.

Maggie squared her shoulders and stepped up to the podium, resting both hands on the edge and looking straight into the camera. A teleprompter stood next to it, but she wouldn't use it. Americans didn't

need another canned speech right now. They needed the truth, straight
from their president.

"Five . . . four . . . three . . ."

Breathe. Control the moment.

Maggie held her head up, and the press secretary flicked two fingers.

Live.

The door to her left exploded open, and O'Dell barged in. Before she
could react, his big arms wrapped around her shoulders and pulled her
back toward the hallway. Other agents swarmed in around her, and the next
thing Maggie knew, she was barreling toward the residence, Sanger and
Coffman stumbling alongside her.

"What's happening?" Maggie demanded.

O'Dell pushed her ahead, looking over his shoulder as Secret Service
agents shouted at the press and locked down the West Wing. "Bomb threat,
ma'am," O'Dell said. "We're taking you to the PEOC."

Back to the bunker.

Maggie crashed into the elevator with the others. She saw Agent
Jenkins move to join them, but O'Dell held up a hand.

"I've got her! Double-check the perimeter."

Jenkins looked confused, but before he could answer, the doors rolled
shut, and they rocketed downward.

"What are you doing?" Sanger snarled, dusting off his thousand-dollar
suit coat as if it were coated in anthrax.

"Protocol, sir," O'Dell said. "We'll secure you with the president until
the threat is neutralized."

Sanger glared, but he said nothing more as the doors rolled open. Two
Secret Service agents greeted them at the tunnel leading to the presidential
bunker, and both ran the fifty yards to the steel door. A third agent waited
there, a submachine gun slung across his chest. O'Dell stood at the door
and motioned Maggie inside, followed closely by Sanger, Yellin, and
Coffman.

"There's another agent inside," the man with the submachine gun said.
"We're closing the door!"

Maggie barely cleared the threshold before the massive vault door
began to close. O'Dell stood close to her elbow, looking over his shoulder as

the airlock hissed and sealed. The bolts slid into place with a dull thud, and everything was suddenly very quiet.

Maggie tore her arm free and glared at O'Dell. "What the *hell* is happening?"

O'Dell didn't answer. He avoided her gaze, then turned toward the hallway without comment.

"O'Dell! What's happening?"

"This way, ma'am," O'Dell said, still walking.

Maggie shot Coffman a glance. The chief of staff looked rattled and disoriented, offering no guidance. Maggie marched after O'Dell.

Her bodyguard stopped at the entrance of the main conference room, putting his hand on the door and hesitating again, then he pushed the door open, exposing a dark room on the other side.

"O'Dell?" Maggie said, her voice dropping.

"In here, ma'am. It's okay."

Maggie took one step inside, squinting into the darkness. The room was perfectly still, but near the far end of the table, a soft orange glow shone like a beacon, and she smelled cigarette smoke in the air.

"Who's there?" Coffman snapped, shoving past O'Dell with Sanger in tow.

Coffman found the light switch, and the room flooded with intense fluorescent light. The room was almost empty, with nothing save a long conference table surrounded by chairs filling the center. The cigarette smoke Maggie smelled wafted toward her from the far end of the table, just beyond a battered laptop and two muddy boots, propped up on the table like it was a fence rail. And behind those boots, leaning back in his chair with a cigarette clamped between two fingers, sat Reed Montgomery.

49

Reed lifted the smoke to his lips and took a long tug, staring at Maggie without comment. Gray smoke plumed around his head as the four people standing just inside the door stared at him like he was a ghost. "Hello, Maggie," Reed said. "Or I guess it's Madam President, now."

Maggie shot a look at O'Dell. The bodyguard dropped his gaze a little, probably feeling guilty for setting his boss up.

Reed understood. He just didn't care. "You should all have a seat," Reed said. "We aren't going anywhere."

"What's going on, O'Dell?" Maggie sounded more angry than panicked, now.

"Just have a seat, ma'am." O'Dell's gaze switched to Coffman and Sanger, and the iron returned to his posture. "You, too. Both of you."

Sanger indulged in a long, weary sigh, as if he were a kindergarten teacher surrounded by brain-dead children. He adjusted his suit as he settled into a chair, then gave Reed a long-suffering smile. "So, who are *you*?"

Reed sucked on the smoke.

Coffman seemed to wake from a daze and shoved a chair out of the way. "Who *is* this?" he demanded, pointing at Reed and shouting at O'Dell.

"I'm the monster in the closet," Reed said, rolling the smoke between his fingers. "The ghost of inconvenient truth. The man who makes problems go away. Right, Madam President?"

Maggie settled into a chair with graceful ease. "Sit down, Jason."

Coffman spluttered. "Wha . . . what's going on here?"

"Sit down, little guy." Reed kicked a chair out from under the table and stabbed at it with the cigarette.

Coffman reluctantly sat down.

Reed dragged on the cigarette, then exhaled through his teeth.

"I don't believe you're allowed to smoke in here," Sanger said, his voice the cultured honey of an Ivy League education and a nine-figure bank account.

Reed laughed. "You know, I believe you're right. You have to excuse me. Rough day at the office, you know?" Reed flicked the smoke, and it spun across the polished mahogany of the conference table, stopping only inches from Sanger's lap.

He didn't so much as flinch.

"Lance Sanger, right?" Reed said. "CEO of Flashpoint Defense."

"That's right."

"I knew some of your people, once," Reed said. "Back in Baghdad. They raped one of my Marines and choked her to death."

"I'm sorry," Sanger said.

"I doubt it. I doubt that report ever crossed your desk. But that's okay. I dealt with it myself. You know, I was in Baghdad this morning, also. Or this afternoon. I really can't keep up with the time zones. Know what I was doing there?"

No answer.

"I was on my way home . . . from Turkey."

"Wait." Coffman leaned across the table. "You're the black ops guy?" His face ran with sweat, his eyes darting anxiously from Reed to Maggie and then to Sanger.

"No," Reed said. "I'm the guy sent to find *this*." He slapped a key on the laptop, and speakers crackled. The room filled with the sharp screech of alarms, punctuated by calm voices calling flight commands, followed by the most famous word in aviation history . . .

"Mayday! Mayday! *Air Force One*, multiple engine failure, experiencing uncontrolled descent. Repeat, we have lost all lift."

The tape ground on, and Reed lit another cigarette, blowing smoke at the ceiling as the final excruciating moments of the president's plane played for the room to hear.

And then nothing. Dead, brutal silence.

Reed shut the computer and looked at Maggie.

"You said you couldn't find it," Maggie snapped.

"I lied," Reed said.

"Why?"

"Lots of reasons. I'll get to that. First, I wanna talk about this." He left the cigarette between his lips and dug into a jacket pocket.

O'Dell flinched as Reed's fingers returned with a small piece of brass about two inches long. He flipped it through the air, straight at Sanger.

The CEO caught it deftly and rolled it over in his hand. "A shell casing?" he said with protracted irritation.

"A seven six two by fifty-one shell casing, to be precise. Heard of it?"

Sanger tossed the casing into a nearby trashcan. "Of course I've heard of it, jackass. I sell a few million of them a year. What's your point?"

"We had to hoof it out of Turkey," Reed said. "My battle buddy broke his ankle, so we were looking for a truck. Finally found one, but then some jerk tried to snipe us. Took a minute to deal with him, but guess what I found when I did?"

Sanger rolled his eyes. "Seven six two shell casings?"

"Damn, you're good. And isn't that strange?"

"No, it's not strange at all. You were waltzing through a war zone and stealing cars. Maybe you didn't know this, but there's a freaking *army* of Iranians massing on that border."

"Oh, I'm well aware. Had a little brush with them, also. But the thing is, Sanger . . ." Reed dropped his feet off the table. "They don't shoot seven six two. That's a NATO caliber. An American caliber. Iranians shoot Russian crap."

Sanger lifted a hand toward the ceiling. "So? Maybe they captured one."

"Maybe. Except . . . I almost forgot . . . that jerk I killed? He was white."

Coffman bolted to his feet in a sudden bluster. "We don't have time for this!"

Reed looked to Maggie, challenging her to challenge him.

Maggie motioned to Coffman's chair. "Sit down, Jason."

Coffman spluttered but sat.

Reed spoke to Sanger. "Rough few years for you, huh?"

"I don't know what you're talking about," Sanger said.

"Oh, sure you do. Sliding dividends . . . stalling growth. Your personal portfolio has taken quite the hit since the de-escalation of hostilities in the Middle East. After all, Flashpoint makes its money on conflict. There's not a lot of profit in peace."

Sanger laughed. "Is that what you think?"

"Nope, that's what I know. A buddy of mine pulled your entire financial profile. Not just the legal stuff, either. Those bank accounts in the Caymans? All those off-shore investments? Man, Sanger . . . That stuff runs dry when the bullets stop flying."

A hint of color tinged Sanger's cheeks, and his lips twisted into a tight line.

"This buddy of mine," Reed continued. "Man, he's good. Of course, he saw the headlines about Flashpoint personnel deployed into Kuwait. Record-setting response time, too. Kinda made him curious, so he did some digging. Know what he found?"

Sanger didn't answer.

Reed grinned. "He found deployment orders dated from three weeks ago, ordering a surplus of troops to assume private security duty in Saudi Arabia. Only hours from Kuwait."

"How about that," Sanger said, his voice low.

"Right place, right time, I guess," Reed said. "But then, with profits sliding, it's hard not to imagine how eager you were to deploy into Kuwait. Thirty-five hundred contractors, plus support staff and vehicles . . . That's one heck of a payday."

Sanger's jaw twitched. "I serve the *country*, sir. My only ambition is to keep us safe. To keep people like *you* safe!"

"I keep myself safe, usually from men like you. But even as bad as this stinks, coincidence isn't enough to find you guilty. You may be a warmonger, but unfortunately, that isn't illegal."

Sanger lifted his chin. "So, screw off—"

"But that's when my buddy dug a little deeper," Reed continued. "He started looking at things like the Brandt campaign—things like shell companies and campaign contributions. That's where he found all those fragmented donations of yours. Twenty million dollars poured into Brandt's election war chest—*well* over the legal limit."

Reed pointed the cigarette at Sanger. "Seems you had quite the vested interest in seeing Brandt elected. I guess you wanted somebody in Washington who could stir up a little international instability for you, huh? Pitch you a few juicy defense contracts. And when that didn't work out, you killed him for it, you blackhearted pig. Knocked his ass right out of the sky. I mean, I have to hand it to you. It's a hell of a win. You got rid of Brandt and triggered a war, all in one move."

"This is absurd!" Sanger snapped, slamming one hand on the table.

Coffman jumped, but Maggie didn't move. She sat with her arms crossed, her gaze fixed on Sanger.

"William Brandt was my *friend*," Sanger spluttered, spraying saliva across the table. "We knew each other for *years*. Yes, I donated to his campaign. Maybe a little too much. Sue me!"

"I'm not that kind of prosecutor," Reed said.

"Oh yeah? What kind are you?"

"This kind." Reed flicked the cigarette away and dropped his hand beneath the table, resurfacing in a flash with a Glock 19 clamped between his fingers, the muzzle pointed dead at Sanger.

O'Dell freaked. He shoved Maggie back and pressed himself in front of her, his hand dropping beneath his coat and producing an identical pistol in the flash of a second. "Drop the gun!" O'Dell screamed.

Reed ignored him, his attention fixed on Sanger. "Nice work bringing that plane down right on the border. With Iranian tensions so high, of course everybody would think they did it. That's why you sent your man to kill me in Turkey, right? Can't risk anybody listening to that flight recorder and hearing reports of 'engine failure.'"

Sanger pointed a trembling finger at Reed. "You're out of your mind. I never touched that plane. It's the most secure aircraft in the world!"

"Sure it is. But somebody has to maintain those engines, and federal contracts are public record. Guess who managed the construction of the brand-new *Air Force One*s? Barrier Aerospace . . . a sister company of Flashpoint Defense."

Sanger's face washed white.

"Like I said, Sanger. That buddy of mine? He's good."

Reed laid his finger on the trigger. "It's a tidy little scheme. I'll bet you probably controlled Vice President Gardener, also. So, you were set for a successor, but then Brandt pulled a fast one on you, didn't he? He set Gardener up. Had him ousted for some petty scandal and rushed Trousdale through the nomination process before you could stop it. Because if there's one thing Maggie Trousdale is known for, it's fighting bottom-feeding scum like *you*."

Sanger didn't respond.

Reed laughed. "Man, I've got to tell you . . . When they asked me to take this job, I really wanted to say no. If I knew it would end with an asshole like you in my sights, I might've done it for free." He cocked his head. "But there's still something missing, you know? I mean, how did you know about Brandt's flight plan? How did you know where to tell your man to find me in Turkey? Somebody had to tip you off, right? It's simple math. Only two people outside of Trousdale knew the details of my mission. The chairman of the Joint Chiefs"—Reed pivoted the pistol to point at Coffman—"and *him*."

The chief of staff blanched, sweat streaming down his face like a waterfall. He threw his hands up and kicked his chair back from the table. "I didn't do anything, I swear!"

"Well, it wasn't Yellin," Reed said. "The man is a four-star general. A war hero!"

"We don't know that." Coffman licked his lips. "He might be a warmonger, too!"

Reed laughed. "Nah. Officers like Yellin play politics, sure. But it's a second language for them. When they lie, they do it to protect their people. Real politicians—people like *you*—they lie for themselves."

"I didn't do it!" Coffman shouted.

Reed pulled the trigger. The Glock cracked like a bullwhip, and blood sprayed from Coffman's thigh. He stumbled back, and O'Dell screamed for Maggie to get down, brandishing his pistol.

Reed ignored O'Dell as Coffman slouched against the wall. "You've had a great year, haven't you? That buddy of mine found two million in cash and one amazing beach house . . . all in Grand Cayman."

Coffman held up both hands, wheezing against the wall. "You're . . . going to prison!"

"Been there, buddy. They kicked me out."

He pulled the trigger again. Coffman screamed and crumbled to the floor, clutching his right shoulder. Maggie shouted, and Sanger scrambled back.

Reed kicked Coffman's chair aside and jabbed the pistol at the writhing chief of staff. "*Talk!*"

Coffman gasped, tears slipping down his face. His hands shook as he looked at Sanger, then he just broke. "I worked for *years*! I gave *everything* for Will, and he couldn't even keep his promises. I was supposed to be on his cabinet. I was supposed to have a career!"

"Coffman!" Sanger shouted. "Shut up!"

Coffman's face turned hard. "Yes, it's true! It's all true. I hope Brandt's burning in Hell!"

Sanger bolted to his feet, his hand flashing beneath his jacket and appearing a split second later with a knife. He hurled himself sideways toward Coffman, but long before his first step, O'Dell's pistol erupted in a storm of shots, blowing Sanger back against the wall and ventilating his chest with a patchwork of red dots.

Coffman launched himself off the wall toward Reed, his face a distorted mess of tears and smeared blood.

Reed took a calm step back and fired from the hip. The Glock spat fire, and Coffman collapsed across the conference table, a hole drilled right between his eyes.

50

Maggie lay huddled against the wall, her hands trembling despite herself. Adrenaline surged through her veins as she surveyed the two bodies slouched over the floor, draining crimson into a growing pool.

O'Dell stepped in front of her and trained his pistol on Reed. "Drop the weapon!"

Maggie scrambled to her feet and pressed herself against the wall as a phone on the conference table began to ring. Reed surveyed the bodies, ignoring O'Dell, then casually disassembled his Glock and dropped it on the floor.

"Hands up!" O'Dell demanded.

Reed pocketed his hands and nodded at the phone. "Somebody should answer that."

Maggie hesitated, her hands still shaking. She looked from the bodies to the door. "They're calling about the shots."

"They never heard the shots," Reed said. "This place is nuclear-blast proof. No way they heard a couple handguns. They're calling because we locked them out."

Maggie's shock at the sudden eruption of violence submitted to anger. She lifted the phone. "Yes?"

"Ma'am! Are you okay?" It was Jenkins.

"Everything's fine. We'll be right out."

She hung up before Jenkins could object, then looked to Reed. "What the *hell*?"

O'Dell pressed forward, brandishing the gun. "On your knees!"

Reed kicked at Coffman's limp form, but the chief of staff didn't move.

"What do you expect me to do with this?" Maggie screamed.

Reed shrugged. "This city runs on lies. I'm sure you'll think of something."

Maggie's hands began to shake again. She wanted to punch something, but the rapid sequence of events she'd just been subjected to left her frozen to the floor. "You expect me to believe this?"

"Wolfgang is emailing you evidence," Reed said.

"Wolfgang? How is *he* involved?"

"He's my research buddy. A damn good one too, as it turns out. All those fancy degrees paid off."

Maggie ran her hand through her hair.

Think. Take control.

The phone rang again. She ignored it as O'Dell stepped around the table, still leading with the gun.

"How did you get that in here?" O'Dell said, kicking at the disassembled pistol strewn across the floor.

"I borrowed it from the guy in the closet," Reed said, tilting his head toward the hallway.

"What guy?"

"The other Secret Service agent they put in here. Don't you remember?"

Maggie had forgotten about there being another agent in the bunker.

Freaking Montgomery.

The phone shrilled again, and she yanked it up. "*What?*"

"Ma'am, it's Yellin. We need you in the Situation Room, ASAP. We've spotted Russian attack subs closing on the Persian Gulf."

Maggie hung up and jerked her head at O'Dell. "Come on. We've got another fire to put out."

"What about him?" O'Dell demanded, jerking his head toward Reed.

"Bring him with us. He's not leaving my sight 'til this mess is cleaned up."

O'Dell glowered at Reed, then motioned to the table. "Lean over."

"Seriously?"

"Seriously."

Maggie hung by the door as Reed stretched over the table and O'Dell completed a full pat down, producing nothing but a pack of cigarettes and a lighter. O'Dell kept them both, then holstered his pistol and shoved Reed toward the door. "Let's go."

Reed navigated around the blood but stopped over Sanger's body. The former Flashpoint CEO lay slumped against the wall, half a dozen well-placed bullet holes obliterating his chest. The knife lay on the ground next to him, coated in his own blood.

Reed toed the weapon, rolling it over in the fluorescent light. "Ceramic," Reed said. "Won't set off metal detectors. You guys should really conduct full-body checks."

O'Dell pushed Reed toward the door. Maggie flipped the light out behind them, casting one more glance at the lifeless bodies.

The enemy is within.

The heavy vault door swung open, and a storm of agents surrounded her, led by Jenkins. "Ma'am! Are you all right?"

"I'm fine. Did you clear the bomb threat?"

"There wasn't a threat, ma'am," Jenkins said. "We're not sure what happened."

Maggie shot Reed a sideways glare. She had a pretty good idea exactly what happened. Reed only shrugged.

They took the elevator back to the ground level, then marched down the corridor to the West Wing. The press had been sequestered to the briefing room by the Secret Service, and there was nobody to block her path to the Situation Room, where a new storm awaited her.

The full panel of Joint Chiefs was present, along with Gorman, National Security Advisor Nick West, CIA Director Victor O'Brien, and enough aides to choke out the oxygen and make the big room feel like a closet.

Maggie took her seat at the head of the table and signaled for Reed to take an open chair. "Everybody shut up!" She turned to Yellin. "Highlights, please."

Yellin retrieved his laser pointer and directed it at the screen. A map of the Middle East was spread across it, pockmarked with flags and symbols. "The entire Russian navy has put to sea. We're tracking three Russian Kilo-class fast-attack subs closing in on the Persian Gulf, with a support fleet of frigates steaming northwest out of the Indian Ocean. Most of these are guided missile boats, similar to what Moscow has deployed into the Mediterranean."

Yellin kept his voice measured, but he couldn't disguise the urgency in his tone. He traced the path of the attack subs and missile frigates with his laser pointer, then moved it north. "We're also seeing increased Russian air activity over the Caspian Sea. They're running air-to-ground attack exercises using an assortment of fighters and bomber aircraft."

Again, the laser pointer pivoted north, into the heartland of Russia. The map adjusted to follow it. "In mainland Russia, we're monitoring troops massing outside of Moscow, along with additional naval deployments into the Arctic." Yellin lowered the pointer and looked to Maggie. "The entire Russian military is mobilizing, ma'am. They're ready for war."

"What about Iran?" Maggie said.

"Still massing troops near Hormuz and Kuwait," Yellin said. "Enough to secure the entire region in a matter of hours."

"What's the latest out of Tehran?" Maggie directed the question at CIA Director O'Brien.

"Same story, ma'am," O'Brien said. "All reports indicate Iran is prepping to seize full control of the Gulf."

"This isn't a theory anymore," Yellin said. "I need your immediate authorization to deploy troops directly into Kuwait and move additional naval assets into the Arabian Sea."

"No." Gorman stood from her chair, craning her neck to make eye contact with Maggie. "Ma'am, please. If we escalate this, we lose all chance of a diplomatic resolution. Let me get President Nikitin on the phone. We can still stop this!"

"It's too late for that," Yellin growled. "If you could've stopped this, you should have done it by now."

"I can't de-escalate while you pour on the heat!" Gorman said. "I need *time*."

"Well, you're out of time. The whole world's out of time!"

A phone rang, and National Security Advisor Nick West answered it. His face drained white as he hung up. "That was the Pentagon. Three of Russia's boomers just went deep off the coast of Hawaii."

"Boomers?" Maggie demanded.

"Missile subs!" somebody shouted. "My God. They're headed for the West Coast!"

Chaos erupted like a chain of firecrackers. Everybody started shouting at once, West returning to the phone while Yellin called for Maggie to authorize the deployment, and Gorman continued to plead for a de-escalation.

Maggie sat frozen in the chair, staring at the map. All those little dots represented warships, aircraft, and troop deployments—enough to trigger the greatest war the world had ever seen. The war to end all wars. Armageddon.

And she had to decide . . .

Maggie gripped her chair arms as Yellin called over the chaos again.

Authorize. Deploy troops.

"Ma'am, *please*," Gorman said.

Another phone rang. O'Brien argued with West.

All Maggie felt was the electric nerves of adrenaline surging through her system. There was only one option left. "General Yellin, you have—"

Reed spoke just loud enough to cut her off. "How much is a liter of gas in Moscow?" He slouched in a chair halfway down the table, staring at the screen. Nothing about his body language reflected any of the tension or chaos around him. He looked ready to sip daiquiris next to a beach.

Everyone swiveled to stare at the dusty man with the battle scars.

"What?" someone snapped.

"Gasoline," Reed said. "What's it going for in Moscow?"

"Who are *you*?" West demanded.

"He's with me," Maggie broke in. "Answer his question."

West consulted an iPad and did some tapping while the room remained hushed. "About ninety-eight rubles per liter," West said. "Five bucks per gallon, give or take."

"And how much was it this time last week?" West shot Maggie an irritated look. She snapped her fingers, and he consulted the iPad again. "About half that," he said.

"Quite the price hike," Reed muttered.

Yellin growled a curse. "Who *is* this guy?"

"He's The Prosecutor," Maggie snapped.

Realization dawned over Yellin's face, but he still ignored Reed. "What does it matter what they're paying for gas?" he said. "They'll be paying a lot more if we go to war."

"Exactly." Reed pivoted his chair to face Maggie. "A *lot* more."

"What's your point?" she said.

"My point is, they're yanking your chain. You should yank back."

"Son, there's enough naval firepower in the Arabian Sea to wipe our Fifth Fleet off the map," Yellin said. "Does that look like yanking chains to you?"

"It absolutely does . . . when it's this obvious."

Yellin spluttered, but Maggie held up a hand. "Speak."

Reed gestured to the screen. "None of what they're doing adds up to an imminent attack. When you pick a fight with the biggest guy in the bar, you don't call ahead and tell him you're coming. You sneak up behind him and knock him out with a baseball bat." Reed picked up a laser pointer and highlighted the attack subs in the Arabian Sea. "This is what I'm talking about. These Kilo subs. Do we always know where they are?"

"Not always," Admiral Turley admitted.

"Of course not. Because they're designed to sneak. But now, somehow, you know where three of them are, all bearing down on your fleet. Making a lot of noise, if I had to guess."

Maggie looked to Turley.

He nodded reluctantly. "That's not incorrect, ma'am."

"Right," Reed said. "Because they're not trying to sneak up and hit you. They're trying to rattle you. And what about all these training exercises over the Caspian Sea? Who ties up that many aircraft for *training* when they're about to go to war? You train before war, not during." He moved the laser pointer to Moscow. "And all these troops massing in inland Moscow. Massing for what? A U2 concert? If you're about to deploy troops, you don't pile them in a field. You move them to airports and seaports, right?"

"Those boomers went *deep*," Yellin snapped. "Do you know what that means? It means we'll lose track of them."

"Which clearly has you rattled," Reed said. "Point Moscow."

"If we lose them, we can't prevent a surprise attack."

"Sure you can. They have to ascend to launch depth to fire, right? You have submarine nets and all kinds of tracking systems near the coast. And anyway, if Russia was planning a nuclear war, why would they mass their fleet and their infantry? That just gives you a big fat list of targets. Like Pearl Harbor."

Reed dropped the laser pointer. "You wanna know what I think? I think this whole *Air Force One* fiasco gave Tehran an opportunity to push their weight around, and they're exploiting it. Moscow is following suit to test the waters with the new administration. After all, if Iran can get away with locking up the Gulf, that's good for Russia. They get along with Iran. They'll probably get cheaper oil while driving up prices for us. It's all a game, really, but they can't play it forever. Not at five bucks a gallon. Their economy can't take it."

"What are you saying?" Maggie said.

"I'm saying you should call their bluff. Will Saudi Arabia follow your orders?"

Maggie looked to Gorman, who seemed flustered and disoriented, but she nodded. "I think so. They're scared out of their minds right now."

"Great," Reed said. "So, order them to immediately freeze all oil exports until further notice."

"What the hell?" West shouted. "Do you have any idea what that'll do to our economy?"

"Wreck it, long-term," Reed said. "But it's not a long-term tactic. Just long enough to send prices in Moscow into the stratosphere."

"That won't work," West said. "Our prices will rise just as fast. They'll see right through it."

"Doesn't matter if they see through it. It'll hurt just the same. You can minimize the damage on our end by suspending federal fuel taxes and opening the reserves. Let Moscow know we can play this game all summer."

"You're poking the bear," Yellin growled. "You don't poke him unless you're ready to kill him."

"So, get ready." Reed shrugged. "Deploy some boomers. Send more troops to Baghdad. Whatever. But I'm telling you, I've dealt with a lot of bullies in my day, and there's no bigger bully on the planet than Russia. The only way to deal with them is to show them who's boss."

"By jeopardizing our economy?" West said. "They know we'd never do that."

"They know *you'd* never do that. But they don't know Maggie from Adam. For all they know, she's a lunatic, ready to run the nation off a cliff if they don't back down. Make this a staring contest, and I'll bet good money Moscow blinks first."

"How does that help us with Iran?" Maggie asked.

"Iran is a dog off the leash," Reed said. "Make Russia put them back on the leash. They won't attack without Russian support."

"How do you know that?" Yellin said.

"Because if they were that bold, they would've attacked already. How long have they been massing troops? Why give us so much time to ship Marines to Iraq? I'll bet Moscow has been holding them back."

Maggie looked to Gorman.

The secretary was busy chewing her lip in an uncharacteristic show of nervousness. "I think he may be right, ma'am," Gorman said. "And if there's even a chance, it's worth the shot."

Yellin made a fist on the desk, but he restrained himself from another outburst. Instead, he only faced Maggie and shook his head.

Reed remained slouched into the chair, arms crossed, relaxed. Maggie wondered if he truly felt that calm, deep inside. She wondered if he was thinking about Banks and what he'd do to protect her if he was wrong. She watched the blips on the screen and thought about the end of days. Then she nodded to Gorman. "Get Saudi Arabia on the phone. It's worth a shot."

51

The Oval Office
26 Hours Later

Morning sunlight streamed in from the Rose Garden, cascading over royal-blue carpet and warming Reed's skin. He laid a hand over his face, trying to pretend it wasn't morning and that he didn't need to wake up. The couch he lay across was comfortable. He wondered how many presidents had slept there and if he was the first civilian.

Probably.

The sun brightened slowly, and Reed lifted his head. He didn't want to wake up. Extreme exhaustion had dragged him deep into black sleep for hours on end, eventually replaced by vague dreams. He didn't remember much about them except for one person, wrapped in his arms, looking out over a backyard littered with brightly colored toys. He didn't see a child, but he knew there was a little boy or girl. The child looked like its mother, and knowing that was the best part of the dream.

Reed swung his bare feet onto the floor. The room was empty, and his back ached. Actually, his whole body ached. Long experience had taught him that there was no better way to learn about every random part of your body than to get into a firefight. Bones and muscles you didn't know you had screamed in pain the next morning, but in a strange way, it was a good feeling. It meant he was alive.

Reed rubbed his eyes with the heel of one hand, then yawned and looked at the clock on the wall. Just after six a.m. He wondered if there was coffee nearby. Or better yet, whiskey and a smoke.

He pulled himself up with a grunt and walked to the window, pushing aside the curtain to stare into the sun. The Rose Garden was gorgeous, full of elegant rosebushes, all perfectly manicured. Reed knew he should feel the gravity of where he was standing, but somehow, it just felt like another Sunday morning.

The phone on the presidential desk rang, startling him. He turned toward it, but just then, the door swung open, and Maggie appeared. She wore the same dress she'd worn in the Situation Room, with her hair pulled back in a ponytail. Reed never thought she was a particularly attractive woman, but then again, he tended to feel that way about people he didn't trust.

Maggie scooped the phone up. She listened for a moment, uttered a couple of "uh-huhs," then hung up and dropped into her chair. Her forehead fell against her hands, and she breathed deeply. Reed watched and waited, hands in his pockets.

"Russia blinked," Maggie said. "They're recalling their forces. Tehran has opened communication, also. Your crazy scheme worked."

Reed felt none of the pride or thrill he knew he probably should. The strategy he outlined in the Situation Room made sense to him, but he was fully prepared to be wrong. He was fully prepared to take Banks's security into his own hands.

Maggie lifted the phone again and hit a button. "Can we get some coffee, please?"

Reed resumed his seat on the couch, interlacing his fingers behind his head. Maggie sat across from him, and a moment later, a waiter with a trolley pushed into the office and poured them steaming cups of rich black coffee. No whiskey. Reed drank in silence from the china cup as Maggie ignored hers and just stared out the window. For a long time, they just sat, enjoying the warmth of the sunrise and the momentary peace.

"I asked about Turk," Maggie said. "They say he's doing well."

"I know," Reed said. "I called last night."

"Tell me about Wolfgang. When did you bring him in?"

Reed poured himself another cup. "Right before we left for Turkey. I had a nagging feeling I might need somebody to sniff around. Turns out, I was right."

Maggie sipped coffee, and Reed noted the black bags under her eyes. He remembered reading a headline about how Trousdale had just turned thirty-five—barely old enough to be president—but she looked a lot older. This place really aged you.

"Why did you lie to me?" Maggie asked. "About the flight recorder."

Reed pondered his answer. The truth was simple, really. "I didn't trust you. There was nothing at the crash site to indicate a missile hit. After that guy tried to kill us on our way back and I found the shell casings, I felt like I was being set up. So I wanted to hold my cards."

"It would've helped to have the recorder," she said. "It might've kept this thing from spinning so far out of control."

Reed shook his head. "Nah. If Coffman heard you had the recorder, he would've reported to Sanger, and they would've found a way to cover it up. Maybe kill you. Why do you think he was carrying that ceramic knife, anyway?"

Maggie stared into her coffee. Her shoulders drooped a little, but Reed knew she had to feel good about the overall outcome. World War Three, averted. For now, anyway.

"What do you expect me to do about those bodies?" she said.

Reed shrugged. "Like I said before, this place runs on lies. And it seems O'Dell will do pretty much anything for you. I'm sure you'll figure it out."

Maggie set the coffee down and walked to her desk. She returned and slid a small notecard across the table. Reed picked it up and ran his thumb across the presidential seal on the face, then he flipped it over and read the single line of text on the other side.

I chose you for this moment. Trust no one. The enemy is within. —W. J. B.

Reed snorted and flicked the card across the table. "Real pit of vipers around here."

"Seems so. Seems you saw through it."

"Wolfgang did the research. I just put the pieces together. Honestly, it's hard not to blame Brandt."

"He sacrificed himself," Maggie said.

"Like hell he did. He fell on a grenade, maybe. But a real sacrifice would've been exposing Sanger for what he was, or at least giving you more heads-up than a cryptic note."

"I suppose you're right."

The relaxation of warm drinks and respectful chitchat quickly faded, now replaced by icy stillness.

"I'll take my pardon now," Reed said.

Maggie set her cup down and folded her hands in her lap. He thought she looked presidential. Poised and collected.

Another politician.

"I'm not sure you've earned it," Maggie said.

Reed laughed. "Well, I just saved your butt from global chaos, all while exposing traitors snuggled up next to you like house cats. I'd say I've earned it."

"You also gunned those traitors down in my freaking basement. That's the thing about you, Reed. You always create just as many problems as you solve."

"Kind of my brand, which you knew when you hired me. Now, let's see it. Or do you plan on backstabbing me again?"

Maggie pursed her lips, waiting a moment. She walked back to the desk and returned with a pen and a folder. She flipped the folder open, exposing a single sheet of paper printed with the presidential seal, followed by a brief body of text. Maggie uncapped the pen and adjusted it between her fingers, then let it hover over the signature line.

Reed waited, unconsciously holding his breath. He saw his future with Banks where he wasn't a fugitive on the run, always looking over his shoulder and sleeping with one eye open. He could be a real husband. A real father. A normal, everyday guy.

He felt a lump in his throat, and Maggie looked up.

"Banks is pregnant, isn't she?"

Reed said nothing.

A dry smile crept across Maggie's face. "I thought so," she said. "You're going to make a terrible father." She dropped her gaze, and the pen glided across the paper, leaving smooth lines of blue. Maggie finished with a slight flourish over the E, then capped the pen and closed the folder. She handed it to Reed. "Congratulations, Reed. I hope you enjoy it."

Reed drained his coffee and accepted the folder. He flipped it open and scanned the sheet.

EXECUTIVE GRANT OF CLEMENCY

REED DAVID MONTGOMERY

A FULL AND UNCONDITIONAL PARDON

He closed the document and gave Maggie a short nod. As he approached the door, he heard her stand.

"Don't go too far, Reed. We won this round, but I may need you again."

Reed put his hand on the door. He thought about Banks and the house he was going to buy her and the music room he'd build for her to fill with guitars. He thought about decades of peace and quiet without the stress of gunfire and lies.

He turned back. "We're done, Madam President. You'll never hear from me again."

Maggie stood with her head held high and her shoulders a little slumped—the picture of exhaustion and executive composure, all at once. She met Reed's iron gaze with calm acceptance and nodded.

But as he turned back to the door, Reed knew she didn't believe it. And someplace deep inside, neither did he.

52

The house was a rental, not a purchase. It turned out that buying a home required credit, a job history, and a whole load of things Reed knew nothing about. But the quiet Birmingham suburb sat on rolling hills under the shade of towering hardwoods, and it was the last place Reed remembered having a home as a child. It felt like the perfect place to start a family.

He paid the lease entirely in advance, using most of what remained from the Diablo hit, then used the rest to buy furniture and take Banks shopping for pots and pans—domestic things, she said. Reed thought you only needed a few, but Banks selected a cartload, and it made him think he'd need another job soon.

A legitimate job.

Reed had no idea how to find that, but he still had enough cash to think about it for a while, and right then, all he wanted was to be with Banks all the time.

Maggie's parting gift to the young couple was to have the Department of Defense ship the battered Camaro back from Honduras, and Reed parked it in the one-car garage and thought about a full restoration. His father's car deserved that much.

The backyard was small, barely large enough for a little patio and a barbecue grill, but Reed liked it. He placed a couple outdoor chairs in it and sat next to Banks, sipping good beer and holding her hand as the sun slowly sank through the trees. Banks's belly now rode her lap like a bowling ball and got a little bigger each day. She held it when she thought he wasn't watching, and every couple of weeks, they piled into the Camaro and rattled down to the doctor for checkups.

Medical bills . . . something else he had to pay for legitimately.

Banks squeezed his hand and leaned her head against his shoulder as she breathed softly. Her skin had resumed the rosy red of health after a few months back in the States, where they were well fed and had plenty of medical care. She looked good again—vibrant and strong.

Best of all, she smiled a lot more, and that made it all worthwhile.

"Promise you'll never go away again," Banks whispered.

Reed touched her head, gently brushing hair behind one ear. Her words sank in, and he wanted to promise her. It seemed like an easy thing to say, but when he opened his mouth, the words didn't come out. They felt frozen in his throat, and no matter how hard he tried, he couldn't lie.

He kissed her head instead and whispered, "I need another beer."

She grunted and pulled herself up. "I'll get it. I've got to pee anyway. Again."

She waddled inside, and Reed watched her go, a smile tugging at the corners of his mouth. Pregnant with swollen feet and not a lick of makeup, and easily the most gorgeous woman he'd ever seen.

He settled back into his chair and scooped a rolled copy of *The Birmingham News* off the ground next to him. He wasn't sure why, but something about having the local news delivered to him on the daily felt domestic. He remembered his father reading the paper every day and figured that until he understood what it meant to be a suburban dad, this was a good place to start. Only, the headline on the front page wasn't local news—it was international.

"TERRORISTS CAPITALIZE ON TROOP BUILDUP. NINE MARINES KILLED."

Reed sat forward, knocking his beer off the armrest as he scanned to the subtitle of an opinion piece, two columns down.

"WITH A CORRUPTION-FIGHTING HERO IN THE WHITE HOUSE, WHO WILL PROSECUTE INTERNATIONAL THREATS?"

Reed crumbled the paper into a ball, tossing it aside. He rested his face in both hands and tried not to think about Turk's words in Iran:

"Some things never change."

He thought about Iraq. He thought about all those young soldiers stationed there, so far from home. Just trying to do their jobs.

In his mind he saw a bomb detonate and nine Marines flung into the dirt, blown apart, screaming for their lives. And he knew . . .

He was never going to be a suburban dad.

FIRST STRIKE
THE PROSECUTION FORCE THRILLERS Book 2

Nine nations hold nuclear weapons.
What if a madman seized control of one of them?

Reed Montgomery's retirement is doomed to be short-lived. After the CIA receives intelligence from deep inside North Korea of a startling new weapon, President Trousdale green-lights an illegal mission to extract the informant.

Reed and his Prosecution Force are tasked with infiltrating the hermit kingdom, under cover and off the books. They won't have backup, and if they are discovered by North Korean authorities, Washington will disavow them.

But there's no question they'll take the mission. Because from inside Pyongyang, rumblings of war are echoing across the west. And with a superior nuclear weapon, those rumblings are no longer empty threats.

The Prosecution Force is on the clock. Failure is not an option.

Get your copy today at
severnriverbooks.com/series/the-prosecution-force

ABOUT THE AUTHOR

Logan Ryles was born in small town USA and knew from an early age he wanted to be a writer. After working as a pizza delivery driver, sawmill operator, and banker, he finally embraced the dream and has been writing ever since. With a passion for action-packed and mystery-laced stories, Logan's work has ranged from global-scale political thrillers to small town vigilante hero fiction.

Beyond writing, Logan enjoys saltwater fishing, road trips, sports, and fast cars. He lives with his wife and three fun-loving dogs in Alabama.

Sign up for Logan Ryles's reader list at
severnriverbooks.com/authors/logan-ryles

Printed in the United States
by Baker & Taylor Publisher Services